W9-CPN-828

Praise for

WHEN THE
SUMMER
WAS
OURS

"A sweeping, heartbreaking love story about how the smallest of choices can change our fates. Set against the backdrop of war and revolution, *When Summer Was Ours* is an artfully written story told with deep compassion. Historical fiction fans will love this book!"

—Julia Kelly, author of *The Whispers of War*

"A gripping story of a passionate, illicit love affair torn apart by decades of brutal inhumanity and secrets. Through unimagined journeys of self-discovery and determination, the characters must find within themselves the courage not only to endure but to once again reach for the impossible. A heart-wrenching, vivid novel of love, war, and loyalty written in Roxanne Veletzos's trademark style of unapologetic honesty and lasting devotion."

—Genevieve Graham, bestselling author of *The Forgotten Home Child*

"In this heartbreaking, powerful story of unrequited love, Veletzos draws us into Eva and Aleandro's enduring love affair that spans half a century, from WWII Hungary to 1950s New York and the Cold War, in which their personal upheavals and triumphs are artfully intertwined with those of history. Veletzos's beautiful and well-crafted novel, in lush sensual prose, opens the deep chambers of the heart to show the choices and regrets and the secret hopes we all carry within us."

—Alexis Landau, author of *Those Who Are Saved*

"A remarkable story of love, suffering, and second chances, told in immersive prose. With its rich setting and bittersweet twists of fate, *When the Summer Was Ours* drew me in and kept me wondering until the final page. I highly recommend this original and moving World War II read."

—Ellen Keith, bestselling author of *The Dutch Wife*

"*A Tale of Two Cities* meets *The Nightingale* in this luminous wartime love story that sweeps readers from an impoverished Romani camp in Hungary at the brink of World War II to the Siege of Budapest, and on to the New York art scene during the Cold War. Tenderly drawn and lyrically told, Roxanne Veletzos's unforgettable characters show us the political is always personal, art is both transcendent and fragile, and courage is the ultimate weapon against injustice. Transportive and moving, *When the Summer Was Ours* is haunted by the violin music of the Romani people and a love that endures through war and devastation."

—Laurie Lico Albanese, author of *Stolen Beauty*

"Like the gypsy music that is at the center of this wonderful novel, *When the Summer Was Ours* is a lyrical and deeply moving story of star-crossed love during World War II in Hungary. Eva is a complex heroine and her ultimate fate is bittersweet and rewarding at the same time. Book clubs will love this intimate tale of courage and sacrifice."

—Anita Abriel, internationally bestselling author of *Lana's War*

"A sweeping story of love and forgiveness. You won't want to put this book down."

—Diana Giovinazzo, author of *The Woman in Red*

ALSO BY ROXANNE VELETZOS

The Girl They Left Behind

WHEN THE
SUMMER
WAS
OURS

A Novel

ROXANNE VELETZOS

WASHINGTON
SQUARE PRESS

ATRIA

New York   London   Toronto   Sydney   New Delhi

WASHINGTON
SQUARE PRESS

ATRIA

An Imprint of Simon & Schuster, Inc.
1230 Avenue of the Americas
New York, NY 10020

First Washington Square Press/Atria Paperback edition August 2021

WASHINGTON SQUARE PRESS / ATRIA PAPERBACK and colophon are trademarks of Simon & Schuster, Inc.

For information about special discounts for bulk purchases, please contact Simon & Schuster Special Sales at 1-866-506-1949 or business@simonandschuster.com.

The Simon & Schuster Speakers Bureau can bring authors to your live event. For more information or to book an event, contact the Simon & Schuster Speakers Bureau at 1-866-248-3049 or visit our website at www.simonspeakers.com.

Interior design by Lexy Alemao

Manufactured in the United States of America

1   3   5   7   9   10   8   6   4   2

Library of Congress Cataloging-in-Publication Data

Names: Veletzos, Roxanne, author.
Title: When the summer was ours : a novel / by Roxanne Veletzos.
Description: First Washington Square Press/Atria Paperback edition. |
New York : Atria Books, 2021.
Identifiers: LCCN 2020055003 | ISBN 9781982152130 (paperback) |
ISBN 9781982152147 (ebook)
Subjects: LCSH: Family life—Hungary—Fiction. | World War, 1939–1945—
Hungary—Fiction. | GSAFD: Historical fiction. | War stories.
Classification: LCC PS3622.E437 W48 2021 | DDC 813/.6—dc23
LC record available at https://lccn.loc.gov/2020055003

ISBN 978-1-9821-5213-0
ISBN 978-1-9821-5214-7 (ebook)

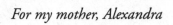

For my mother, Alexandra

WHEN THE
SUMMER
WAS
OURS

Part I

HAUNTINGS

1

Sopron, Hungary
Summer 1943

*A*s the Budapest streets with their clatter of trams and hurried pedestrians began to thin out, Eva César reclined against the cool leather of her father's town car and let out a long breath. Two hours from now, she would be on her family's country estate in Sopron with nothing to do but soak in some much-needed sun, bask in Dora's glorious cooking, and tackle (at last!) the three biology books she'd tucked inside her valise under layers of clothing like boxes of stolen chocolates.

It had been a maddening spring, filled with endless parties and dinner outings, and a steady stream of thank-you notes to write for the gifts arriving in elaborate packages for her upcoming wedding. She'd unwrapped each one nonetheless, feigning delight, filled with an undercurrent of annoyance that with Europe at war, she should be receiving such lavish gifts.

Endless bibelots, crystal napkin rings, stained glass vases large enough to fit all the flower bouquets in Budapest combined. All, she imagined, would be stored in a pantry somewhere, collecting dust after the wedding. She wouldn't have much use for them in her new life with Eduard.

The planning of the wedding itself had felt more like the negotiation of a peace treaty, obliterating any time at all she might have had for reading. Even the dress fittings (all six of them) she'd come to regard as a weekly trip to the dentist. At the last appointment, she did her best not to slouch, or tap her foot, or swat the tiny flies that seemed enthralled with the bursts of tulle and lace on her shoulders. She'd had the overwhelming urge to push past the seamstress hovering at her feet and flee. Didn't this woman with a mouthful of pins and the concentration of a mathematician understand what was taking place outside the rosewood-paneled walls of her shop? Didn't she know that while she insisted that every pearl on her five-foot train should be fastened at exact intervals, men were trudging through trenches without proper boots, dying in the Russian snow?

Then she'd spotted a recent newspaper folded in three on the low table near the sofa strewn with patterns and rolls of silk, and she realized, of course this woman knew.

Everyone in her family's circle knew, yet they all seemed intent on looking the other way. Everyone other than her dear Eduard seemed far more consumed with the fact that chocolate éclairs had vanished from Budapest entirely, or that the Széchenyi Baths had become overcrowded. No one was concerned that tens of thousands of Hungarian soldiers had been killed at Stalingrad, with the new year still in celebration.

Poor Eduard. As her car moved through the streets, Eva pictured him at that very moment, his head bent in concentration, pushing his round wire glasses back on the bridge of his nose as he extracted a piece of shrapnel from a soldier's shoulder. He'd planned to join her in Sopron until late in the spring, when what remained of the Hungarian Second Army had retreated from the Eastern Front and wounded soldiers began pouring into Budapest hospitals by the thousands.

Of course, she had agreed that he should stay for as long as he was needed. Besides, here, under her father's nose, their every movement and conversation would be observed, their every word measured. There would be no Sunday strolls on Andrássy út, their arms intertwined, exchanging views on what might come to Hungary if its alliance with Germany was to continue. No coffee and Gauloise cigarettes at the brasserie across from Heroes' Square, where he would give her a detailed account of the latest tourniquet he'd applied, and how, just as he was preparing grimly for an amputation, it had managed to stop the blood flow and save the doomed limb. Or how a bullet could enter the body in a way that endangered no organs then splay under the skin like a trick flower pulled from a hat.

As the car turned into the main highway and began closing the two hundred kilometers that stretched between Budapest and Sopron, she sparked a cigarette, and thought with some amusement of the day when her fascination with anatomy began. She was eight years old, and on that Christmas Eve, among other gifts, she'd been presented with a brand-new set of pencils and a coloring book. She sat at the kitchen table later that night with her book and a cup of hot chocolate provided by one of the servants. There, among the clattering of pots and pans and plates being scrubbed, she opened it for the first time and wondered in that first instant if her uncle had picked it up from the bookshop by mistake. It was a drawing book, but there were no flowers to fill in, no clouds or castles. There, in all its glorious form, Eva glimpsed the naked human body for the first time.

Not just the body, however, but all it contained in its secret corridors, intricate maps of systems she never knew about. As Eva stared at the illustrations opposite the blank pages she was to fill in, she marveled that her own body contained such complexities. That underneath the quiet smoothness of skin, blood pumped through mazes of veins; that everything from the muscles in her neck to the tendons in her toes was all connected in one perfect constellation. All night she'd spent copying the illustrations— the tendons, the arteries, the organs, shaped like some strange exotic fruit. She hadn't noticed when the sun had come up nor that her breakfast tray lay untouched on the armoire.

It was only when she met Eduard years later that she was able to confess this obsession to anyone. She went to a friend's birthday dinner out of obligation as much as boredom. She expected the usual meaningless chatter as she stood around alone smoking a cigarette, then she overheard the conversation taking place just on the other side of the fireplace. She didn't mean to eavesdrop, but then she saw that the woman in the duo had grown quiet and was looking at her in perplexity. The man, too, noticing the distraction, had glanced over his shoulder. There was a sort of gentility in the premature silvery strands at his temples, an earnestness in his clear blue eyes as he turned to her fully.

"I'm sorry," Eva found herself explaining. "I'm just waiting for someone. Please don't mind me. I didn't mean to interrupt."

"You're not interrupting in the least," said the man. He

held out his hand, and a tiny, amused smile that seemed at odds with his formal gesture appeared at the corners of his lips. "I'm Eduard."

"Eva," she replied as she shook his hand, hoping that taking a drag of her cigarette in tandem would convey some mild disinterest. But she was interested, not necessarily in the way he looked, which was not exactly unpleasing, but in what she'd heard him say only moments earlier.

"You're a doctor with the Red Cross. I'm sorry." She found herself apologizing again and wished that she hadn't. "I couldn't help overhearing. That, and . . . well, mostly everything else. So it's true, then. Our regent means to disentangle Hungary from the war. And he's already promised the Americans and the Brits to hold back fire on their aircraft." She took another drag of her cigarette, which shivered slightly between her fingers. "Incredible, isn't it, but is it sustainable? I imagine Herr Hitler will not take this kindly."

"True," said Eduard after a long pause. He looked at her as if suddenly observing her from a different angle. "But tell me . . . Eva. Why would someone as lovely as you be interested in tracking political maneuvers?"

"Why not?" she said, tipping her chin in defiance and tossing back the rest of her champagne. "Even someone like me"—this, she said in clear irony—"does not wish to see the Nazi flag flutter on Castle Hill."

They ended up leaving the party together, grabbing a late-night drink. In the dim lights of the tavern he insisted on, Eva noticed how alive he was talking about his work, which had begun in earnest even before he finished medical school. It occurred to her that perhaps he couldn't afford to take her to a place better—he'd earlier mentioned with surprising openness the school debts he'd been struggling to pay for years—and she felt warmed from within with something like enchantment, or perhaps admiration. To her own astonishment, she'd placed her hand on his.

Later, he walked her home in a drizzle of rain, passing the darkened storefronts on Váci utca. The quietness of the night, with its faint sound of streetcars, seemed to embrace them in an intimate way. In front of her home, just just a stone's throw from the Operaház, he paused on the sidewalk to take in the tall windows and ornate baroque facade, and she squeezed his arm, as if to indicate that this, like anything else, was ordained by something that had nothing to do with them. He'd kissed her cheek and departed in a hurry, his shoulders scrunched against the October wind, shaking the mist from his hair as if to dispel the evening, which might have been no more than a dream.

Four months later, they were engaged. She knew it was rushed, yet ever since his proposal, when he declared that her presence in his life had spurred in him a desire to rise to the highest planes, a similar feeling had awakened in her as well. She was twenty, after all. Twenty, and he, perfect in every way. She couldn't have hoped for a better match. Besides, in the short time they'd spent together, she never became more certain of one thing: with this man at her side, she could shape her own future. She could make of it what she wished—and that, above all, had filled her with great exhilaration.

———

The car, Eva realized with a start, had turned from the main highway, and began its upward climb on the smaller road leading up to the villa. She hadn't noticed the time pass, yet here she was, on a land that belonged to a different world, with its lush trees and the calmness of a simple life, and all the colors of a Cézanne painting. At the end of the long driveway, after they'd gone through the main gates and the villa revealed itself from the shade of oaks, she opened the car door and, before stepping out, she inhaled deeply. The Sopron air always smelled of fresh-cut grass and rain even at the onset of summer, that nostalgic, comforting air of her youth.

Despite the chauffer's protests she pulled her own valise from the trunk, and as she slammed it shut, a familiar voice greeted her from the top of the stairs. Dora, her summer governess, was hovering under the arched door, breathing heavily as though she'd run a mile from the kitchen.

"Oh, my dearest, you're here!" she sang in her quivery voice, fanning her plump, ruddy cheek with one hand while balancing a platter of her legendary baked strudel on the other. "Oh, but look at you! Soon to be a madame! Oh, come here, love. Let me see you, my beauty."

"My dearest Dora, hello!" Eva shouted, laughing, running up the steps. "You're back! You don't know how happy this makes me." Dora lived in town, but every summer while Eva visited, Dora reinstalled herself at the villa even though Eva had long stopped needing a nanny. If anything, they'd become close friends over the past years, and Eva couldn't wait to see her year-round.

"You know, I think this will be a summer of great adventure for us," Eva said now, kissing Dora's flour-dusted cheek even though she couldn't think of anything at all adventurous between now and early September. Taking a hearty bite of the strudel, she walked into the house with it, letting the powdered sugar scatter into the air like dust dancing in a slant of light.

In the vast windows, the sun had already dipped beyond the hills, bathing the vineyards in shades of amber and gold, and she paused in the living room doorway to take it all in. This peacefulness, this splendor. Would it last? For how long? Sopron, she thought, after this summer, may never quite belong to her in the same way again. She turned and went up the staircase, thankful that at least for now, for two more weeks, while her father was detained in Vienna, the Sopron of her childhood belonged just to her. It was only hers and Dora's, and she intended to enjoy every languid, unadventurous moment.

2

THAT ENTIRE WEEK AFTER HER ARRIVAL, the first thing Eva did in the morning was to pull open the shades and let in the sunshine and fresh air. Still in her pajamas, she turned on some soft music, sipped her coffee, walked barefoot through the hillside, picked grapes from the vines. She ate them right there on the spot, not bothering to wash them, relishing in the sweet, tangy taste, then slipped down to the kitchen and helped Dora prepare a meal. The tomato vines in the vegetable patch by the kitchen had exploded in huge, plentiful fruit, and she would bring them inside in a basket along with some fresh thyme, which had sprouted unexpectedly on the side of the wall. Alongside Dora, she would slice the tomatoes and a loaf of dark bread, flatten the glistening cloves of garlic into a paste with the blade of a knife. More often than not, they ate right there at the kitchen table. Such simple pleasures. She had no idea how she'd survived without them an entire year.

Afterward, she lingered, cleaning dishes, even though it was obvious she was just getting in Dora's way. Back in Budapest, her life was too busy to let her mind wander aimlessly, but here, away from the bustle of her everyday life, memories of her mother would startle her in their vividness. There, on that green sofa facing the fireplace, after the house quieted, they would tell stories sometimes until dawn, making up silly improvisations that had them both bursting with laughter. And out on the veranda, on those same wrought iron lounge chairs facing the valley, she and her mother would stretch out under the sun and listen to opera on the radio while her mother French-braided her hair. It seemed odd to remember such minute details when the larger, more vital moments of their lives were a blank. She didn't remember, for instance, the sound of her mother's voice, but she remembered the bright shock of her red fingernails parting her hair in segments and working them into a plait as *The Marriage of Figaro* drifted into the vastness of the valley.

To keep the melancholy at bay, Eva was happy to drive down into town with Dora in the late afternoon, when the height of the heat broke. In truth, she would have much rather walked, but Dora seemed oddly fragile these days, tiring too easily as she dusted around the house or hauled in flowers from the garden. In the past year, she'd gained weight, and the constant ruddiness in her cheeks concerned Eva, even though she didn't want to worry her by bringing it up. Instead, she tried observing her with a cool eye, to detach herself from her own alarm, often wondering if poring over those anatomy books more than ever since meeting Eduard was causing her to imagine things.

Regardless of Eva's objections, Dora insisted that she do the shopping in the market alone, so Eva would install herself at an outdoor café, order a light refreshment, and delve into her books. There was still so much that she didn't know, so much to learn if she would have a chance at a nursing school. The idea had never become more solid than in the past weeks. She hadn't told Eduard yet of her plans, but she would soon, after the wedding. Everything began after the wedding, after the war. She did not want to imagine that it would go on beyond this summer, beyond what her new life would be.

On this particular afternoon, a week after her arrival, she was sipping a lemonade when a dark-haired boy, no more than nine or ten, appeared at the side of her table. He stood before her, barefoot and snotty-nosed, swaying on his heels. Eva smiled and held out a chocolate mint, which had come with her drink, but the boy didn't take it. Before she could reach for her purse to extract a few coins, he was dashing across the square, his feet slapping the cobblestones. It was a moment before she realized her satchel was no longer next to the glass.

"Goodness," said a stunned Eva to the waitress behind her, who'd witnessed the whole thing and stood there with hands on her hips. "That was swift. Unfortunately, you see, I'll have to find my companion before I can pay you. Or I can come back tomorrow. I'll make good on it, I promise."

"Those goddamn gypsies," spat the woman in reply. Picking up a few empty plates and glasses from adjoining tables, she walked back inside, shaking her tightly wound curls in disgust.

Eva had almost laughed, wanting to say that he was just

a boy. Sopron was full of hungry gypsy boys. She'd seen them all over Budapest, too, sleeping under awnings, selling flowers in the middle of winter—certainly, they could do with a few *pengös* more than she. Then, with a staggering jolt, the real magnitude of her loss hit her.

———

Some time later, after looking around the maze of alleys radiating from the square for any semblance of the boy, Eva ambled back in tears and plopped herself down on a bench. For the first time in thirteen years, she wept for her mother and for herself, she wept for her lost satchel, which was the only thing she had to remember her mother by. She felt angry, angry with herself for being so careless with the only object she had been able to salvage from her mother's boxed possessions in the days after her funeral. Angry, above all, that in all thirteen years since her mother had died, it had taken this absurd act to unleash her tears. She didn't even have a handkerchief to wipe her nose, so she used the hem of her dress. Then she looked up and, catching a glimpse of the gathering clouds, realized it would begin to rain any minute. She needed to find Dora.

Wearily, Eva stood and scanned the square. There was no sight of her, only a few pedestrians dashing by, a band of musicians packing up their instruments near the Trinity Column, where they gathered to play for change. She shot a look in the direction of the chapel. Often, Dora would go in to light a candle for her husband after she finished her shopping, yet it looked as though the doors had been locked long ago. There was no one nearby, no one other than a tall figure, a man, seated on the ledge of a flower bed at the far end of the chapel.

The first thing she noticed about him was the way he seemed utterly lost in a drawing, the way his hand moved in quick bursts over the large sheet of paper balanced on his knee. He looked like an apparition from another century—his hair a mass of black ringlets grazing his shoulders, his features gathered in such concentration that it almost resembled pain. He seemed not to notice her in the least—then, as if sensing her gaze, he looked up from his drawing and their eyes met. There was nothing unusual about it—strangers' eyes met all the time—but the way he held her gaze, and smiled as if he knew her, made her breath catch.

As if on cue, he tucked his pad and pencils inside a brown knapsack and picked up the other object at his side—a battered violin case—which he hoisted high onto his shoulder. An instant later, he was making his way in her direction in firm steps, smoothing those dark curls from his forehead. There was a fresh carnation pinned to his vest, his matching trousers perfectly pressed despite being somewhat faded. A fiddler, Eva realized. He was a fiddler, like dozens playing in impromptu ensembles all over the Hungarian countryside—probably belonging to the very troupe by the column.

"Forgive me," he said in a deep and grainy voice that sounded amused more than apologetic. "I've startled you. I didn't mean to."

Eva gave a brisk smile. Did she appear startled? Certainly, she wasn't accustomed to being approached by random strangers—fiddlers, least of all. Up close he looked like no fiddler she'd ever seen but more like a count in a Dutch painting.

His face was a play of contrasts, his mouth square yet as full as a peeled plum, those dark eyes soulful but alert, lit from within. She took in the trace of a smile, the playful glint in the walnut eyes, and a mortifying thought crept into her. *God.* No doubt, he was good-looking in a rough, exotic sort of way, but just glancing in his direction couldn't have given him the impression that she was interested in him.

"You didn't startle me in the least," she said flatly. "I was just going. Can I help you?"

"Nothing would be more pleasing, miss, than to require your help," he replied, his smile widening to reveal a tiny chip in an otherwise perfect set of teeth, "but I think *I* might be able to help you."

"Oh?" Eva glanced at the case on his shoulder. "Well, as much as I'm sure you are wonderful with that violin, I haven't a single coin, you know. Truly, I wish I did. But you see, it can't be helped."

At this he said nothing more, only reached inside his knapsack and extracted an object that he tucked quickly behind his back. Then with a slight flourish, slowly, as if he intended to draw out the moment, his hand extended to her and Eva couldn't help giving a tiny gasp. There in his hand was her mother's satchel.

Instantly, she was on her feet, stunned more than confused. "I don't understand. How did you . . . ?" A heat rose in her cheeks, and before she realized what she was doing she ripped the satchel from his grasp. "What is this? Is this some kind of a game? Did you help that boy steal it? Did you?"

It was his turn to flush, violently, as if she'd slapped him. "Steal? No, miss, I assure you I did nothing of the sort. I don't steal. I would have returned it to you sooner, except that I didn't want to disturb you. It seemed like you needed time alone, so I didn't want to . . . to interrupt your thoughts. Go on. Check to see if the money's still in it."

Eva frowned and bit her lip and looked inside the satchel. The money was there, intact, rolled up in a cylinder precisely as she'd left it. The blood in her cheeks spiked all the way to the tops of her ears as she realized he'd seen her crying, then wiping her nose on her dress. And now she'd managed to insult him. Part of her wanted to run, part of her wanted to explain what this satchel meant to her, to tell him how she'd never been able to weep for her mother and what he'd witnessed had been a monumental break—a cleaving of a shell she'd spun around her grief since she was a girl. But he was a stranger after all—how could she say such things to a stranger—and she'd behaved no better than the waitress at the café. In the end, all she could manage was to withdraw a few bills from her satchel.

"I'm so sorry. Here. For your trouble. Please take it."

She shook the bills at him, once, twice, but he wouldn't take them, and eventually her hand dropped away.

"More? Sure, I can give you more. You can take it all. Take all of it."

Again, she was fumbling with her purse. It was impossible to get it open now; in her fluster she'd knotted the strings too tightly. All of a sudden, his hand was on hers. It was a light, casual touch, meant to calm her, yet she felt it shoot like an electric current from the tendons in her hand through the full length of her arm.

"I was happy to help," he said, withdrawing quickly, as if he, too, was stunned by his own brazenness. "You looked so distraught back there at the café, and I thought, no one should be so unhappy. Not all of us Cigánz are in it for a few *pengös*, you know."

"Of course not. I never meant to imply . . ."

Now her heart was pounding, but she couldn't think of what else to say and looked down at the ground, where a line of moss snaked through the cobblestones. The silence stretched. Nothing was happening at all yet something was. She could feel his eyes on her, burning through the space between them. Was it with expectation? Or—judgment? Straightening her spine as if she was pulling herself up to her full height, she met his fixed stare, held it, and a staggering, terrifying thrill coursed through her. Then the moment passed. He took a few steps back, tipping his head to her, and it came to her with some slight panic that he was going.

"Wait! But why . . . why then would you want to help me?"

A bright, easy smile reignited in his face. "That boy in the market—let's just say you are not his only victim today. I'm Aleandro, by the way. Your knight in shining armor. Your savior." His arm swept downward theatrically, as if he was bowing at the end of a performance, just as thunder broke—one long boom, followed by a shorter, more intense one. "Don't get caught in the storm, miss," he said, gesturing lightly to the sky; then he turned and departed in the direction of the Fire Tower, the violin case thumping against his back, his head raised to the clouds as if in welcome.

The storm had already come, fat raindrops darkening the cobblestones, which he traversed in quick, long steps, passing the café where the waitress was stripping the oilcloths from the tabletops and farther on, where a side street forked away from the piazza. Just before rounding the corner, he turned and looked straight at her one last time. Then he was gone, and Eva stood there for a long moment fixed in place. Without knowing, she pressed the hand he'd touched to her cheek and held it there, despite the rain, which started falling down in pelting sheets.

3

THREE, FOUR DAYS IN A ROW, Aleandro had been drawing the girl in the square. At times, it felt somehow wrong, as if he were stealing something from her, but what harm was there in it? It was the only hour in his long day when he felt unburdened, free. There were no demands of him here in the cool shade of the church, no brothers to feed, no fiddle to play, no one to answer to. It was only him and his charcoals and this face, this Botticelli face that inspired his hands to move as never before.

When he first set his eyes on her all of five days ago, she stopped him in his tracks. She was beautiful, there was no denying it, but he'd seen plenty of beautiful women before. Unlike girls of her age, there was no flirtatiousness in her walk—she walked straight and powerfully, with purpose, a bit like a man—even though everything about her was feminine, the honey-blond tresses reaching down to her waist, the small feet inside the red sandals, the slender calves.

At the café, she sat at a table under the geranium balcony and took off her sunglasses, and her eyes were yet another enigma. Were they blue or dark? Dark, he thought at first, like ink dropped in a glass of water; blue, he thought as her gaze drifted up to the sky. Definitely blue, the intense aquamarine of a sea where it meets the horizon. In the end, it didn't matter the color. They were the largest, most luminous, most striking eyes he'd ever seen. Right then and there, he dropped his knapsack at the base of the chapel and reached for his notepad and pencils, forgetting where he was going.

Since Aleandro was a child, drawing and painting had been his everything, his ballast, his joy, his companion. Yet, since his parents had died two years prior, the responsibility for his brothers, the worry to provide for them, had brought with it a lack of inspiration that had persisted like an incurable illness. The summer before, he'd given it up altogether, although he still carried paper and charcoals wherever he went. He could never let go of it entirely, couldn't accept that perhaps it had been a momentary phase in his life, yet each attempt of late left him more disillusioned than the last. To be able to draw again! To fall back into it with such ease! As he watched his hands move over the parchment, he nearly wanted to weep.

And she kept surprising him. Each day, she came bearing small trinkets for the scampering kids in the square—butterscotch candies, stickers, ribbons for the girls. She would ruffle their hair, laugh with them, then she would continue on to that same café with a book under her arm, her heels striking the cobblestones as if to defy the quietness of the piazza.

He couldn't imagine what she read every day in those massive books of hers, only that it had to be good, very good. A whole hour would pass without her lifting her eyes from the pages, tapping her foot under the table, chewing absentmindedly on her fingernails. *Love stories*, he decided, and smiled to himself broadly.

On this last day, he was capturing the slope of her shoulder reclined against the wicker café chair when a flurry of movements drew his eye away from the paper. A disruption of sorts. It took him but an instant to grasp what was happening, and then he was on his feet, chasing the little vandal—a boy of about the same age as his brothers he knew from the gypsy town. It wasn't the first time he'd seen him rob in broad daylight, nor the first time that he'd shaken the life out of him, threatened to take him straight to the police. But never before had he acted with such will, such sheer determination.

Halfway back to the square, finger-brushing his curls, he imagined her surprise when he brandished her purse. To actually have a reason to speak with her! He couldn't stop smiling. What he didn't expect was to find her no longer at the café but on a nearby bench under an alcove, weeping quietly into her hands.

For a few moments he stood there like a four-year-old lost in a park, staring at the purse in his hand, and after some contemplation, he tucked it inside his knapsack. Not knowing what else to do, he made his way back to his usual spot, and while he waited, he took out his supplies and began drawing again.

He should have placed the satchel down next to her and gone, but a shard of light broke through the clouds, catching the gold in her hair, and he had to keep drawing. And what happened next—well, what happened next would cause him to spend many nights in bed tossing around.

There had been no words of gratitude, only a feeble attempt to push some money into his hand, and he'd never felt more conscious of the shabbiness of his clothes, of his dirt-caked fingernails and the stench of poverty emanating from his every pore. Yes, it was easy to see himself through the eyes of someone like her, and he'd departed in a hurry, swallowing his humiliation and what he recognized, even though he'd never felt it before, as the cold sting of heartbreak.

And yet, despite the voice in his head that wouldn't stop mocking him, that night after his brothers were asleep, he took out his sketching supplies and went down by the fishing pond with a lantern and began a new portrait of her. From underneath the strokes of his pencils, her face came to him once more, not perfect, no, not at all, but the eyes! Those eyes were captured in near perfection, and he was there with her again in the square under the clouds. This time he painted in her hair the red carnation he'd envisioned extracting from the buttonhole of his vest and handing to her. It was nearly dawn when he fell asleep in the grass with the etching of her face folded against his chest.

4

IN THE FIVE DAYS SINCE THE incident in the town square, it seemed that Eva's expectation of a quiet summer had gone completely off course. Her father had returned early, and to her dismay, not alone, but with an ensemble of guests. There were two families, one belonging to the director of Creditanstalt Bank in Vienna, whom he hoped to charm enough to fund his latest wine export venture. The other belonged to a distant cousin whom he'd run into by chance during his stay at the Imperial. Six people in all—a boy of ten with skinny legs and glasses who seemed perpetually pinned to his mother's skirt; two women in their forties who spoke to each other with a polite affection that did not meet their eyes; her uncle, Janos, a quiet man who spent the entire day with his nose in a paper smoking a pipe; and her cousin Isabel. Isabel, who was two years younger but carried herself as though she were twenty-five.

The last thing that Eva had wanted was the company of this girl—not only because the last time she'd seen her was at her mother's service and couldn't help being reminded of it whenever she entered a room but also because she seemed entirely incapable of enjoying one silent moment. Not one. Every minute was filled with unabating chatter, about how Vienna had become such an awful bore, how the air-raid sirens wasted everyone's time since nothing was happening at all, how the latest New York fashions, now with Paris under German rule, were all the rage. She'd practically begged, begged Eva to show her a picture of her dress, unfinished as it was, and gasped, flushing with pleasure and what Eva thought was some envy, tilting the photo against the window and studying it from every angle as if she could somehow conjure it into a three-dimensional existence.

"To marry in this dress." Isabel swooned while Eva lay on her bed with her nose in a book. "My goodness, Princess Elizabeth herself would be green with jealousy!" She plopped herself down next to Eva and pulled the book away from her face. "So, tell me," she said, glancing at Eva over the top of the pages, her hair wound up in pink ribbons. "Tell me about him. About your intended."

"Oh, surely my father has filled you all in during the drive from Vienna. He approves, it would seem, although I'm certain he'd happily marry me off to the highest bidder." She swallowed back a tinge of bitterness. "At least now he won't have to worry about me not dressing properly for his associate dinners or blurting the wrong thing, or generally causing gossip among those society ladies he's always trying to impress. He more than approves."

"Uhm," said Isabel, not really listening. She scooted herself up to the top of the bed beside Eva and pulled a pillow behind her. "So I hear: promising doctor, great family; however, I gather only marginally well-off. Oh, yes, and I hear his grandfather was a baron, sometime, oh, I don't know, during the Napoleonic Wars, or something."

"The Great War," Eva corrected. "You know, the war twenty years ago in which a Serbian prince was murdered, which was then blamed on the Germans, which then eventually led to the mess we're in now. That war." She looked at Isabel for a nod of understanding, but Isabel's expression was deadpan. She only wanted to hear about the groom.

"Well, he's . . . wonderful," Eva said finally, because in fact, there was no other way to describe Eduard. Instantly, a thread of anxiety tugged at her. For nearly a week it had been there, simmering in the depths of her stomach. She didn't allow herself to pay it any attention, although she knew well enough why it was there. That fiddler, with his black eyes, which seemed to pierce through every layer of her. Perhaps, after all, it was good that Isabel had arrived to provide a distraction, for Eva could no longer return to the town square in the afternoons. Not if she had any sense.

"But this calls for a party!" Isabel exploded, making her flinch. "We must celebrate! I know he's not here, I know, but we can still celebrate! I can help you plan it!" She squeezed Eva's hand and squealed as if she were to help out in the preparation of the royal wedding. "How else are we going to spend the next two weeks till I go back to Vienna? At least it will pass the time! It will give us something to do!"

"No," Eva said, shaking her head. "No, no, no. No more

parties. I had enough of that before leaving Budapest to last me ten years. And besides, there is plenty to do. I can show you how to garden. There is a lovely vegetable garden that I helped Dora plant two years ago, and you should see it already! Or I can show you some incredible things in my medical books. Did you know, for instance, that if our blood vessels were laid out end to end, they would go around the world four times?"

Isabel was gone from the bed, dashing through the door, her heels clattering through the hallway.

"Papa!" Eva heard her shout. "Papa! Uncle Vladimir! I've just had a brilliant idea! Brilliant!"

───────

It was to be a quiet affair. Just the eight of them, *eight*, yet as Eva watched from her bedroom window all the cars queuing up in the driveway, she knew it wouldn't be anything of the sort. All day long, Dora had been running around wringing her hands on her apron, fretting that the lawn was still to be mowed, that the chairs had not been placed in the garden in a way that would invite a late-night chat, or a drink, or a smoke, that the oven wasn't heating to optimal temperature, that the butcher was yet to deliver the ground meat for her stuffed peppers. Behind her agitation, there was a flare of satisfaction to be in charge of a proper affair, to prove that she wasn't just a cook or a nursemaid, after all. The cake, which had arrived in a huge pink box, was hauled from the delivery car by two men and carried into the house as gingerly as a newly concocted model of the Tour Eiffel. Then her dress was delivered as well, not the wedding dress, but a long, floral lamé number that Isabel had taken upon herself to order.

In her room, where Eva was finishing getting ready, she could hear the voices of arriving guests through the open window, the pop of champagne bottles going off in near tandem and then being propped in ice buckets on the terrace to keep them cold. She finished rouging her mouth in a deep crimson, examined her own image in the mirror, wiped off some of the lipstick with a tissue, blew out a bubble of air through her smeared lips. One more week and the house would be hers again. All she had to do was be patient. Isabel, after this evening, would sleep all day. That thought alone gave her enough motivation to walk downstairs and into the hubbub of activity already in full swing in the foyer.

No more than ten minutes into the dinner, however, Eva lost her patience. She sat staring at the lemon wedges garnishing the roasted fish on her plate, taking small sips of water, waiting for the inevitable. Next to her, her father was frowning into his glass and helping himself to the wine carafe again. Seated on his left, Uncle Janos was addressing him in his usual mild tone though waving his fork around as if directing a small symphony. She was only mildly surprised when her father slammed his fist on the table.

"Vladimir, please, calm down," Janos said, touching his sleeve at the elbow. Her father pulled away, then refilled his glass again.

"Horthy!" he spat. "Do not speak to me, Janos, about what a nationalistic hero he is! A patriot, ha! He should follow the examples of Mussolini, Kemal—men who are molding their countries, not driving them into ruin by refuting the Reich's wishes. Those are great men! Those are men to admire for their commitment to a new Europe! Not this excuse for a leader, this utter imbecile."

Janos stared glumly at his hands. "I was only suggesting, Vladimir, and please hear me out, that his job can't be an easy one. To balance our national sovereignty with Hitler's wishes, it can't be accomplished easily."

"Don't you see, my dear Janos," Vladimir retorted in a somewhat calmer tone, which seemed to suggest that *dear* meant *dim*, "our national interest, our Magyar interest, cannot be unaligned with that of Germany. We all want the same things. We all want a world order of racial purity, of—"

"That's enough," Eva found herself saying. "Please, Papa. That's enough. You promised me that you wouldn't talk like this anymore." She closed her eyes and breathed out through her nose. "I'm leaving."

She was halfway up from her chair when his hand descended on her forearm, squeezed it. She didn't expect it. Not that he wasn't rough with her once in a while—she'd been accustomed to his terrible moods since she was a child, but never in public. Never at a party where they were the center of attention. She looked at his hand, glared, but he only tightened his grip and forced her back down in her chair. Her face pounded with shame. Everyone had seen it. Even Isabel, suspended as she was in the middle of a sentence, her face still partially turned to the woman with a huge diamond necklace and a beehive of hair seated next to her. Vladimir, too, noticed the looks, the trailing voices, and withdrew his hand.

"Oh, but I nearly forgot! Dora!" he shouted across the room in the direction of the door. "Dora, where's the entertainment?"

Dora rushed to his side, head bowed, no doubt beet red under her bonnet. "You said after dinner, sir, that they should wait until the dessert was served—"

"Oh, for God's sake," Vladimir snapped. "Bring them in at once! What do they need, a written invitation?"

"Right, of course," Dora said and made herself swiftly invisible.

———

They came in through the door behind Eva, several figures in dark jackets with an array of instruments. If Eva didn't turn in greeting or pay them any attention, it was because she was somewhere else altogether. She had never been less in the mood for entertainment, for having to continue to smile, for having to be anywhere near her father. Her father, who'd disrespected her, humiliated her, treated her like an errant child.

"Ah, here they are—at last, they've appeared!" she heard him say to someone across the table louder than was necessary. "Such an honor! I'm assured they are the best damn band in all of Sopron. You wouldn't know it from the look of them, right? Surely they could do with a few tips, ladies and gents! Those coats, dear God, were they resurrected from the labor service?"

It was only when she heard that voice—"We are ready when you are, sir"—that she turned in her chair and a swell of heat rolled through her body. She felt self-conscious all of a sudden, of her hair, which had been done up in an exaggerated coil and fastened on one side with a diamanté comb, of the terrible light gold dress, which made her look like an overgrown goldfish. She wished she'd worn something brighter, less makeup. She wished that she'd left her hair loose.

Hello, Eva thought she mouthed. He tipped his head to her, made that same sweeping gesture from the square, smaller, less conspicuous—something only she would understand, which made her laugh. She laughed a little too loudly. She wanted to say something back, but was too stunned to see him, and so she only smiled, too long. It was only when her father stood from his chair that she was forced to redirect her gaze to the length of the table, to the glint of crystal and silver, which seemed too bright in her line of vision.

"Ladies and gentlemen, before we get on with the music," her father said, tapping his wineglass with his signet ring as he swayed a little at the edge of the table, "I would like to make a toast! To my daughter, Eva, whose happy engagement we have all gathered here to celebrate. As you are all aware, our esteemed groom could not be here with us this evening, busy as he is attending to our brave soldiers and whatnot, but I know I speak on his behalf when I say this is a most joyous occasion. Most joyous! May the two of them live a very long and happy life. To Eduard and Eva! *Egészségedre!*"

"To Eduard and Eva!" repeated all twenty guests in unison, clinking their glasses and raising them in Eva's direction. *"Egészségedre!"*

For a long moment, she couldn't look at the fiddler, then she did again, and saw the understanding seep into his gaze. It grazed past her, to the terrace door, to the grandfather clock, then to the violin at his side, which he lifted heavily. He placed it under his chin, positioned his bow, still as a statue, his hair slicked back with brilliantine, the hollows in his cheeks like shallow spoons. Serious now, the jaw stern as he motioned toward the others to begin.

"Ready? On three."

And begin they did, slowly at first, each of the three violins joining the *notà* in intervals, working around each other in a dance of sound, building their rhythm. She saw him close his eyes, flying with the music, no longer there in the room, no longer in any place where he could be reached. The other violins slowed, dropped off at the next break. Then it was only him, taking it higher, faster still, his face twisting with the sound, with what she imagined was joy, and the love of it.

"My God," the woman with the diamond choker gasped. "They're spectacular." But as she said this, Eva saw that her eyes were only on one fiddler. Her bejeweled, plump fingers came up to the hollow of her neck, where the matching diamonds sparkled, then traveled a little farther down, to the top of her cleavage, where they pressed slightly against the powdered skin, as if to steady the pulse there.

The maestro nudged Aleandro, pointed with his chin in an almost imperceptible way in her general direction. For a moment nothing happened, nothing changed, but then the maestro circled back around and nudged him again, this time with his elbow, whispered something in his ear.

A look was exchanged—sternness on the maestro's part, protest on Aleandro's—then he broke from the trio and made his way slowly across the room, working the bow faster, faster still. The woman reached into her purse, extracted something, flashed it in a nondescript way—either for the spectators or perhaps for the fiddler—and he moved closer, so close that she could now touch him. The woman leaned back in her chair so as to enjoy the full performance, her chest rising and falling.

There was a sound, a terrible scrape, which Eva realized with horror was her chair. The music tapered off, and all the eyes in the room fell on her. The room spun. She was trembling, so she stood and stepped away from her chair, nearly tripping on the edge of the rug.

She laughed, something that to her sounded more like a shriek. "Please excuse me, I'm not really in the mood for music tonight. I've really got a terrible headache. Please don't mind me. Enjoy your night."

Then she walked from the room, fighting the urge to run. On the other side of the door, she leaned on a wall, pressed her fingertips into the hollows of her eyes.

5

N O MORE THAN TWENTY MINUTES LATER, the band was asked to pack up and shown out by an impersonal valet who walked them through the bowels of the house and a long kitchen lined with polished cabinets and marble counters. Leading the way, with the maestro lamenting behind him, Aleandro was thinking about the girl, feeling as though a new window had been slammed shut on his heart. He didn't think he'd see her again that night. Then the door opened to reveal her standing there on the lawn under a light post, smoking a cigarette. Her back was turned, and she was no longer in her sequined dress but a drab pair of pants, an oversize shirt untucked, something silk, shimmering in the light. He wanted to continue on, to keep walking down the path along with the others, but she startled and turned, and he couldn't pretend he didn't see her. Instead, he told the others he would catch up, that they should go on without him, which they did, grumbling under their breath.

"Hello, Eva. It's Eva, right?" he said when they were alone, and she turned her face away a little, and her hand holding the cigarette rose up, stayed suspended as if she was deciding whether to take a drag or stomp it out in the grass. Her expression, though, was not impassive; it was as if she was asking something of him, and when she began walking into the depths of the lawn, he followed her. On a bench abutting the gates at the far end of the estate, they sat under a pergola with an overflowing trumpet vine that obscured them from view.

"I find myself at a loss for how to explain my behavior around you," she said with an honesty that took him aback. "I don't know why I left that way, but I do know that the evening was cut short on my account. And I feel terrible about it, Aleandro. I do. Because you play beautifully."

"It's really quite all right. It was your party, after all."

"But I do owe you an apology," she said. "Not just for tonight but for the time in the square. You see, that satchel, it has a very special meaning to me, and . . . well, what you did was perhaps one of the kindest, most thoughtful things anyone has ever done for me. And so yes, an apology is quite necessary. Can you forgive me?"

What could he say? His words fled him entirely. She was engaged (God, she was engaged!), and she owed him no explanations, but he was so touched by this that he couldn't help reaching for her hand, feeling his heart slide into a happiness that rose inside him like a crashing wave.

To his utter surprise, she didn't pull away but kept her gaze pinned on the span of the garden, blowing ringlets of smoke into the darkness, and he knew he had to say something to make her smile. The whole thing seemed far too serious. As if they'd reached the end of something, and he didn't want it to end.

"It was really nothing. As I said in town, I was very happy to help. As for tonight, well, if I had known it was you that we were hired to play for, I would have worn a better suit. My English wool tux, or something a little less assuming. Perhaps just a Hungarian number I had custom made. I have quite a closetful."

She not only smiled but laughed. She laughed, and to him it was like jumping into a clear blue stream in the height of summer.

"Well, perhaps you might return for a repeat performance someday."

"Sure. You can always give me a ring for one of your galas in Budapest."

She pretended to ponder. "No, I'm afraid that won't be possible."

"No?" he said, now quite seriously. "And why not?"

"You in Budapest? I fear you'd cause quite a stir at the society parties."

Was he mistaken, or was there a trace of jealousy in her voice? It emboldened him enough that without thinking, he blurted, "You know, back there . . . that woman. I didn't know that the maestro would insist . . . that . . ." God, he had to shut up before he spoiled everything.

"Well, you play that violin with such heart," she went on to his utter relief, which turned into disappointment as she extracted her hand. "How nice it must be to make a living doing something you truly love."

"The violin?" said Aleandro, trying not to lose his focus. "Oh, yes, thank you. When I play it's like . . . like falling into a different world. Same as when I draw. I suppose I am lucky in that regard, even though I fear being a fiddler isn't the most lucrative of vocations."

"You draw?" He hadn't meant to bring it up; it had merely slipped out, yet now he could sense in the darkness that she was looking at him in a new way. "Well, how wonderful. I've been coming here since I was a child, and the beauty of this place never fails to astound me. I wish I could sketch or paint it myself, but I haven't the talent for it."

"Oh, it's just something I do on occasion, a silly hobby, really . . ." He was about to tell her that it was in fact people that he enjoyed drawing more than landscapes, when they were interrupted by a sudden noise from the villa—voices, something that sounded like the shatter of glass. A wash of light spilled onto the lawn.

"You should go," Eva said. "They've come out to the terrace."

"Yes. I'm sorry that I won't be able to walk you back."

"No, no need to walk me back. I'll stay here a little while longer."

"Are you sure? You'll stay here alone, in the dark?"

"Alone?" She seemed faraway repeating it. "I come out here at night all the time. Precisely to be alone. This is the only spot on the entire grounds that belongs to me. It's my own secret corner." She smiled, somewhat wistfully, lovely in the shimmering ribbon of light. "Well, good night, Aleandro."

Reluctantly Aleandro stood, lifting his violin case from the foot of the bench. On a sudden impulse, he reached for her hand again and this time brought it up to his lips. "Sweet dreams, Miss Eva."

Then he walked through the grass along the length of the gates, willing his legs to carry him, thankful to intersect the graveled driveway at a point where he couldn't be seen.

———

All the way back to the shanty town, Aleandro was so consumed with the encounter in the garden that he'd forgotten entirely about his little brother whose fever had not abated for the better part of the week. Then, coming up the road, he spotted Lukas in the grass, curled up in a ball near the wall of their hut, and dashed toward him, stumbling along the way on some invisible stones.

"Lukas! You shouldn't be out here!" He scooped him up in his arms and tried to find his eyes, shook him, crushed him to his chest. "You promised me that you would try to rest. You promised that you would stay inside."

"Why, Andro?" Lukas's voice was sleepy, his arms somewhat listless as they went around his neck. "I tried to go to sleep, but I couldn't. It's too hot in there. And you know I can't sleep without you."

Back inside, where the twins were already asleep, Aleandro made Lukas some tea with a few drops of a lemon he'd picked from a yard. He smoothed a slice of bread with some olive oil he'd reluctantly taken from a tavern, watched Lukas take minuscule bites, which he knew were only for his benefit, then hummed him a song as he rocked him to sleep. After placing him in his cot gently, Aleandro took tonight's tips from his pocket and counted them by the window.

Thirty *pengös*. Thirty *pengös* was all that he'd walked away with. It would barely be enough to last him another week or two, assuming the baker's kindness would continue and those half-stale loaves of bread wouldn't be thrown in the trash at the close of the day before he could get there. Not enough for new oil pastels and paper—all of which he'd soon run out of altogether—not now, surely, when all that remained of his savings would be spent on food for the children. Not enough for aspirin, either.

Perhaps he shouldn't have put such faith in the whole affair; perhaps he should have accepted that other offer to play in Burgenland, to play at a real tavern, a real job that would mean steady pay, relief for his family. Yet he'd wanted to stay in Sopron a little while longer, didn't want to leave this place, his home, and after tonight, after seeing her in the garden, he wasn't sure he'd be able to leave anytime soon. What a fool he was!

That night, he couldn't get a wink of sleep. Couldn't sleep for a whole week after, and as he scrounged whatever he could earn in the town square playing for disinterested tourists, as he endured the cutting remarks of the maestro, who clearly blamed him, too, for the whole botched gig, Eva filtered through every minute of his miserable day. He didn't see her again at the café, didn't see her anywhere in the piazza, and yet he couldn't stop thinking of her, couldn't stop replaying every detail of their moments alone in the garden. How she looked in the soft glow from the terrace, how her hand felt like it belonged in his, and how her laughter revealed a whole world, a world that he'd like to know and never would.

He had to see her again.

But how? And for what purpose? he tried to reason with himself. What would someone like him possibly have to offer a girl like that, even if she wasn't engaged? A word of encouragement, a small reason to smile; what else could there be beyond what they'd already shared?

Nearly a dozen plans he'd concocted in recent nights—all elaborate, over-the-top, likely to get him arrested, and with little chance of success, at that. In his hot sheets, he tossed and groaned into his pillow, praying he wouldn't wake his brothers, who slept in cots next to him. It was hopeless. But tonight, tonight, just as the silvery light of dawn began to trickle through the window, a fragment of a thought came to him, piercing his state of half sleep.

The sketch pad of her portraits—there in her hands. But how could he not have seen it before? How could he not have thought of it sooner?

Later, he would tell himself that he should have stayed in bed, that he should have pulled a pillow over his face, that he should have gone for a swim, but in that moment, none of those things would have been possible. Already in his mind he was walking down the path under the glow of the moon, back toward the manor, guided by the vision of her looking upon what had been born of his hands.

———

It was still dark when he reached the villa. Around the tall iron gates, he slithered like a nocturnal cat, concealing his shadow from the garden lights, marveling once more at the sheer size of the estate, the vast windows and stately entrance, the statues of polished stone scattered throughout the garden. The stone bench on which he and Eva had talked was nearby—if he could only find it. *Her secret corner.*

Fumbling in the darkness, he thrust his hands through the tight iron slats and the brambles of rosebushes, searching for the surface, not minding the thorns scratching his skin. At last he felt it: the unmistakable roughness of limestone under his fingertips. Reaching farther through the shrubbery, he placed the sketchbook upon it, then disappeared as quickly as he had come, the blackness enclosing around him, drawing him further into its folds like a protective cloak.

6

*A*T PRECISELY FIVE O'CLOCK, LIKE EVERY morning, hours before a single stirring would emerge from the rooms upstairs, Dora dragged herself from her bed and made her way down the hallway to the kitchen, where she put on a kettle and dropped a bag of Earl Grey in a mug. Still in her robe and hair wound in curlers inside a net, she slipped through the back door and into the vegetable garden, where she sipped her tea at the wrought iron bistro table she had set up for herself under the olive tree. She relished the stillness, the white roses moist with dew swaying like tiny phantoms in the yielding darkness, the night breeze caressing her cheek in a cool whisper.

It was a busy time. The cleanup effort after the banquet—which had been left entirely in her hands after the temporary staff hired for the occasion had departed—had dawdled endlessly, and Isabel had been asking constantly for freshly pressed skirts and ribbons, changing three times a day, dragging in girls she knew from whatever corner of the province for tea or a game of cricket.

It was not that she minded Isabel (at times her joie de vivre injected the home with a much-needed energy) but rather that Eva, in the flurry of all that activity, seemed to have disappeared. Most mornings she didn't even come down for breakfast and slept until Dora went to her room and wrenched open the curtains. Then she would be out on the veranda with her books, sunglasses perched on her nose to hide her gaze, which seemed always pinned not on the pages but on the contour of the hillside or the vastness of the sky.

How strange she'd been this summer, Dora thought. Ever since she'd arrived more than three weeks prior, she'd been removed, taciturn. Even their conversations about the vegetable garden, which they'd planted together (their *joint work of love*, as Eva had described it only the summer before), were met with only mild interest. And that bothered Dora the most, this new distance between them, which had been in the past reserved for others, the space that Eva created around herself like a fortress that couldn't be breached.

In the months after Mrs. César's death, Dora came to think of Eva as her own child. During that long summer, not a word of tenderness was addressed to Eva—only commands, which Eva had met with a silent obedience. It made Dora's blood boil. *Sit, go upstairs, brush your hair, brush your teeth.* Mr. César himself was hardly able to meet her eyes during those weeks, and his sister, who'd joined unexpectedly, regarded her with a thin, immutable smile, as if waiting for her to finish recounting whatever story so that she could be sent on her way. No one seemed to consider that the girl, too, had suffered a great loss, that perhaps she needed a kind word or a smile, a set of arms to embrace her. The only available ones, it seemed, had been Dora's.

The day she packed Eva's luggage to go back to Budapest, Eva burst into tears.

"Don't send me back," she begged. But what could she say, Dora remembered fretting, as Eva spread herself out on the bed and buried her face in a pillow. At the end of the season, the villa would be closed, the furniture draped in sheets, and Dora would return to her home. Surely they couldn't stay here, in this vast empty space, just the two of them, and besides, Dora needed to get back to her steadier restaurant job, which she worked outside of the summer months. But the way Eva had looked up from the depths of the pillow shattered Dora's heart, and in the glimpse of a moment, she'd made her decision.

Later that afternoon, perched on a damask chair across from Mr. César and his sister, she explained that it could be done. That Eva was in no shape to return to Budapest, where only three months earlier she'd seen her mother's casket lowered into the ground, and that besides, now that Dora's home was empty as well, she could take care of her through the fall, if they didn't mind having her stay. It had seemed like a preposterous proposition, downright ludicrous, and Dora had expected a definitive no, perhaps even a stern admonishing. Instead, the pair exchanged a long look. Mr. César looked in the fireplace, then looked again at his sister, and in that single look, it seemed as if a decision had been made.

"If you're sure," the sister said, leaning against the fireplace and wrapping her woolen cardigan tightly around her. "We will pay you, of course."

A week later, Dora took Eva to her one-bedroom home with the leaky roof and noisy pipes on the outskirts of Sopron, and as the leaves fell from the trees later that year, then the frost came in an overnight storm, there was no sign of her father. It wasn't until the following summer that he returned, not with the sister this time, but with a lady friend, a tall, exceedingly slim young woman with a minuscule, upturned nose and large gray eyes who looked upon Eva as though startled to learn of her existence.

She did end up going back to Budapest at the end of that summer, fifteen months after she'd arrived. And in all that time spent together, Dora, in her heart, had never been more convinced that Eva had been sent to her by God to rebuild life again. Life again in the wake of loss, love that was still possible beyond a beloved husband, a beloved mother.

Perhaps—Dora considered now, finishing her tea—it was the engagement that had caused this recent change in Eva. Now that she was soon to be married, Eva needed no nannying, nor mothering; what she needed was her independence. Still, Dora couldn't help feeling that there was a deeper need in Eva, something that couldn't be assuaged—and Dora's inability to fill it as she had in the past deeply unsettled her.

She looked up at the horizon, which was beginning to lighten, and she stood, lifting herself heavily out of her chair. She began walking back toward the house, when she heard a sound behind her, a rustling of sorts. A bird, or several, she thought at first, but then she heard footsteps. She raised the lantern up to her face but couldn't make out anything beyond the glare, and a tremor of panic shivered through her.

"Who's there?" she shouted in the direction of the sound.

"It's me, only me," came the voice, and Dora breathed out with relief.

"Eva, sweetheart, what on God's earth are you doing out here at this hour? You gave me a fright!" On further thought, her eyebrows creased into a frown. "Please don't tell me you're smoking cigarettes before dawn now!"

Eva emerged from the shadow in quick, quiet steps, not in her robe but rather in a chiffon floral dress with a golden locket at her neck—both of which, Dora recalled with a flinch of surprise, were from the night before.

"I . . . I was just getting some air," she explained. "Not smoking, I promise." Even in this light, Dora could see the flush in her cheeks, an alertness in her eyes, which seemed out of place, given the hour. There was something in her hand, something that Eva drew behind the folds of her skirt.

Eva said nothing more, just walked past her to the iron table and sat down. She didn't speak for a while. She placed on the table what Dora saw now was a journal. Shivering, she drew her feet up on the chair and wrapped her arms around her knees, her eyes pinned on the object.

"You know, Eva," Dora said, sitting back down in her chair and reaching for Eva's hand, "you can talk to me about anything. Darling . . ." What could she really say? How strange she'd been acting? How strange it was that she was here beside her at dawn, in last night's clothes, at that?

"Is it the wedding, Eva?"

"The wedding?" Eva looked up, surprised. "No. I was just out for a walk. What makes you think that?"

"Sometimes weddings . . . they can be straining. One like yours, especially. But you know, it will be behind you soon. You mustn't let it consume you so much. If you can find a way to see beyond it, I think, it will not seem so scary. And, dear Eva, you know I'm here to help." She scooted in closer and smoothed Eva's hair behind her ear. "Whatever it is, you know you can trust me. So talk to me, darling."

"I do trust you, Dora, of course I do. You are like my own mother. But it isn't the wedding." Eva turned her head away and looked out across the emptiness, across the graveled path, the darkness.

"What is it, then, love?" Dora squeezed her hand. "Your happiness is all that I care about. You know you can tell me anything."

"It must be all this heat. It's . . . it's been draining me. I can't sleep well, that's all. But thank you, Dora. I know you are here for me. And I love you for it. I love you so much."

Yet even as Eva said this, she lowered her eyes and pulled that pad of paper from the table, close to her chest as if to protect it. Then she stood and went into the house, slipping off her heels at the kitchen door, closing it softly behind her.

7

A FEW MINUTES AFTER THE UNEXPECTED RUN-IN, Eva slipped inside her room and locked the door, then threw herself on the bed. Under the light of the lamp, she flipped through the sketchbook, seeing that what she'd glimpsed on the garden bench (she had in fact been sneaking a cigarette before sunrise) was not a mirage. It was her, all right, in each of the charcoal drawings. At least half a dozen of them, although not exactly the way she saw herself in the mirror when she combed her hair to a gloss or fastened pearls in her ears.

In the first portrait, there was a deep crease between her brows as she bent over her book at the café, her bitten fingernails she normally hid inside silk gloves gripping the cover. In the other, her eyes, darkened to a shade of polished steel in fine graphite strokes, stared hauntingly into the vacantness of the square after she lost her satchel. The last one had captured her on that same bench in the piazza, but from a different angle: her hair swept over her shoulder exposed the silvery scar over her right eyebrow, which she'd acquired falling from a swing. That scar, above all, which she took great pains to style her hair around, was now the focal point.

To be observed so closely! It was as if she'd been drawn naked, in a way that should have angered her, yet as she looked on, at who she really was and what she tried to hide from the world, from herself even, tears rose in her eyes.

That long afternoon, her gaze stayed pinned on the clock. There was a quick lunch with the guests waiting to catch the three o'clock train. Suitcases were hauled into the great entrance from upstairs as Isabel fretted that she was missing one of her parasols. Someone had brought flowers in from the garden, and the smell of lilac made Eva somewhat nauseous and restless. Restless. She watched the sun soften in the vast windows, then waved good-bye in the driveway, promised Isabel that she'd come to Vienna after the wedding, words that barely touched her ears. Then she was on her old bike, which she'd pulled from the toolshed, knowing that her father was slumped in a chair dozing in an afternoon haze of wine, and that Dora would be too busy cleaning to question where she had gone—and she was riding away from the villa, the wind whipping her hair, the sketchbook thumping in the basket in front of her as she scaled the graveled road.

At the fishing pond where she'd seen others pass en route to the gypsy camp, she sat in a shady patch and waited, watching the half-naked children splash about in the water. A group of women washed clothes, stretching them out to dry on the bedrock, and she felt self-conscious knowing that in their pleasant enough smiles her presence was seen as an intrusion.

She withstood their looks nonetheless, but after nearly an hour she was ready to ride back. It was not disappointment she felt but almost a sense of relief—she had come after all and nothing happened. But as she positioned her bike and checked the tires, she saw him—her fiddler. His eyes, she could see even from this far away, were pinned to the ground, the fiddle strap drawn across his chest, a look of consternation in the crease of his eyebrow. When he saw her, he froze, his hands coming down slowly from the strap and landing at his sides. He was wearing the same outfit from that night at the villa, and seeing him again for what he was pierced the grandiose fantasies she'd been entertaining all day.

Turning her bike around, Eva began walking it the other way, guiding it alongside the edge of the water. She did not know if he would follow. She no longer knew what she'd intended to say at all. She passed the children, through willows that dove into the bank, through the ensuing patch of reed beds, and farther on. At the narrow wooden pier, she stopped and turned to look behind her—and he was still there. Leaning her bike against a tree, she lifted the sketchbook from the basket, held it in her outstretched hands as some kind of an offering.

"These," she began. "They are yours."

She felt slightly off-kilter being so close to him in daylight, the slant of sun falling between them offering a barrier so easily crossed. He walked into it and beyond it, closing the space between them, and she felt herself stepping back, as if reaching for some safeguard that wasn't there. Sensing it, he turned toward the lake, ran a hand through his hair.

"Do you like them?"

"Like them? Yes. But . . . why?" Eva said simply.

"I can't explain why, only that I wanted you to have them. Think of them as a gift."

"A gift?"

"Yes, a gift. Do you not believe in gifts, Eva?"

He turned to her, held her gaze, and in the silence, it seemed to her that a different conversation was taking place. His eyes danced with light, as if no further explanations or reasons were needed, as if any words beyond the ones spoken would only reduce what his drawings meant. They were more than a gift. It was clear in the way he'd drawn her, in the way he was looking at her now, and she knew that she should go. That she should set the sketchbook on the grass and climb back on her bike, ride back to the villa. But she did not move, and she felt some inexplicable sadness or regret rising up within her, which she couldn't push back.

Stepping closer, he reached for her hand, flooding her with the familiarity of the night on the bench. "I don't know why I drew them, Eva. Only that it's something I had to do. And I wanted you to see them. I hoped that you would see in them what I see."

"They are beautiful. The most beautiful things I've ever seen."

"They are true," he said in reply.

And they both looked out to the glassy pond, where a fishing canoe glided solitarily.

As the sunset deepened into a purple haze, Eva and Aleandro sat together in the grass and she told him things she'd never shared with anyone, not even Eduard: things about her life, her family. About her mother's death and how Eva found herself grasping for anything that would keep her alive in her mind, and about her happiest days, when they were still a family, when she still had a mother as much as a father, who, at some point, was lost to her as well. She told him her dreams of becoming a nurse were important to her, because she didn't want to become trapped, like many women of her standing, in a life of idle meaninglessness.

In turn, he told her about the meaning of his art and what he felt when he was drawing. How he hoped that someday, if he applied himself, it might lead him to a better life. He confessed about his parents, who had died two years prior in the typhus epidemic, which had torn through the gypsy town, and his younger brothers, whom he'd been taking care of ever since.

"Look," he said, extracting a battered sepia photograph from his pants pocket. "That's them. My brothers. I carry their picture in my pocket so I can never forget the reason for my existence. And I love them, Eva. I want to be a good father to them, to give them a happy childhood. That is my greatest purpose."

Her eyes misted studying the photograph. They both had wounds, yet perhaps in these moments together, they found some measure of healing, and she set her head on his shoulder.

"Your portraits," she said in the long pause that ensued. "You know that I can't keep them."

"Why? Why can't you?"

"Because I wouldn't be able to explain where they came from. I'd have to hide them in a drawer, and such lovely things should not be hidden. They should be kept in the open."

"Well, perhaps they don't belong on a mantel behind framed glass. But there will be more, and I hope you will at least indulge me by looking at them. No one else has to know of them. Only us."

And she believed it. She believed that those portraits belonged only to him and her, that they were simply a glimpse in time that no one else had seen, nor ever would. And also, she knew that indeed more facets of her would be caught in the strokes of his pencils, perhaps her right now, in the grass next to him. But of this she couldn't approve openly, and without further word, she got up and fetched her bike. As she rode off, she knew he was watching her, and her heart in that moment never felt fuller.

8

HE Sopron estate, with its optimal sun exposure
and stark change in temperature from day to night, had
every advantage to produce some of the best wine in all
of Europe. Sándor Bartok decided this as he strolled through
the province that late afternoon. Now that his son and wife
had departed along with the others for Vienna, he could finally
tackle the reason for his visit, and the afternoon seemed like
the perfect time. It hadn't taken him long, after all, in those
very first days after arrival, to see that a grape-export business
here would bring in a small fortune. Three hundred acres of
vineyards packed with the tightest, most translucent, most
perfect grapes that he had ever seen—and that aroma! In each
grape he tasted, it was as though a different bottle revealed
itself, and the variations—from dry, to sweet, to dark—had
made him nearly giddy with excitement.

He was not a man of rash decisions and wanted to see the full land for himself. Besides, the more he reflected on Vladimir's proposition over the past week, the more he began to see how myopic it had really been. So much more than grape export could be mined from a land such as this. Over the past two nights in particular, his vision had expanded from a modest label to one not so modest, if he was willing to open his pockets wide. Twenty thousand bottles—no, fifty—could be produced every year. He'd practically designed the label in his dream: the lush view from the veranda faded in sepia tones, his name, Bartok, in gold lettering as if emerging from the depths of the hillside. Fifty thousand bottles carrying his name, competing with even the most pretentious ones from the Loire Valley or Bourgogne.

The only thing dampening his vision—and the other reason for this prolonged promenade—was to see for himself the gypsy camp near the estate, which was less than ideal. All he could hope for, as he walked on through the rows of vines then down the small gravel road toward the dreaded site, was that things would settle themselves of their own accord quickly. It was about time that Hungarian authorities stopped dragging their feet and followed the example of his own country. As far as he was concerned, these gypsies were no more than vermin who could only be counted on to steal from the cellars. The sooner they were all rounded up and transported east, the better.

He strolled farther on. Perhaps it was there, on that very bank, which the gypsies insisted on polluting with their rags and filth, that he could set up his wine cellars—if all went his way by the time the papers were signed.

Yet he had come a little too late in the day, he realized, too late to survey the full activity to his satisfaction. Only two figures hovered on the edge of the pond, their silhouettes a blur in the flare of brightness reflected in the water. They looked like something he sometimes spotted on the covers of his wife's romance novels—both slim, young, striking—although in this tableau, unlike in those covers, they were not intertwined in a swirl of passion. Only their heads were bent together as if they were sharing a confession. The girl threw her head back and laughed, and that was when Sándor saw who it was, and withdrew in the shade of a tree.

A little while longer he watched them. It was her, all right. Vladimir's daughter. He had to stifle a laugh, recalling her at today's lunch, tapping her foot under the table, pressing her lips as he complimented her on her dress, and how she'd looked away from him in the middle of the next sentence, offering him her beautiful profile as if it was enough contribution to what he was saying. And here she was, sitting in the meadow like a common peasant, with her feet stripped of shoes. And with a man, no less—a man who was surely not her fiancé. No, far from it. A moment longer Sándor studied him, the wildness of his hair, the dark skin and threadbare shirt.

He turned away in disgust. Of course, he might have gone to her, presented himself, admonished her as he might his own daughter. But he would do nothing of the kind.

He smiled as he departed quietly in the other direction. The ache in his bones lightened at what he could only see as an advantage. An advantage in his negotiation with Vladimir.

July 20, 1943

My dearest Eva,

I speak from the heart when I say that Budapest without you is like a dreary day in winter with no promise of sun, or warmth. The things that I've seen, Eva, in the past weeks fill me only with desire for a different decision, if one could have been made.

They say that forty thousand Hungarian boys were killed on the Eastern Front and that sixty thousand more are now prisoners beyond our borders. That the ones who have made it home are the lucky ones. Though how can they be lucky, I often ask myself, how, when they arrive in such a state? Some have been dragged through the snow across the border crossing, some arrived wearing no shoes and with wounds festering behind soiled bandages. Nearly all of them suffer from dysentery, and there is little I can do for so many of them. I look into each pair of eyes, hold each boy's hands, lift water to his lips. I tell him he will be all right, that he must be strong, knowing well enough that at sundown, when I return for my rounds, a different soldier will occupy this very same bed. And I weep, Eva, I weep when no one is looking.

When I leave the hospital at midnight, Budapest unfolds calmly, though it is a heavy calmness. Horthy holds strong against Hitler's wishes for mass deportations, although with the latest news out of Poland, I'm gripped with a terrible fear for what might still come. A colleague of mine suggests that if he is to continue along this path, a full invasion of Hungary is likely. Words of pessimism, which I choose not to believe.

Certainly, with such disastrous losses at the hands of the Red Army, Germany cannot sustain this madness much longer. It is what I pray for, what we all pray for.

How are you, my darling? I haven't heard a word from you since you left. Perhaps in Sopron, away from all this, you do not want to hear of such things. I do not blame you, but honesty is what we've promised each other, Eva, and I know that any other words beyond these genuine ones would only worry you. All I can say is that in the dreariness of my days, my thoughts of you and our wonderful spring together console me. In my dreams I am there at your side, walking the vineyards with you, hearing your voice soft in my ear telling me, as you did on our last evening together, that you love me. Please write, dearest.

Yours,
Eduard

9

THE LATEST LETTER FROM EDUARD WAS still on Eva's nightstand, unopened. In the four days since it arrived, she'd picked it up and set it down more than a dozen times, unable to read it. At some point, she considered sending back a letter of her own, explaining that the wedding arrangements had been made in haste and she needed more time. He wouldn't be happy, but he would understand in his generous, kindhearted way, and once she was free of the impending event, she would figure out what to do next. But figure out what, exactly? Whatever it was that she felt for Aleandro, it was all so very new and fragile, as easily breakable as a porcelain cup. And could she really give up Eduard? Could she give up the life she'd envisioned for herself with him, her dreams for the future?

Still, despite her endless consternation, for the third night in a row she slipped out at half past ten and made her way to the edge of the estate, where Aleandro would wait for her near an abandoned wine cellar, which had become their meeting place. The first two nights they went no farther—they just sat in the grass and he showed her his latest work under the dim light of a lantern—but tonight, he did not bring his sketchbook.

Rather, they walked farther through the field of high grass to the top of the hill opposite the villa, from which she could make out the faint contour of the gypsy camp. To the left of the clustered rooflines and garments strewn on crisscrossing lines, a spark of light bloomed in the darkness. A bonfire, Eva recognized, as they kept walking closer.

Twenty-odd figures were gathered around it—women with babies in their laps, older children roughhousing, men playing cards and passing a flask around, laughing—and she was struck by the beauty of the scene, knowing that in the circles of her life dominated by propriety and etiquette, she would never know what it was like to share such closeness. A fiddler—the elderly one she recognized from the villa—launched into a ballad, a soft, tremulous melody that seeped through her like a warm liquid. There were words in the gypsy dialect, which Eva didn't understand, and she hesitated going any closer.

"It's all right," Aleandro said. "I promise. You don't have to be afraid."

"I'm not afraid of them. Not any more than I'm afraid of you," Eva said haughtily, and he laughed. "It's more that . . . well, it doesn't seem right. I don't think they will like it."

"There are no rules here, Eva. Here, there is only freedom. Freedom, and the magic of the night that belongs to us all. You'll see."

Yet she wasn't entirely wrong, for as they emerged into plain view, the voices and the music trailed off.

"This is Eva," Aleandro announced. His words hung in the air listlessly, and Eva took a step back, but Aleandro grasped for her hand. "She is my friend. And she came to hear you play, not to see you stare. So come on, let's get on with it. Let's show the lady how we play among ourselves."

With some murmurs of disapproval, the figures around the fire finally resumed movement and the *notà* picked up again. Someone handed her plum brandy in a rusty tin cup, as if daring her to drink it, and a little girl scooted herself closer to her mother to make room, still regarding Eva suspiciously.

Next to Aleandro, Eva sat, pulling the folds of her skirt tightly around her. There was a guitar playing now, a rich, raspy voice joining it, the quick, rhythmic clapping of hands, the metallic thump of a tambourine. Closing her eyes, she tipped her head back to the stars, then somehow she was on her feet again, her hand in Aleandro's.

It was like no other dance she knew, so she let him lead her. She stumbled and laughed, and he pulled her closer, his arm tightening around her waist. She tried to focus on her feet, but all that she was acutely aware of was his hand on the small of her back, there, where it burned through her dress, and the hardness of his shoulders under her fingertips. For an instant she closed her eyes, overcome with the brandy and his proximity, and when she opened them again, he was staring down at her. All she had to do was tilt her chin up to him and his lips would be on hers.

A boy launched himself at his legs. It jolted Eva, broke the spell, and with her heart still pounding, she watched Aleandro bend down to pick up the boy.

"Sweet Jesus! You sneaky little rascal! What are you doing here at this hour? You scared me half to death!"

The boy only gave a raspy little laugh and Aleandro lifted him onto his shoulders. From above him, the boy beamed at Eva. He had beautiful eyes, exactly like Aleandro's, large and dark, endless in depth. That smile, she thought, it was the most beautiful smile she'd ever seen on a child.

"Well, who's this?" she said. "Let me guess. Are you Lukas?"

"Ah! You know me! You know my name!" He leaned down and whispered in Aleandro's ear, even though it was loud enough that Eva could hear. "Can we bring her home, Andro? Tamás made soup. Maybe she's hungry. She looks awful skinny. But real pretty. She's prettier than in your pictures."

"Soup?" said Aleandro, quirking an eyebrow. "Well, I don't know. Besides, you should be sleeping." He gave Lukas's leg a firm tap and set him back down on the ground. "When are you going to start listening to me? Just a week ago you were burning up like a cinder and now you're running around at almost midnight. I told you before, I told you a dozen times: if you're going to get your strength back, you need to rest!"

In reply, the boy stretched his arms over his head and pushed himself to a handstand, wiggled his spindly little legs in the air, then came back up with a triumphant smile. "See? I'm strong again. Now can we bring her?"

"No, Lukas, I don't think she's hungry at this hour . . ."

"I'd love to come," said Eva. "I'd love to come! Thank you for your invitation, Lukas. As it turns out, I'm famished. And I'd love to meet your brothers."

There wasn't any soup. It was all a ruse, and all Aleandro could offer her in a hurry was water and a drop of overly sweet home-made wine, but it hardly mattered. At the small wooden table, she sat with his brothers who were drawing pictures of their own with some old pastel bits, as if to compete with Aleandro. There was only a lantern on the table, the nubs of coloring sticks no bigger than pencil erasers—a treasure trove. They fought over them, fought with such fierceness that Aleandro threatened to throw all the colors into the pond if they didn't quit.

"I'm sorry, they can be very unruly sometimes," he offered to Eva, then a little louder in their direction: "Downright rebellious! Tonight, it seems, especially!"

"Oh, they are fine, Aleandro." Eva laughed, as the boys were now poking one another under the table with their feet. "They are lovely! And who would have known, such budding little artists?"

She was tempted to blurt out that she could buy new pastels for them, and for Aleandro, too, but knew he would find it insulting, and she wasn't going to go back there again. Instead, she rose from the table and pushed through the threadbare cloth that separated the kitchen from the rest of the space. "Did I tell you that I'm an artist, too?" Silence greeted her from the other side. She poked her head through. "No soup, but I see you have lemon and garlic. And some leftover bread. And, from what I can gather here, some rosemary and olive oil." She held up the little tavern jar and the bunched herbs. "And do you know what you get when you mince all these things together? No, maybe you don't. So you're in for a treat."

She glanced at Aleandro, saw him smiling widely in the same way Lukas had smiled at her at the fire earlier.

"Don't move," he said. "Stay like that for just one moment longer." Then he reached for one of the pastel bits and a sheet of paper on the table, and as she stood in the partition holding the jar and the herbs, he drew her.

———

Their meetings after that night were no longer contained solely to the hours after dark. Her father (to Eva's great relief) was absorbed in business, and he spent entire afternoons in his study or entertaining that awful man he hoped would become his partner. Often Eva would go into town and watch Aleandro play, not minding Dora's warnings and endless reproaches. Later they'd walk back together to the gypsy camp, and she would fill him in on things she was learning in her anatomy books. He in turn would talk about his art, which seemed to preoccupy him a great deal lately.

"This painting I do," he told her one such afternoon. "It feels urgent, like it demands to be heard. But often I think, is this just an indulgence? A foolish dream? I mean, I should be focused only on caring for my sweet brothers, Lukas above all, whose health has been fragile since he was born. Yet I want my brothers, my people, to be left with a legacy, and my drawings may be all I can offer. I want to leave something of significance behind; I want my brothers to know that they were raised in a beautiful culture, a place of love and acceptance. That, to me, is equally important."

Wiping wetness from the corners of her eyes, Eva nodded. She had to admit that she, too, was growing fond of his brothers. She liked their openness, their toughness, their acceptance of her. Loved the way they doodled alongside Aleandro as he sketched her at the pond, the way they carved all of their names inside a giant heart on a chestnut tree after Aleandro had shown them how to do it. They wanted to be like him. And the others looked at him the same way in the gypsy camp, where lately, they walked together unabashedly. She'd never in her life seen someone so willing to help out his neighbors—chop wood, carry buckets of water—not out of obligation but because his people were everything to him. And they loved him back. They loved him enough to tolerate her presence, to ask her what she wanted them to play at the bonfire, to let her inside the folds of their customs, which they protected so dearly. Even if it was just for the moment, they did it for him.

All this time, Aleandro still did not kiss her. Sometimes the desire to touch him, to be in his arms and press her lips in the dark, shallow groove at his throat, was unbearable, yet she knew that they'd be crossing a fault line that couldn't be uncrossed. And it frightened her. It frightened her as much as the fact that summer was slipping away.

———

One afternoon, instead of going into town to find Aleandro, Eva headed directly toward the gypsy camp. She knew that Aleandro's brothers would tag along with the other children to the pond in the afternoon, and hoped she could find Lukas. Her father had left for Vienna just an hour earlier and would be gone until the next day, which opened the window for what she had in mind. Still, she had to hurry. The day was almost over, and the stables back at the estate would be closed soon, the horses brought in for the evening.

It was Lukas who spotted her first and came running up to her, shaking droplets of water from his black curls, pulling up on the band of his oversize shorts, which had no doubt belonged to his brothers.

"Eva, Andro's not back. But"—he held up a finger in a very adult sort of way, which she imagined she'd learned from Aleandro—"I, Lukas, is a great entertainer!" He pondered. "If you wait here for Andro, I can sing you some songs! Or! I can teach you cartwheels. Cartwheels are fun!"

"They are," she agreed. "I love cartwheels! But, you know, today I thought we'd do something different."

"Different?"

"Yes, sort of an adventure."

"Ah, adventure!" His eyes widened with excitement. "Yes, let's do adventure! I love adventures."

"Well, come on, then," Eva said, clasping his tiny hand. "You always said that you wanted to ride a horse. And I've got one just the perfect size for you."

A half hour later, she watched the way Lukas smiled seeing the pony, the way his face beamed with joy and how he kissed its moist nose, caressed his mane. He had no shoes on, but when he scaled the horse, it was with confidence, curling the soles of his feet close to the pony's flank to keep him in place. He leaned his whole body against him as if melting with him.

"He likes me! Don't you, boy?" Another noisy kiss landed between the pony's ears.

"Go slow, Lukas," she told him, holding on to the pony's

reins. "He is young like you, and you will need to ride him slowly. You will need to let him trust you."

They went around the pen, in a brisk trot at first, then in a gallop, stirring dust. A squeal came from Lukas, even though she told him that they needed to be quiet, to not draw attention. But she didn't care. All she cared about was this moment of happiness she was making possible for a boy whose parents had died, who only had a good meal on occasion and was prone to fevers, yet loved life.

At sunset, after returning the pony to the stable, Eva walked Lukas back to the camp. It was a warm, beautiful evening, and as they ambled through the vineyards and grass bathed in gold, Eva found it impossible to keep up with Lukas's enthused chatter. She'd worn her favorite summer dress—the same red dress she'd worn in the square when she and Aleandro had met—but the hem had become caked in mud, and she knew there wasn't enough time to go back to the villa to change. Her hair had also come loose from its French braid, but her skin was warmed by the sun, and after all, she hardly thought that Aleandro would notice. Still, she wanted to look pretty tonight. She wanted to look her best when she delivered her news.

"Today I became a man!" Lukas interrupted her thoughts. "I harnessed him good, didn't I? Did you see how that big ol' horse listened to me?"

"A pony," Eva corrected as she ruffled his hair. "A pony, just like you!"

He beamed. "That pony, is he yours?"

"Yup. He's mine, all right." She bent down to find his eyes. "And perhaps, Lukas, if you can give me a little time to arrange it, I could bring you back to see him soon."

"Tomorrow!"

"Well, maybe not tomorrow, but soon, Lukas, soon. Anyway, it's good to have things to look forward to, don't you think?" Eva said as they came up the hillside.

Then she saw him, saw a figure approaching, and she knew it was him. Aleandro. He, too, saw them and rushed in their direction. Putting one arm around Eva and the other around Lukas, he led them through the final stretch of the valley toward the bonfire already in bloom, and all the reasons Lukas was offering why tomorrow was an ideal day to return to the stables scattered around Eva like dust blown from a palm.

———

After the bonfire, after the usual brandy and songs, after the children had been brought home and tucked into their beds, Eva and Aleandro strolled through the darkened valley. The fire had long gone out and the air smelled of pine and honeysuckle, and he was unusually silent, no more than a shadow beside her. All night he'd been looking at her a bit strangely, although not less lovingly, his gaze shifting often to Lukas with something she couldn't quite read. She was glad she could be alone with him at last. Glad she could tell him what she was thinking, what she'd been thinking all afternoon. Yet it was him who spoke first.

"Thank you, Eva. Thank you for what you did today. For Lukas."

"It was really nothing. I know how much he hates that all the horses in the camp are too big for him to ride. I hope you don't mind me not asking you first. Truly, I wanted to, but there was no time."

"Of course not. To see Lukas in such high spirits, how could I ever mind? It's just . . ." He stopped speaking. Stopped and lifted his hand up toward the breeze as they walked. "Do you feel that? Do you feel the change in the air?"

She did. She, too, had felt it for several days. "Aleandro, I've been meaning to tell you . . . I don't think I'll leave for Budapest as planned. Not yet. I can delay maybe until the end of September, October even . . ."

He halted. Turned to her slowly, with effort, as if willing his whole body into the movement.

"Eva."

A slow breath. "Yes?"

"Tell me about him. Please. We talk about everything else but him. So tell me what he is like. I need to know."

It was so direct, but she liked this about Aleandro, liked that he didn't mince words, and she also knew he had every right to ask. She couldn't pretend that Eduard wasn't here between them in these stolen moments, that things had not already gone too far.

"He is . . ." she began, weighing how much to reveal or to hold back. "He is not like many people I meet in my everyday life. He loves his work as a doctor, much as you love your painting or your violin, and he's generous, kind. He respects me. I suppose that's what I like most about him. He treats me as an equal, and always would."

"And you will marry him. You will go back to your life eventually and marry him. Whether you delay leaving here or not."

What could she really say? What assurances to give?

The truth was that she had no idea what she would do in the fall. Her whole world felt as though it was splintering before her. "Look, Aleandro, this is so very new, so . . . unexpected. I didn't expect any of this to happen." She held her hands out to him as in a plea. "I don't know, honestly, what I'm supposed to do."

Again silence. He didn't try to comfort her; rather, he drifted farther into the depths of the valley, into a place that was apart from them, and she couldn't bear this distance between them. It was she who came to him and draped her arms around his waist, burying her face in his back, inhaling his smell. He smelled of beer halls and fire, he smelled of Sopron, of home. Whatever stood between them, nothing would alter this simple truth.

"I don't know what to do, Aleandro," she repeated against his shirt, tears rising in her eyes. "Please tell me what I should do."

Turning to her, he took her hand and they resumed walking. There was an oak, a sturdy trunk a hundred years old, and he drew her against it, with her back to his chest. She felt his fingers below the clasp of her necklace, tracing an invisible line over her sunburned shoulder, slowly, as if to imprint its curve. Then he spoke. Softly he spoke into her ear:

"You know exactly what to do, Eva. There is nothing I can give you, nothing at all beyond a small measure of happiness, and in our world, that's hardly enough. If you stay, there's a good chance that you'll regret it someday. And I don't want regret between us."

"But how can I leave now? And what about your brothers? What will happen to them?"

"The Romani, you know, we are survivors. But you have a bright future ahead, a wonderful life that I can't offer you." A pause stretched, Aleandro steeling himself for what he would say next: "So go. Go now, Eva. Please. I'll stay here and watch you go. I want to remember you like this, in your red summer dress."

For a long moment, she didn't move, couldn't move, and she remained against him, her heart thundering against his chest in this great empty valley where there was no sound now, no glow of fire. She knew he was right. There would be no place for them in this divided world. She didn't belong with the Romani any more than he belonged in her world; they'd both been stealing time. Still, she couldn't accept that this was the last time she would see him, couldn't imagine what it would be like to wake the next day knowing they wouldn't meet again.

When she finally forced herself to step away, she couldn't look at him, and kept her back turned as she walked off, shivering in her thin dress. After a few steps, she broke into a full run, back to her old life, her sandals in her hands, the soggy earth underneath her feet. Halfway through the valley, she could go no farther, and she sank into the grass, letting her tears flow.

10

SHE HAD BEEN SO CAREFUL. So careful to leave the house unseen, to not leave behind a trace of her absence, to lock the front door. To disguise fatigue into preoccupation, to conceal the torment of her heart behind smiles. So when her father called her into his study the next morning, the last thing she expected was to be confronted with proof.

Four photographs in all. All black-and-whites, blurry, taken with a cheap camera. All lined up in a neat row in front of her, cataloging the trail of her deceit.

"It's not what you think, Papa."

"Not what I think?"

"No."

She couldn't tell him that, in fact, it was over—that these photographs meant nothing now and how her heart, seeing them, was raked fresh with regret and longing. He had changed her, changed something fundamental in her, and even though she would never see him again, the whole thing was serious indeed, more serious than he could imagine.

"I've sacrificed everything for you, Eva," her father shouted. "I've given you the best of everything. I've raised you to be a lady! A lady, Eva! And this is how you repay me? By disgracing me? By compromising my reputation, our family name?"

He scooped up the photographs and scrunched them in his fist, shoved them in her face. "Look at these! My very own daughter, running around in plain sight with this *parasite*! I know what he is, Eva! I saw the way you looked at him at the party, while everyone no doubt laughed behind your back! Laughed at you, at me."

"Papa, please try to calm down—he's only a friend," she tried to reason. Her father was still in his robe, unshaven, something unhinged in his gray eyes, which normally regarded her with a glassy, impersonal aloofness. There were papers strewn on the rug near the desk, a shattered crystal tumbler, a picture of her mother in a silver frame—which she bent down to pick up.

"Leave it!" he roared. "Don't you dare move from that chair, Eva!"

"Why don't you go up and change and we can talk about this a little later," Eva went on in that same mild tone even though she was shaken with fear. "I'll have Dora put on some coffee and clean up this mess and we can talk a little later."

"Dora? Oh, no, no, my dear, Dora isn't here. I sent her home just an hour ago. While you were sleeping off your lit- tle . . . escapade, I threw her out of the house. She's gone. She's never to come back."

"What are you talking about?" She couldn't blink suddenly, couldn't breathe. So this was how he would punish her. He would take away the only person in the world who cared for her. "Papa! How could you? Dora had nothing to do with this! Nothing! You had no right!"

"No right? Oh, I had every right! Every right, when you comport yourself with no regard for anyone but yourself and your cheap little whims, with no regard for me or even for your fiancé." He paused. "When my own associate throws it in my face as a bargaining chip meant to demean me. Dora covers for you! She enables you to behave like a whore!"

She stood, still under his enraged gaze, and steadied herself on the edge of the desk. Then without further word, she turned toward the door. All she saw was the oak paneling with the squares of stained glass; she just needed to reach and walk through it. She was nearly there when he came for her. His hand gripped her hair, yanking it, and his open palm struck her face. She was crying, yet she knew she had to remain still, very still. A single movement would only provoke him more. Provoke him to do a great deal worse.

He forced her to turn, shoved her forward into the depths of the room. She stumbled but regained her balance and as she did, something unleashed inside her. All her angst, and guilt, and heartbreak, and humiliation bundled inside her into a tight vortex and exploded from her. She straightened her dress, tucked her hair behind her ears, and wiped her tears.

Then she said aloud the words she'd been dying to say ever since her mother had died and her father had become this stranger, this person who reeked constantly of gin and spoke about racial purity, whose bitterness and contempt was born out of cowardice. Cowardice to face his own loss.

"And what are you, Papa? Don't you see the way that people look at you? Don't you know what *you* have become? If I've soiled your reputation, it was at least for something good, something that filled my heart with all that you've denied me, all that you've made impossible for me to gain in any other way." She gave a laugh. "A whore and a drunk. That makes us a perfect match. Now get out of my way!"

She knew what would come, didn't care in that moment about anything at all. She closed her eyes, perhaps even smiled. And still, she hadn't expected the full force of it. All she was suddenly aware of was his fist colliding against her cheek, the spinning of the room, and the surface of the door as she slid down the full length of it. And a pinprick of blackness expanding in her field of vision, growing as an approaching meteor. Engulfing her.

11

 LEANDRO KNEW SHE WOULDN'T COME. YET here he
was for the second night in a row, leaning on a large
oak near the wine cellar. It wasn't hope that pulled
him back, but more that he knew a decision of his own had
to be made. She would go on with her life, marry, think of
him someday with pleasant detachment—a transient attraction in the final weeks before her marriage that had been, after
all, mostly innocent. Eventually, even that would fade, but for
him, it would always continue—beyond this night, beyond
this summer. Here in Sopron, there would always be her.

And so he would say good-bye to their meeting place, to
all they'd been to each other, to the town he'd intended to leave
before Eva had come into his life. There was nothing to keep
him here now, and he'd already delayed too long. So he would
pack up his brothers and head out on the old, familiar road

he'd traveled in another lifetime with his parents, when it was only the three of them. How he missed that road.

For a little while, Aleandro sat against the tree, letting his mind drift back to those early days of his life and all they contained: starry skies, open fields with scorched grass, hawks gliding through the golden translucence of sunsets. Through it all, the sound of hoofs beating the gravel, day melting into night, towns opening on the horizon, towns fading. They were the travelers, they were their own gods, they were masters of their destiny. They were free, as he hoped to be again.

In daytime, as they closed the distance between villages, his mother had made medicinal potions from herbs she collected along the way, and he would sit alongside his father as he guided the horse-drawn wagon. The sun beat down mercilessly, making him light-headed, and they passed the time talking. There were stories about the taverns in which his father played, about where their music came from, and Aleandro often picked up his violin and played for him. "Like this?" he would say, and his father would lean in closer, or ask him to move to the other side of him to hear him better. "You are getting there," he would tell him, although the way his face beamed with pleasure was enough encouragement for Aleandro to keep sliding the bow over the strings.

In town markets, his mother sold her potions while he accompanied his father to the taverns. It was in those early days that someone had spat the word *Cigányok* at him and he asked his father what it meant. "It means you play from the soul," his father explained, even though Aleandro knew that it meant nothing of the kind. He'd heard it thrown in his father's face, too, despite the beautiful sounds that emerged from his violin, but by then his father, still young and towering, could no longer hear those words. He couldn't hear anything anymore.

They settled on a small patch in the green belt by the pond near Sopron where one of the caravans had set down roots a few years prior. Here in Sopron, they ate freshly caught fish around fires, and danced night after night, and Aleandro played with the children he'd only watched from a distance throughout the first ten years of his life. It was no longer just the three of them but other families like theirs, families willing to share so that Aleandro wouldn't go hungry. His father couldn't play the taverns anymore, couldn't repay them for the food, so he rolled up his sleeves and returned the kindness in the only way he could. One morning he came back with a sack full of tools that he'd bartered for work from one of the land farmers and began building. First there was their own hut—no more than a one-room wooden structure with a tiny sink and a butcher block cut from strips of wood he'd used for the siding. The other men joined quickly, and by next summer most of the families had moved out of their wagons, and the horses were now kept in a shed during the rains.

It was in those days, when they all worked from dawn to dusk, that Aleandro began making drawings for his father, filling the spaces of words he no longer grasped. The way the walls would intersect inside, the way alcoves could be carved in the corners for sinks, baby cots. He was twelve by then, and his mother taught the camp children to read and count money, to keep their heads low against taunts and hurled stones from the non-Romani children in town, to make themselves immune, invisible. He never could understand how so much hatred could exist in a place that cradled such beauty. But inside the inner circle of his life, there was beauty indeed—music and dancing, and many arms to embrace him.

It was the closest to a regular life that Aleandro had ever known, yet after a few years, he began missing the adventure of the open road. One day he picked up his father's rusty violin and headed out on the road again. He was fifteen, restless with youth, and the sky that had always been his roof in summer drew him with the promise of something new.

He followed more or less the roads he'd known as a child. He was good enough at the violin, even though he dreamed of drawing those houses and began drawing churches and beer halls, then after some time, only the people that gathered under those roofs. At Lake Balaton, he joined a flamenco group and was bewitched by the lead dancer—a girl much like him, with ripe lips and melancholic, liquid eyes, whose ample hips molded around the sound of his violin, and to whom he lost his virginity later that night. Many such nights followed, yet she was much older than him, and the way she ignored him during the day, despite the fevered whispers of the night, made him see what he was to her.

One morning he left again and kept moving, past rows of houses on swollen banks and rivers that led him to new places, places he enjoyed discovering as much as leaving. There were more taverns and a few other women not unlike the dancer, and the years passed unbeknownst to him, until he was twenty and word caught up to him about what was happening in Sopron.

Nothing prepared him for what he found when he returned. His mother, ill with typhus, barely recognized him. He couldn't bring himself to ask about his father, but in his heart, he knew what had happened before he stepped through the door. He knew. Later, an elderly woman from the village brought in three children—twin boys of about five or six and a younger one, no more than a toddler, with a similar mass of curly, dark hair and huge eyes that pierced his chest.

She'd been taking care of them, she explained to him. For his mother. For *their mother.*

For the rest of his life, he would never forget the relief washing over his mother's face when he promised her that he would stay. He took her place and loved those boys as she had; he protected them. For two years after he'd buried his parents, he kept his promise, and he would continue wherever life took them. Burgenland awaited, Vienna after that, maybe, and the open road in between, their steady companion.

The road had always been his one constant, and he was ready for it again.

———

Aleandro inhaled deeply now, imagining the villa where Eva slept peacefully, maybe relieved or perhaps a little sad, already moving past him. It was late, nearly midnight, and he needed to save his strength for tomorrow, so he got on with the final task of the night. It didn't matter to him that he would draw in the darkness—it was only a rough sketch he intended, a memento of his last moments here. But as he took out his pad and began, he did not continue past the first strokes. Rather, his eyes focused on the flutter of white, there just at the base of the valley, no more than a few hundred yards away.

A dove, he thought for an instant, then realized that it couldn't be—it was too low. Straining his eyes in the darkness, he watched it a bit longer as it continued to expand and take shape.

Eva. She was still at a distance, and Aleandro stifled the urge to run to her, to crush her to him. To crush her in order to prove she was real. Instead, he stood there and watched Eva come toward him the same way he'd watched her depart two nights earlier and he had to steady himself on a tree. Only when she got closer did a stab of shock slice through his stupor.

"Eva. Eva, what happened?"

He stared at the proud expression on her face, which he knew so well and worshipped, at the deep shadow the size of a plum on the marble skin of her cheek. There was a fissure in the corner of her lip, which she touched protectively, as if to conceal it, then a glint of relief sprang into her impenetrable gaze and she rushed into his arms.

"I'm sorry," she murmured in the collar of his shirt. "I was hoping to find you. I didn't know where else to go, and I needed to find you. I needed to see you."

"My God. Eva, look at me," he kept saying, but she would not. She was shaking, and all he could do was draw her closer, hold her tightly as he knew she needed, even though he, too, was shaking with fury. He would kill whoever did this to her. He would, and he said it out loud. "Just tell me who did this to you, Eva. I will kill him. I will kill him with my bare hands."

"It doesn't matter," Eva said, lifting her cheek from his chest and gazing across the darkness. "These bruises mean nothing to me now. There are worse wounds to heal. These bruises have set me free."

Later, Eva recounted what had happened at the villa—the photographs of their time together, the open palm that had split her lip, the fist that had turned the room to blackness. How afterward she found herself in her room with the door locked and knew it was futile to bang on it or shout out. There was no one to hear her now. There was no one in the house but her and her father. The next night she climbed out of the second-story window and crawled down the bougainvillea vine, not caring that she might break her neck. She never wanted to see her father again, she declared, her face twisted with anger, with humiliation. She would never go back. She could never go back to any life that included her father.

She broke into tears saying it, as if putting it in words made it real, and so he took her hand and led her inside the wine cellar, their meeting spot, where on the concrete floor he laid out the blanket they'd always kept there, lit the kerosene lamp, and set his sketchbook down in a corner.

"Here, lie down for a bit. Rest," he said and sat down beside her, pulling her head in his lap. "You don't have to go back, Eva. You are safe here. We can stay here as long as you want."

They didn't speak for a while, and the silence between them agitated him more than her tears. Moments ago, he was convinced he would never see her again, and now she was here with him and there wasn't a thing he could do to ease her pain. In a way, it was worse than losing her.

"Eva, come with me," he found himself saying. "We will leave in the morning with my brothers; we will get away from this place. I will find a way to take care of you, Eva. Besides my brothers, you are all that matters to me in the world. Come with me."

She didn't answer at first, and he realized how absurd his proposition was. How could he take care of her? How, when he could hardly take care of himself, of his brothers? And hadn't he encouraged her to return to Budapest? Yet now he couldn't imagine another man soothing her, holding her. And it was *him* that she'd come to—not her fiancé, nor her friends, not even Dora. *Him. He* was meant to protect her, to love her, to keep her safe.

"Have you ever been to Burgenland?" he continued, fueled with sudden hope. "It's not far from here, on the other side of Lake Fertö, in Austria. It's a place much like this, but I can get work there. I've already been offered a steady job playing at one of the taverns, and there will be enough for a while, enough until we can figure out someplace else to go. Anyplace that you want, Eva. I will take you wherever you want to go."

Still no words from her. She was motionless, not a muscle stirring, and for a moment he thought she'd fallen asleep, so he went on stroking her hair. Eventually, he lay down on the blanket next to her, aching with his own exhaustion and the weight of his thoughts. They stayed like that for a while, their bodies curved like spoons, the light from the kerosene lamp casting their shadows on the barren walls, dancing demons.

"Are you all right?" he whispered when she suddenly shifted away from him and sat up. Her fingers on his lips kept further words from coming. In the weak light, her hair was diffused in a halo of gold, and her fingertips on his mouth stirred something deep inside him. He searched her eyes, but he couldn't see them. Couldn't see them in the backwash of light.

"I will come with you, Aleandro. I will."

Swept with disbelief, with happiness, he could not hold

himself back any longer, so he kissed her, cautiously at first, with more tenderness than passion, then more deeply. She tasted of tears, and he thought he'd never known such a sensation of pain and sweetness, and how much better it was than what he'd imagined. He buried his hands in the silk of her hair, drew her beneath him, and kissed her again, kissed her warm mouth and her neck, and the base of her throat, where her pulse raced.

He loved her, he was in love with her, he adored her, he would remember murmuring incoherently. Did she say that she loved him, too? He couldn't be sure, for his head was swimming. Perhaps it was only a sigh, or the crickets outside in the hush of the night, singing. For a moment he was sobered by the thought that she was merely acting on impulse, that he was taking advantage of an emotional moment and he drew back from her, closing his eyes. Releasing her.

It was not the end. When he opened them, she was still there, kneeling beside him. As if in a dream, he watched her undo the tiny shell buttons on her dress and it slid away from her shoulders, easily, without resistance. He stared at the staggering beauty of her, the tiny breasts and the crescent beauty mark low between them, wanting to ask if this was what she really wanted.

Then her hand was on his, lifting it to her burning cheek, and it was more than he could take. More than a man, nearly twenty-three years old and bursting with love, could take. When he reached for her again, it was hungrily, without reservation, without fear.

12

FIRE. HIS EYES SNAPPED OPEN, HIS nostrils filling with the acrid smell. In the silvery light of early dawn, he breathed in deeply, hoping he was mistaken. Beside him, Eva slept peacefully, her pale arm draped over his bare chest, her breath slow, warm in the space between them. Taking care not to wake her, he untangled himself from her and sat up, all of his senses shooting back into his body like a great thunderbolt. He fumbled around, groping for the kerosene lamp, but he couldn't find it. The lamp had long burned out in the night.

"Don't go."

She was awake. Her arm came around his waist, and she pulled him back on their blanket, laughing a little, her lips moist on his shoulder. "Don't leave," she said, and it took all his strength not to fall back beside her, not to drown in her beauty and the scent of her skin once more.

"My love, I'm not going anywhere. I'm coming right back. I just have to check something. It's probably nothing, it's probably just . . ."

A thought smashed into him like a tidal wave, causing a small, involuntary cry. It was only a filament of a thought, something unformed, yet it eviscerated the night's dream.

"Eva," he said now, more insistently, pulling his shirt over his head, struggling to get his boots on. "Eva, do not leave here. Wait for me." He leaned over her now, his lips nearly touching hers. The bruise on her cheek had deepened, become more violent, and he brushed his fingers over it lightly. He hated leaving her, never wanted to leave her again, and yet he couldn't tell her why. He hoped he was wrong. God, how he hoped he was wrong.

"I'll be back before you know it, all right? I'll be back in a flash, I promise. Please don't go anywhere."

There was no time to wait for her answer as he bolted out of the cellar.

Outside, a terrible orange halo billowed out over the horizon, the air a blanket of suffocating smoke. His heart pounded. He couldn't see more than two feet ahead of him, and the air grew thicker as he approached the shanty town at a full run. It was only when he got closer that the sight halted him, making him falter. He couldn't believe what he was seeing; it was impossible to take it all in. Moments ago, he was in Eva's arms, and now this.

More than a dozen huts had caught fire like they were

made of flimsy paper, the rooflines a row of crumbling embers. Cypress trees a hundred years old had erupted like matchsticks, tongues of black fumes lapping up to the sky, as if intending to consume the heavens themselves. It was the height of summer and the grass dry, and the flames were racing through the reeds. People—his people—were running in all directions, disoriented, screaming, the horses were whinnying inside the shed. Someone released them, and in a matter of seconds, they trampled past him, a wild herd headed for the hills. One of the horses toppled and couldn't get up; it lay there in agony. No one saw Aleandro; no one called to him for help. He was invisible.

He pounded on the door of his hut. A shallow flame slashed from the base of the structure toward the roofline, and he knew that he didn't have much time. Rivulets of sweat poured down his back, gathering in his waistband, trickling down his legs. He pounded again, launched his foot into the door, shrieking his brothers' names. There was no movement in the window, nothing but stillness, darkness, and the air trembled in his blurred vision. He kicked the door harder, alternating feet—left foot, right foot—and finally it gave way.

"Lukas! Tamás! Attia!"

By the hearth there was a slight movement, a stirring. Coughing, holding the collar of his shirt over his mouth, he stumbled through like a blind man. "My God," he heard himself shout. "My God! What are you thinking?"

He had found them. Three pairs of eyes stared at him, as if he were an apparition, as if he had come too late to do anything but watch the fire come in through the walls. They didn't even seem aware of his presence even though he shouted at them, shook them, shouted again.

"Let's go now. Get up!" He grabbed Lukas first, heard him whimper as he twisted in his arms, and this single action seemed to shift something in the others, to snap them from their stupor. In near tandem, they rose with their arms linked, holding on to each other.

"That's right, that's good, don't be afraid! I will get us out of here, do you hear me? Here, grab my hand, Attia! Good, that's good. Now hold on tightly to your brother's, and don't let go. Yes! Keep your eyes on me, only on me!"

Outside, more flames, more smoke. But the smoke was a blessing, for it didn't allow them to see. They couldn't see what was happening, but they could smell it; he could smell the burned flesh, and it made him weak with nausea. Everything was a dream, a nightmare from which he couldn't wake. He carried buckets of water, threw them onto the grass between the huts. A chicken caught fire; it scampered past him and toppled to the ground in a sickening burst of flame. The ground underneath him was a river of fire. He doused the bottoms of his trousers with water. He was choking, trying to pull air into his lungs.

He did not know how long it lasted, how they were able to contain it, nor how much time had passed since he'd left Eva. Time lapsed, lost all meaning. He was sitting on the charred ground among the ruins, covering his face with his hands. Shadows moved past him. He drew his hands away, and they were black, covered in soot. Soiled with the loss of everything his father had built.

Yet he was alive. He moved his hands around to prove it.

He was alive, and he pushed himself from the scorched grass and went to look for his brothers down by the water, where he'd delivered them, knowing they would be safe. When he saw them, he ran to them and pulled them into his arms, and then he was weeping out loud—weeping into their shoulders and their tiny chests, whispering their names and what he thought was a prayer.

———

"What happened?" he asked Tamás and Attia sometime later, as they sat together in the grass, still too weak to move. "What happened last night while I was gone?"

He didn't really expect them to know, but the way they looked at each other and lowered their eyes jolted his tired heart. They knew something, of that he was sure. "Tell me, boys!" he insisted. "It's all right. You are safe now. What happened?"

"There was a man," began Tamás, almost fearfully. "He came 'round looking for you. He banged on some doors and did a bunch of shoutin' and cursin', but no one could tell him where you were, no one would really speak to him, so after a while he gave up and left. Then some other men came, 'bout a half hour later, on horses, carrying rifles. Everyone just ran inside, and we did, too—we locked the door twice as you taught us. Then we smelled fire. But we stayed inside. We stayed inside 'cause we knew you'd come. We knew you'd come to get us."

"You did good," Aleandro mumbled, even though he felt punched in the stomach. "But tell me, Tamás, this man who was asking for me, what did he look like?"

There was a hesitation: "He was . . . older. Had kind of grayish hair and he was wearing a leather vest."

Then Lukas spoke: "I seen him before, Andro, driving up the road in a black shiny car to the big house on the hill. The one over there. Where Eva took me to ride the pony."

A scream. Aleandro couldn't push it back, couldn't stop himself even though he knew he was frightening his brothers when they'd been frightened enough. Another came, and another. He was screaming, for he knew now, with the clarity of a dying man, what had eluded him all along.

The fire had been set for him. It was the price to pay for his love.

Eva was not there when he returned with his brothers. The cellar was empty. Only the sketchbook was there, near the kerosene lamp in a corner, the blanket folded neatly beside it. All around the vineyard he searched for her, calling out her name, plunging through the rows of vines, cutting himself on the barbed wire, shouting out, imploring: *Eva, answer me! Eva, where are you, where are you, where are you?*

The sun had dipped below the hillside. It would be dark again soon, and there was no more he could do. He was spent, so he stretched out in the grass with his arms splayed wide, his gaze pinned on the sky, though he knew no stars would shine tonight.

Eventually, he returned to the cellar where his brothers waited, picked up Lukas, and began walking. No wagon now, nothing to carry them but their feet and his will to lead them.

The two other boys followed silently, and they made their way toward the winding dirt road that cut through the province. Not looking back, he led them along at a brisk clip, not too fast, for they needed to save their energy. Not too slow, either, but steadily, toward the two-lane road, four, five kilometers away. If they could get there, there was hope. If they could get there, they would continue on toward the Austrian border, follow the very same route he'd envisioned they'd be taking with Eva.

Two days later, they were walking still, the little one on his back, his other brothers slightly ahead now, passing a flask of water between them, kicking stones. They were walking toward the horizon; they were walking to Burgenland, his sketchbook with the portraits of her tucked against his heart. All that kept him going was a single thought, a single conviction. Once he knew his brothers were safe, he would turn around and come right back for her. For Eva, for his love, he would return if it cost him his last breath.

Part II

ROADS

13

W HENEVER EVA LOOKED BACK ON THOSE early days upon her return from Sopron, she would recall a general vacantness, a long stretch of indistinguishable hours punctuated only by the hum of the traffic below. The pale wallpaper with its silver and gold stripes, the rumple of sheets on the bed that Eva hadn't bothered to straighten in days, the perfume bottles sheened in dust on the dressing table next to the thank-you notes she'd once intended to write—all blending into the darkness and coming into focus again. From her bedroom window she noticed the tinge of gold in the treetops lining the wide thoroughfare below her window, pupils in school uniforms carrying their lunch pails and clarinets, a thickening of pedestrians returned from the summer holiday. The first rain came down in a torrent, and she watched it in the same impassive way, tracing the rivulets on the glass with her fingers.

She saw practically no one, hardly left the room to grab some food from the kitchen when she was sure that the house was empty. Only Dora called her once in a while, and she would run to the phone hoping for news, but there was nothing new to convey, nothing but the grimness Dora had delivered the first time: the gypsy camp had been burned to the ground. There were casualties, but some had been able to escape unscathed. The portion of land had been bought by a wine merchant (a friend of her father's, rumor was), and it was being razed. No one had seen a sole fiddler in town since.

"Please, Eva," Dora would conclude, "please try to put the matter out of your mind. It does no good to dwell on it, my child. Try to forget."

Yet how could she forget? How? To know that she had been the cause of the fire seemed a burden impossible to carry. It seemed impossible to bear it here, alone, in this apartment with its massive Florentine furniture and slabs of marble, which had always seemed small to her on return from Sopron, yet which now had the effect of a tomb.

She could have left anytime. The door was no longer locked; she could have walked out into the street and away from this life, which in some way still contained her father. But she couldn't. If Aleandro was somewhere out there, still alive, perhaps he would come to look for her here. She recalled telling him in their time together that on a clear night she could see the lights inside the opera house from her terrace. *The building two blocks away, guarded by two marble statues. My father, it seems, must dominate even the ostentatiousness of Andrássy út.*

And so she would wait.

Her father had tried several times to make amends. He'd brought her a ruby pin one day, set the velvet box containing it outside her door. Another day, there was a leather journal and a beautiful Montblanc pen.

She put them out on the hallway table with only a few words written inside the first page:

I will never forgive you.

The letters from Eduard, which had come at first in a steady stream, had dwindled as well and eventually stopped. The only trace of his prior ardor to speak with her rested in a pearly white box on the windowsill, withered—a coffin for those roses, for what their lives might have been.

Then she realized one day that she was waiting to no avail. She was waiting for a ghost.

Even if Aleandro managed to escape from Sopron, the fire had changed everything between them. She saw that now, clearly. What had they ever been anyway but a temporary madness? What else did the silence prove? Soon however, thoughts about that night abated. All that consumed her now was the nausea in the pit of her belly that came like the tide one morning, stirring her from a deep sleep.

It had passed as easily as it came, then returned again in the afternoon. The morning after, she vomited until the tears streamed from her eyes, even though her stomach contained only the glass of water from the night before. Again, it happened before dinner. Again, the next day. She considered it to be a virus, nothing more, but her medical knowledge far surpassed her wishful thinking, and soon she could no longer deny what she already knew in her heart.

———

That night, she'd called an old friend, a brash girl with bright red lips and a mass of glossy curls whom in another life had dragged her into a bar for the first time, and confessed to her that just three weeks earlier she'd managed to solve what she referred to as a "female problem."

"All French women are doing it," Eva recalled her saying, adjusting the top of her blouse in a way that evoked cheers from a group of soldiers at the other end of the bar. "And why should we deny ourselves the same pleasures as men? Why should we endure the greater consequences when they come and go as they please?"

At the time, she found her casual demeanor about the matter distasteful enough that in the months after her engagement, she'd managed to avoid her entirely. Now, as she dialed the number, her fingers trembled so violently she could barely complete the numbers on the rotary dial.

"Hello, Julia? Yes, yes, it's me, darling." She struggled for an even tone, her hand fisting the cord so tightly it might have drawn blood. "Yes, yes, I know it's been a long time. A very long time. But I'm calling now because I'm in a bit of a bind. And, well, you are the only person on earth I could turn to. It concerns something of a personal nature. And I'm counting on your discretion. Much, of course, as you've been able to count on mine."

After she'd written down the address, she stuffed it in the dressing table drawer and slammed it shut. Then she sat down on the brocade green stool and sobbed into her hands.

The building was, as Eva might have imagined, not located on a wide thoroughfare but on a narrow backstreet in the seventh district, lined with dilapidated windows overfilled with chipped flowerpots and undergarments hung to dry. She stopped in front of the address she'd written down, confirming that this redbrick building with its glass-fissured door was indeed the right place.

Her heart surged with paralyzing fear, but—she reminded herself—what choice did she have? What choices at all were available for girls like her, without a husband or a profession, without the support of a family, without any means of income? For, surely, once her father found out, he would disown her. Not that she minded so much for herself, but how would she support a child? No, there was no other way, and after silencing the meek inner voice that had been telling her to turn around since leaving home, she pushed through the door.

The stairwell reeked of an overpowering combination—cat urine, fried meatballs, cleaning fluid—so she held her breath as she took the stairs to the first landing and knocked on a maroon-colored door. There was no answer, and then she noticed the sign on the door, which read *Reception Inside*, and she let herself in. It was no more than a vestibule arranged to give the impression of a waiting area. The only furniture comprised two stiff wooden chairs and a dusty glass table with coffee mug stains and fashion magazines with curled edges. The carpet, dark green and discolored in places, she realized, accounted for the cat urine stench—and she breathed into the crook of her elbow, willing her stomach not to revolt.

"Name?"

She turned and found herself looking up at a mountain of a woman sporting a turban and green housecoat that was oddly almost the same shade as the carpet. In her hand there was a hunk of bread lined with slices of pork fat. Her lips glistened under the fluorescent lights.

"Eva," she said, averting her eyes from the flat, disinterested stare. "Eva César."

"Did you bring the money?"

"Yes, as you asked."

"All six hundred *pengös*, then?"

"Yes."

"Well, now, that's a first. This way, please."

She was led through a dank corridor and down another flight of service stairs at the end. A door opened to reveal a basement room with a sidewalk window. A chair similar to the one in the waiting room was accompanied by a metal cot stripped of all linens, a rough woolen blanket rolled up at the foot. Next to it, there was a standing tray on which some objects lay hidden from view underneath a white towel.

"I . . ." Eva began. She turned to the woman, scrunching her purse to her chest. From somewhere in the building she could hear loud voices, a couple arguing, a baby crying. "I don't know if . . ."

"Don't worry, dear," the woman reassured her, her gaze roaming lazily over the tailor-cut coat as if considering if she should have charged more. "The doctor is quite good. Now, what you need to do is to set your things down"—at this, she pointed to the chair, as if instructing a two-year-old—"all of your clothes is what I mean, every last stitch, then lie down on the bed and pull the blanket up to your shoulders. After he is done with the examination, he will proceed right away. Afterward, you can stay for two hours. Then you are on your own. Questions?"

Eva began again, feeling hazy. "You see . . . I fear that I haven't really thought this through. I haven't. I didn't quite have the time." She laughed loudly, shrilly. "Can I just take some time and maybe come back later?"

Then she was running. She was through the door, flying up the steps, scaling them two at a time, and through the hallway, where the terrible smell assaulted her again. A small cry escaped her throat as she emerged into the daylight.

Outside, she found that her knees couldn't carry her farther. She sat on the edge of the sidewalk, thinking miserably that she had just wasted the last of her personal savings. Bending over her knees, she vomited into the street.

———

On the streetcar, later that afternoon, Eva sat in the back, away from the other commuters, tucked her valise under her chair, and leaned her head against the window. Beyond the glass, Budapest stretched like a lazy old cat—cobblestoned streets and old Gothic churches, parks with grass coming back to life after the hot summer, Edwardian flats much like hers, windows. Endless windows, beyond which life would unfold tomorrow precisely as today and the day after that, when she would no longer be here to see it. How easy it was to slip out of one's life, Eva thought. How little she would be missed.

At the train station, she bought her ticket and sat on her

small valise amid all the activity. A little girl caught her eye—she was crying for something, an old toy she might have forgotten at home, and her mother was trying to soothe her with a square of chocolate, which the girl didn't want. The mother picked her up, and Eva felt oddly lifted from her loneliness for a brief second. But she couldn't entertain any thoughts of motherhood or what it would be like to hold a child of her own, so she lifted her valise and walked to the other end of the platform.

On the train, more dwellings, more windows passed in her vision, thinning out, fading. Soon only a dismal collection of cottages with collapsed picket fences and crumbling porches lined the tracks. Then there were no more buildings of any kind, just infinite strips of land and overgrown weeds. On a narrow dirt road, a handful of women in peasant dresses came into view, balancing huge wicker baskets filled with apples on their heads. Beyond them, a red sea undulated in the late evening breeze. Poppies, she realized. Poppies. She was nearly there.

She descended at the station, got in a cab, delivered an address. In the back seat, she kept her eyes closed, not wanting to see this land yet inundated nonetheless with the recollection that had become her punishment: A hand grasping her arm as she stumbled through the haze of the field. The car door slamming behind her, the back seat of her father's Buick. The sheen of fire over the horizon, which had made her scream and pound her fists on the glass. Then, hours later, as they sped through the streets of Budapest, an irrational calmness overtook her. The conviction that he would come for her followed. Then silence.

In front of the shabby door of the cottage, after the cab sped away as if the tip wasn't worth waiting for in this part of town, Eva stood resolutely. The light-headedness from the train had returned, so she sat on the rocking swing on the porch. She traced the faded red roses on the cushion she and Dora had stenciled in the time she'd lived here. Once, this run-down little cottage with peeling windowsills and oak sap peppering the wooden porch had been her safe haven, and perhaps now, for just a little while, it could be again. Emboldened by this thought, she picked up her valise and walked to the door and knocked. It opened finally on the third one, just a crack at first, then widely, and in her relief, she let the suitcase drop to the ground.

"Eva? Child! What are you doing here?" The stupor in Dora's voice gave way to a tone of admonishment as she reached for the porch light and flicked it on. "Eva, I told you not to come here! There is nothing here for you, Eva! Why don't you ever listen?"

"I had nowhere else to go, Dora. Please forgive me, but something has happened. I need your help." Her hands came up to her face. "I'm so ashamed, Dora. So ashamed."

Then she was in the only arms she had ever been able to count on and was drawn inside, into the warmth of the tiny room, with its plaid sofa and threadbare rug, which, she vaguely recalled, had once lined a hallway inside the villa.

14

HE PLANNED TO STAY JUST LONG enough until they could figure out a solution. An answer, if one existed, although as the days passed, it was clear that one wouldn't come. Three weeks had gone by, then three months, and as the first snow came in a downpour, burying for the first time in eighty years the dome of the Fire Tower, Eva knew it was too late to leave. She had written a letter to her father saying that she would be traveling for a while. She was meeting some friends at the Black Sea in Romania, that he needn't worry about her; she was fine. It was enough to keep him from coming to look for her here, and for the time being, this distance was all she needed.

As the last feeble leaves fell from trees in the neighbor's apple orchard, Eva stopped venturing outside altogether, for whenever she did, she couldn't help but be drawn in one of two directions: one was the peak of the hillside on the other side of the train tracks, from which the old gypsy land surfaced down in the valley as a great lake of upturned earth, strewn with garbage and motionless tractors. The other was the town square, where Aleandro's face would crop up unbidden wherever she turned. On cobblestoned lanes that twined through clusters of pink and ochre jewel-box buildings, in doorways and corner parks, through tired taverns' windows, she couldn't help seeking his face. At times it would be no more than a shock of black hair under a hat, the clip of a stranger's walk, or a set of stern shoulders that drew her eye, and then she would follow these figures for blocks, pretend she was studying a store display or a map, pretend she was checking her watch, waiting for someone. Often she would catch inquisitive glances from passersby, be asked at times if she needed help, if she was lost.

She was indeed lost, she'd admitted once. It was the truest thing she had said that day.

It came almost as a relief when her condition became apparent enough that she could no longer go into town, where someone might recognize her. Now she lounged around the cottage in Dora's oversize robe—the only thing that fit comfortably—reading the books she'd brought in her luggage along with a few pieces of clothing too thin for the season. The rest of the time she just daydreamed, chewing her fingernails, while overgrown, barren branches tapped at the windows.

In her fourth month, her state of inertia was interrupted quite suddenly by a kind of euphoria, one that pulled her from a deep sleep. It seemed inappropriate that this seed of happiness should bloom in her heart when nothing about her life was cheerful, but then she'd placed her hand on her belly and felt it again. That flutter. She hadn't dreamed it.

And it was then that Aleandro, her mother, Eduard, even her father and all the losses that weighted her heart lifted and became a faraway constellation from which she saw herself detach like a shooting star.

This was hers, hers to keep, and she knew in that moment that she would not give up her baby. And she realized also, with some surprise, that she'd known this all along.

After that day, she felt renewed with an unbound energy. While Dora worked her restaurant job, she reorganized Dora's pantry, repainted the green kitchen cabinets, polished the pine floors, which sprang back to life under her fervent scrubbing into a surprising art deco motif. Dora had shown her how to knit, and after she was done with her chores she would sit out on the porch in the rocking chair with a blanket regardless of the weather, and watch tiny shapes emerge from the long silver needles: booties, socks no bigger than her thumb, a bonnet she'd embellished with a piping of silk threaded through the edges.

When her fingers were numb from cold, she would retreat inside, make tea, and scour the newspaper headlines, inhaling the scent of press ink, which carried with it the latest from Budapest. Eduard this time, not Aleandro, was there, his attentive, good-natured face coming to her as she read of the escalating tension with Germany and the increasing speculation that it was only a matter of days before Hitler would march in his troops. She was in those moments reminded of their conversations, and the last one in particular before she left Bu-' dapest at the onset of summer.

They'd drunk champagne bought from a corner store under the statues of Magyar rulers in City Park, spending what would be their last evening together before the wedding in the fall. How she missed those conversations now.

Once she'd nearly written to him, then at the last moment, she ended up ripping up the letter. Everything between them had been cut clean like the snap of a bone. She could not interfere in his life now—and she chided herself for this selfish desire to vindicate herself even in this small way.

After some time, even the memory of her time with Eduard retreated and became one with the dust of a life that she had, with the arrogance of youth, believed was irrevocably hers. As she'd done as a child, she shut her heart against all those memories, denied herself any tears. Snow fell silently against the windows and clustered in white kaleidoscopes on the panes, and she watched it come down from the milky sky. All she could do now was wait.

———

Her baby was born on an early May morning after a twelve-hour labor that Eva barely recalled. There had been a doctor, a thin, balding man carrying an enormous case, who arrived in a rush and whose hands as they prodded her belly and between her legs seemed uncommonly strong for such a frail composition. A moist gauze was placed on her mouth, something imbued with an astringent smell resembling turpentine. By then, her pain came in waves so powerful and frequent that she couldn't draw a breath. She couldn't bear to hear her own screams.

"Breech," she recalled the doctor saying to Dora. "I have to anesthetize now in case I may have to remove the child surgically. You understand that I will do what I can, but it may be the only way."

Still she held on, refusing to close her eyes, refusing to slide under. She held on, steadfast, even though she could barely make out the doctor's words, or Dora's pale face looming above her, tapping her cheek. Biding her time, waiting. Waiting to see the tiny face and the wide, startled eyes that rose up above her in hues of sunset-kissed rivers, the color of his and hers melted as one.

"Bianca." She uttered the name that had been her mother's and would now be her daughter's. Then she let go at last, letting herself sink into that dark, sweet abyss.

15

Dachau, Germany

Spring 1944

THAT YEAR, THE ONLY WAY TO mark the time had been with the slant of the sun, the lengthening and shortening of days, the flock of sparrows flying against the gray clouds, the frozen snow, which seeped through the worn soles of Aleandro's boots as he was marched through unknown lands. At each of the stops, time dissolved into the grim tasks he hoped would soon consume what remained of his withered body. He was forced to carry chopped trees, to carry sacks filled with concrete, to clear land mines, to bury dead bodies in ditches with bullets flying from both directions. He was forced to strip naked in the winter daybreak so that his upper arms and loins could be inspected and deemed fit for labor. He was forced to let his own urine flow inside his stiff canvas pants to warm his legs. He was forced to eat snow, while praying that his body would topple right there against the mud-splattered banks like so many others. He prayed for those bullets to find a way to his own heart. He prayed for the madness to come, to drown out whatever remained of his consciousness. And still he kept moving and waking and sleeping as a winter weakened and a new spring turned.

One day, he was loaded onto a new train and there was nothing but the darkness again and the rumble of wheels, the human stench that had become so familiar to him that he hardly noticed it anymore. All he could grasp from snippets of dialogue delivered by a front soldier was that Hungary had fallen under German occupation, and now the future of his country would mirror the rest of Europe's. Here in this boxcar, they were still able to work, to keep themselves alive, unlike the rest of the undesirables of Europe. They were fortunate not to be herded into ghettos, to see their loved ones shot in the streets, to see their babies die of starvation in their arms.

His country had not been the whole of Hungary. It had consisted of a small patch of land, a land of beauty and peace, that had burned down right before him. His country had been made up of three small children and one woman, and a future that had been stolen from him in the blink of an eye. His country had already perished long ago.

At one point, his exhausted mind could no longer take it all in, so he fell asleep scrunched between two other laborers and dreamed for the first time in months. In his dreams, his brothers were still with him. They were still in the forest at Komárom, where they were taken by the SS guards after being captured just three kilometers past the Austrian border. His little brother Lukas had found mushrooms in the ground and held them up in his tiny palms, his eyes wide with glee. *Eat them*, Aleandro told him in his dream, and Tamás and Attia. *Eat.* Then they were all eating, but as Aleandro chewed the mushrooms, they turned into stones. They shattered his teeth, and he looked at his brothers for an explanation, but their mouths were too full. They were choking on the stones, and they couldn't speak. They wanted to speak to him and couldn't.

———

He woke drenched in cold sweat as light flooded his eyes. Shouts in German came from the tracks below the open box-car: "*Schnell! Raus! Schnell!* Get out! *Schnell!*" Two seconds later, he was outside in a sun so bright that it burned through his skull. There was shouting and dogs barking, guns drawn against the glare, a spray of blood across the gravel, already darkened, abuzz with flies at his feet. "Drop your possessions in front of the wagon!" came another order through a bullhorn. "Leave all your possessions and gather at the line! *Schnell!*"

From up ahead, someone kept shouting amid the chaos, and an old man appeared in one of the wagon doors, clutching a paper bag. "Where have you taken my son? Please, let me find my son!" he kept shrieking as guards pulled him down from the train.

Aleandro wanted to reach for him through the crush of bodies, but before he could push his way through, a baton came down on the man's shoulder, knocking him to the ground. Aleandro turned his head in revulsion. He couldn't look, had to place his hands on his ears as the baton hit the man's flesh in a sickening rhythm that slowed and eventually stopped. Then there was only silence, and Aleandro had to fight the bile in his throat.

Flanked by soldiers in black uniforms, they were marched through a massive iron gate, which clanged shut behind them, trapping them inside a large concrete courtyard surrounded by a wall topped with barbed wire. More orders came: *Stop, turn, file into a single line. Stop.* A guard came forward and began counting the men, calling out numbers. Another man scribbled them down in a ledger, asking for verification. When the task was finished, another figure materialized from the shadow of a building—a stocky, shortish officer with a slight limp, bearing several golden medallions at his breast. He paused halfway down the line, and before he uttered a word, his arm opened up in an almost ceremonious way in the general direction of the barracks.

"Your new home. Welcome to Dachau. Quite grand for the Roma people, wouldn't you say? Far cry from the caravan tents, am I right?" He beamed as though impressed by his own wit, exposing a row of tiny teeth and prominent gums the color of skinned salmon.

Just then, near the strip of shade where more guards congregated with bored expressions, a door swung open and a diminished shape like that of a child was dragged through it. Not a child, Aleandro realized, but a man, who was hauled across the courtyard, his bludgeoned feet dragging behind him at unnatural angles. Beneath the watchtower, the guards dropped him to his knees and took four precise steps back. A crackle echoed like a stone dropped in a lake. The whole thing was over in less than ten seconds.

On Aleandro's right, a boy of about eighteen, who had shared his boxcar, began sobbing, and Aleandro, recalling the earlier scene at the train, put his hand down on his shoulder.

"You have to be strong," he whispered. "You can't let them see you weep, do you hear me? If they see it, it will only make things worse."

The boy nodded, swiped his flat palms over his bleary eyes, but the disruption caught the attention of the officer, who began limping toward them with hands at his back.

"Don't worry, my friend," he began, halting in front of them and addressing the boy as if all he intended was polite conversation. "We're not going to shoot you *all*. That Jew, that slime, deserved to die. But for you and your lot, the free-spirited *Romani*"—this pronounced with equal revulsion—"we have other plans."

His eyes snapped to Aleandro. "You, for example. You, with such strong bones, such impressive stature. Such . . . bravado. How long, I wonder, would someone like you cling to life in the medic's chamber when they put the needle into your arm? I do question which disease would be the first to triumph over such youthful vitality. Malaria? Typhus?" Leaning closer, the officer dropped his voice to a jovial whisper. "We won't know, will we, not until our esteemed doctor decides how to carry out his . . . experiment. And in your case, I may want to witness it in person. What do you say to that?"

What would he say? What Aleandro wanted to say, to spit in the face of this cowardly man, was that he didn't care. He didn't care how many poisons they injected him with. He didn't care if they dissected his frontal lobe to study his genetic differences. Everything he loved had been ripped out of his hands, and he did not care if they bled the life out of his veins or fed his flesh to the German shepherds guarding the fence. But he said nothing.

The lack of reaction caused the officer to come even closer, so close that Aleandro could smell the tinge of pine in his aftershave. In the cool Aryan gaze he detected no humor now, nor anger, only a feral, overt cruelty. He held the gaze nonetheless, not looking away. Then, as the officer laughed and pulled a whip from his belt, he realized his mistake. He lowered his eyes, lowered them to those perfectly shined boots, but it was already too late.

"A demonstration!" announced the officer to the rest of the line. "You are about to witness the consequence of defiance." The tip of his whip came up to Aleandro's cheek and gave it a sharp, stinging slap. "Take off your jacket and shirt. Step forward and kneel."

There was nothing for Aleandro to do but obey. He began unfastening the buttons on his coat slowly, feeling the battered lapel. The sketchbook that had carried him through the horrors of winter, through the rains and sweltering sun, was there at his breast, where he'd placed it out of some strange premonition when he was still on the train. Not in his duffel, which he'd been ordered to leave at the tracks.

After he extracted it and placed it gingerly on top of his folded coat, Aleandro straightened up and closed his eyes. He forced his thoughts back to what had become less flesh and blood and more of an ethereal thing. Somewhere between the loss of his brothers at Komárom and now, she had faded from him piece by piece, become just an image in pencil, an icon to pray to. Yet now she came to him so vividly, so clearly, that he let out a cry through his mashed lips. It seemed right that this last vision of her should bring him the end he had prayed for. The end that was now unavoidable.

But the bullet he braced for did not pierce his chest, and when he opened his eyes again, he saw that the officer was holding the sketchbook. There was a new look on his face now as he flipped through the pages, no longer that sinister smile but a stern concentration.

"Are you the one who drew these?"

Aleandro nodded numbly.

"A man of arts, then, are you? Funny, I didn't think your lot were even taught to read."

For a moment longer, the officer seemed to ponder, scratching his smooth-shaven chin with a manicured finger. A moment later, he slammed the sketchbook shut and barked to the group of guards under the awning: "Bring him to me at once."

Then he tucked the whip back in his belt and he limped away in the direction of the gatehouse with the sketchbook tucked under his arm, muttering something that sounded to Aleandro like expletives in German.

16

*B*IANCA WAS SO BEAUTIFUL.

The first few months, Eva couldn't get her fill of her daughter's perfect, heart-shaped face, the pink, oval fingernails that were so much like her own, the way her flower-bud mouth moved around tiny, almost imperceptible sounds while she slept. On the bed she shared with Dora, Eva would curl herself around the tiny shape and press her lips to her smooth, velvet head, inhaling her scent. And her smile! For that smile, she would keep herself awake for hours, for days. She'd heard of mothers being plagued with a crushing fatigue in the weeks after giving birth, but all Eva wanted to do was to bask in that smile. Only her eyes she couldn't glance at for long. Those keen, elongated eyes with thick dark lashes, despite their warm hazel color, were still undeniably his.

The only time Eva slept was when Dora brought Bianca

into town, tucked neatly inside the blue buggy she'd insisted on buying, along with the rocking bassinet they kept by the bed. It was both delightful and astounding to see the way Dora cared for the baby, the way she scrubbed every fold of her pudgy, compact body while managing not to get her head wet, or the way she changed her with the efficiency of a maternity-ward nurse. Often, Eva saw herself as an infant in the care of those sturdy, dependable hands and she would hug the life out of Dora, misty-eyed, overcome with love.

"Such demonstration of affection!" Dora would tease. "Don't tell me, Eva, that motherhood has made you all soft and mushy. Frankly, I never thought I'd see this side of you. Although I like it. I think it rather suits you."

"I'm just saying thank you, that's all, Dora. There's no sentimentality about it whatsoever. I'm just so happy to be here with you."

They would hold each other's gaze, both knowing what the other was thinking. Knowing that for a few brief moments the world outside, and the war that had shredded its heart, could be sealed off, and it was just the three of them, safe still, alive still, inside this cocoon of a home they'd built together.

Soon the news, growing more alarming by the day, could not be kept entirely at bay. Sometimes Dora recounted what she'd overheard in town, or at the restaurant where she still worked six days a week. Rumor was that the Red Army had penetrated the Carpathian Mountains and were now at the Hungarian border. The Allied bombings were no longer contained to petrol fields and factories outside Budapest, but were targeting government buildings in the center of town. More dismal even was what was happening with Budapest's Jews, who had since early spring been forced out of their homes and into yellow-star houses—five, six families sharing a room without electricity or running water. All of them had been forced to turn in their telephones, bicycles, radios, and jewelry, their homes raided by the SS guards at whim.

Even here in Sopron, things had unraveled with dizzying speed. One day when Dora wasn't feeling well, Eva had gone into town for groceries (her first outing since Bianca was born) and had been stunned to see that there was a Nazi flag on practically every building. There were few people wearing the yellow star in town now—most of them had already been taken away on trains to so-called relocation camps—and the ones remaining lived in hiding, sheltered in the basements and attics of the few friends who hadn't turned their backs on them. On her way home that very same afternoon, Eva witnessed rocks and bits of garbage being thrown from windows at a young family. The father had enfolded his toddler boy inside his coat to protect him from the assault. Eva had stood there in the middle of the street, glaring at the shivering curtains, until a wad of spit landed on her own arm. It was the father (shockingly enough) who resurfaced from the end of the block to pull her away by the elbow, telling her that she needed to go home.

"I can't believe it, Dora. Look," Eva said now, lifting the newspaper from the burlap bag as Dora stored the groceries in the pantry and placed a pot of water on the stove. "It says here that in Budapest, those Arrow Cross beasts are killing innocent people in the street, raiding the yellow-star houses and putting them on trains—not just the men, but the women and children now, too. How can this happen? How, when Horthy has promised not to deport? Paris was liberated weeks ago, and it's been just as long since Romania, our neighbor, for God's sake, extricated itself from the war! How can this happen so late in the war when everyone knows that Germany will fold?

"I must do something, Dora! We must all do something, we must speak up, revolt to protect our friends, if it comes to that. We must see what we can do to help!"

"Help?" Dora asked, chopping vegetables and dropping them into the soup pot with a quiet stoicism that infuriated Eva. "What can you possibly do to help? What can any of us do to help? I tell you, Eva, I never thought I'd live long enough to see such a thing, but there isn't much that can be done. Especially not by someone like you. Now that you have a baby to care for, you have to keep yourself safe."

"Safe? How can any of us be safe? This defies any human decency, and as human beings we are obliged to act!"

"I know what's in your heart, Eva. I do," Dora would say. "And I don't disagree. But it's simply too dangerous. Think of Bianca! What would happen to her if you went and got yourself arrested? Or killed? I'm too old to raise her alone. God knows, I may not be around by the time she's ten. Do you want her to end up in an orphanage? Well, do you?"

Nearly every such conversation ended much the same way: Dora would resume cooking dinner, thin-lipped, banging pots around, while Eva tended to the baby or tried to lose herself in her books. Lately, sentences passed in a blur, and she found herself staring at the pages, unable to absorb what she was reading.

It was for this reason, perhaps, that the latest letter to arrive sat on the coffee table for nearly a day, untouched. It bore Dora's name, although the Budapest stamp in the corner made it clear enough that whatever was contained in the pages pertained to Eva. It wasn't the first letter her father had written to Dora. There were several letters in the months after Eva had failed to return from her supposed sojourn at the sea, and half a dozen phone calls as well, during which, Dora, precisely as they'd rehearsed, had assured her father that she, Eva, was just fine, that she was taking some time for herself, to refocus her life. She had moved on from the sea to Sofia, in Bulgaria, Dora explained, and planned on staying the winter at a friend's. In time she would come home, as young people did; he just needed to be patient, and, of course, she'd agreed to keep him informed of further news. It had been astounding, really, how easily her father had believed the whole fabrication (as if wanting to believe it), and for a while the barrage of inquiries stopped.

But this letter was different from the others. This one was marked *Urgent*.

"Oh, for God's sake, Eva," Dora said after they'd both passed it enough times. "Are you going to read this damn thing or not?"

Eva shrugged nonchalantly. "Dora, you know that any news from my father is of no concern to me. I have no interest in reading it. Besides," she added, trying to hold back a small ironic smile, "it says here that it is for you."

With a reproachful look, Dora tore open the envelope and extracted the single sheet of paper and read over the lines. Then, without any expression whatsoever, she handed it to Eva.

"It's not from your father. It's from his lawyer, who's been desperately trying to reach you. He says that if I should hear from you, to ask you to call immediately." There was a slight frown. "I don't know, Eva. Perhaps it wouldn't hurt to make one single call, have your voice heard on the other end. Just for reassurance, yes? Lord knows we don't want your father showing up here unannounced."

"Well, this should be interesting." Eva took the letter and sighed impatiently, scanning the same lines, then headed into the bedroom, where the telephone rested on an old dresser with rusted knobs. "If this is how my father thinks he can get my attention," she shouted through the cracked door, "he is sorely mistaken!"

———

Ten minutes later, Eva emerged back into the living room, her face drained of color. She stumbled to the sofa and picked up the baby from the playpen, smoothing down the edges of her crumpled shirt. Bianca gurgled and happily pumped her fat legs against Eva's stomach.

"My father, Dora," Eva said over the top of the baby's head, hearing her own voice as if from another room. "My father, it would seem, is no longer alive."

It was Dora's turn to pale. "What? What do you mean? This can't be true."

"Hard to believe, I know." She felt faint, and she placed the baby back in the playpen and plunked herself down in a chair. It wasn't sorrow she felt, but shock. "Isn't it? I mean, we all thought that the indomitable Mr. César would live long enough to see himself declared a national hero. Yet it appears that as he was leaving a champagne gala at the Plaza in honor of the Führer, he suffered a heart attack. Collapsed in the street.

Not one person apparently bothered to help him." She swallowed hard and blinked. As if to convince herself, she affirmed: "So, yes, it is true, Dora."

In an instant, Dora was kneeling beside her, taking her cold hands in hers, but Eva couldn't quite anchor herself to the moment. She kept her eyes on the window with its open lace curtains, where a drizzle was falling through the shriveled amber leaves.

"Oh, Eva. I'm so sorry, my darling," Dora was saying. "I know things between you have been strained to say the least, but I hoped that someday, in time, you would find a way to make peace with him. I hoped that—"

"Furthermore," Eva interrupted, only half listening, "it seems that I must go to Budapest. To settle the matter of his assets."

"Budapest?" Now Dora struggled back to her feet, setting her hands on her robust hips. "No, Eva! You are not going to Budapest! Didn't you tell me that there are air raids going on almost daily?" There was a pause, and Eva looked up, realizing Dora wanted an answer, and saw in the crimson of her cheeks that Dora was incensed. "How can you even consider going there at a time like this, with danger lurking at every corner? You're a mother now, Eva, a mother! Haven't we discussed this already? Unless this is just a reason"—she waved her finger around—"for you to get back there so you can meddle in affairs . . . affairs that are none of your concern!"

"Dora! That's not what this is about!"

"No?"

"No! How can you even say that? I'm my father's only surviving relative, and there are matters of finances to be handled.

There are debts, apparently *many* debts, left unsettled, and if I don't make an appearance, all of my father's assets will be frozen. And you know well enough that we desperately need the money! For that reason alone, I must go."

"No, we will manage. We have managed so far, and we will continue—"

"Until when? You've been taking care of me for over a year, and now Bianca, too. How long are you going to keep going at this pace to support us? To see you work as hard as you do just to keep up with bare necessities is eating me up inside. It's killing me, Dora!" She paused for breath and lowered her voice, aware that Bianca had begun to whimper in her playpen. "I will not be an unnecessary burden to you, Dora, not if it can be helped. I will not stand by and see you work yourself into the ground for any mistakes that I have made. So please, Dora. Let me go. If I leave in the morning, I could be back by week's end. Maybe sooner."

Dora went and picked up Bianca, bounced her on her hip, cooing in her ear, and they said nothing further about it. But Eva knew in that ensuing silence the battle was won.

17

THAT NOVEMBER AFTERNOON, AS EVA TRUDGED on foot from the Nyugati station toward the center of town, she found it impossible to believe that this was the same city she'd left just over a year ago. Her Budapest, the Pearl of the Danube, had become a land of debris, of broken glass and despair. She hadn't been able to get a cab and was thankful that her valise was light enough for her to cover the two kilometers to Saint Stephen's Basilica on foot. Along the way, rows of apartment buildings stood as if leaning on one another for the last ounce of support: windows had been blown out or boarded up with wooden planks, and the once-gleaming, unabashed Parisian facades blended under a layer of soot. The parks, usually teeming with people soaking in the last rays of sun, were empty, the flower beds choked in overgrown weeds. At the corner of Szent István tér, she passed her favorite bistro, where as a child she would go with her mother on Sundays, insisting that she be the one to read out loud the day's specials. Now, in that same display case, a sign of a very different kind was posted in black lettering: *Not serving Jews.* Similar signs peppered windows everywhere, like mushrooms after a summer rain.

Minutes later, she entered an art nouveau building and walked up three flights of stairs to a heavy oak door with beveled glass left ajar. It was surprising stepping in to find herself not in a dusty, cramped office but rather a vast apartment with tall ceilings and custom bookshelves. A grand piano stood regally at the center. The lighting, warmed by red silk curtains, gave the sensation of having waltzed into an old boudoir painting salvaged from surrounding ruins.

"Ah, Miss César. Eva. Welcome."

She turned to the booming voice. Behind her stood a barrel-chested, aristocratic man with a shock of white hair leaning on an ivory walking cane. "I'm Igor Georgy." The cane shifted from his right hand to his left so that he could shake hers, gripping it firmly like a man's, which she rather liked. "First, let me extend my condolences. I know this must be very hard for you. It was rather . . . unexpected."

"Thank you, yes, it certainly was. But you did say that I needed to come urgently, so here I am."

"Would you like a refreshment?" Igor asked as he ushered her to a bright red brocade sofa near the window, beyond which the dome of Saint Stephen's Basilica sparkled in the softening light like some uncut jewel. "I have a wonderful peppermint tea that is just the perfect pick-me-up. Surely you must be tired after your journey. Or perhaps you would prefer something stronger."

"I'll take the stronger choice. Thank you."

Igor returned a minute later with two crystal glasses filled with ice and scotch and settled himself in a chair across from her, drawing his silk lounge jacket neatly over his crossed legs. There was a calmness about him, a solidness that set Eva at ease, and picking up the glass she reclined against the sofa.

"Well, how to begin. I know this is a difficult time for you. Let me start by saying that I hadn't seen your father in quite some time, and the state of his affairs was unknown to me."

"Unknown?"

"You see, as I mentioned to you on the phone, your father in recent months acquired a great deal of debt. Don't ask me how—as I said, he'd stopped consulting me long ago, since our interests became . . . unaligned. But the sad news of the matter is that there is a long line of investors who have been left uncompensated. And now, with all this uncertainty, this chaos, they are more eager than ever to mitigate their losses. I hate to have to speak so frankly, but it appears that the Sopron estate will have to be sold. If you can agree to that, at least you'll be able to hold on to the Budapest home. I can make certain of that."

Eva took a long sip of her drink, held the whiskey inside her mouth before letting it slide down her throat. "I'm a bit confused. How can this be? My father had plenty of money. And why Sopron, anyway? If assets must be liquidated, why not the Budapest home instead? Surely it's worth just as much."

"It is indeed. Although it appears that is the one asset that the debtors cannot go after, as technically, it belonged to your mother. It was hers before the marriage, as you probably already know. But Sopron, unfortunately . . . well, I'm afraid there isn't much I can do to salvage it."

Eva set her glass down and lowered her head, stared at the crimson motif of the Persian rug. She loved that villa with all her heart, and once she would have fought the idea tooth and nail. But during the past year, the truth was she hadn't even had the courage to walk up to the gates. It reminded her too much of Aleandro and their night on that bench, when everything had started, when she knew with every fiber of her being that she was falling in love. Dora's home was different, it had always belonged to her, but at the villa there would always be Aleandro.

"All right," she agreed. "I will sign whatever you need me to sign. I assume it's the reason you called me here."

There was a solemn nod. "It will take me several days to draft the documents and initiate the sale. Can I count on the fact that you will be here to sign them?"

"Yes. I cannot stay long, but I will wait."

"Thank you, Eva. Thank you for being so understanding. To be honest, I expected a different reaction."

She shrugged, caught in her thoughts. "These are strange times. It doesn't seem that anyone wants to fight for anything anymore. Why should I? With all the horror out there, with all the injustices committed around us, this seems a small loss, doesn't it?"

There was unquestionably surprise in his lingering gray gaze. "There are injustices everywhere in our world today."

"Yes. And we all choose to ignore them, do we not? A place

such as this"—she swept her arm out to indicate the room and all in it—"I assume is a nice place to shut it all out. Much like my own home over on Andrássy. A grand piano, books to get lost in. We are all guilty of it." She felt raw saying it, bolstered by the drink, unable to keep at bay the memory of a different injustice, so easily brought to the surface, like dying embers stoked into a full flame.

She was startled by the hearty laugh. "How different you are from your father. Even when you were a little girl, I knew this about you. I don't know if you remember me, but I used to visit your home when you were little. Back when your mother was still alive. She was different, too, had different . . . ideas. If anything, it is her that you remind me of."

"My mother . . ." Eva bit her lip, feeling the sting of tears. "My mother would have fought for change."

"And you, Eva, is that what you want?"

There was a long silence. "Mr. Georgy, once I thought that becoming a nurse was the only way in which I could apply myself, make myself useful in this world. But now . . . now, I think, perhaps there are other ways. Much, you see, has changed in my life as well."

"It is possible, you know. To bring about change. Although helping in a time like this . . . it is not for the faint of heart. There are people, Eva, many people who do care. People who are willing to help. If one should really desire it, that is."

No further words were needed as they held each other's eyes in understanding.

"I'm your gal," Eva said, feeling a smile rise up through her chest like a butterfly and land on her lips. "At least while I'm in Budapest. Just let me know what you'd like me to do."

For the next three days, Eva passed the afternoon hours at a small café on Vadász utca in the fifth district, not far from Saint Stephen's Basilica and her own home on Andrássy, sipping black coffee at a barstool facing the window. Waiting. Watching attentively the building across the street with its long rows of windows. Before the war, it had been a glass-manufacturing factory and was now simply known as the Glass House.

She checked her watch. Three fifteen. The usual signal never came past three o'clock sharp, and she was seized that afternoon with a slight panic. Sometimes whole blocks would be quartered off without any warning just minutes after five, and even someone like her, with her typical Aryan looks and perfect papers, would be subject to inspection by the German guards.

To her relief, the signal came a moment later—two quick bursts of light in the basement window, followed by a third flicker. She reached inside her purse, extracted a five-*pengö* note to place on the counter, then wrapped her coat tightly around herself. The interval between the flickering of lights and the opening of the door was precisely five minutes. Long enough for her to pay for her coffee and make it across. Not long enough to draw the attention of any patrolling guards who might be passing by when the package appeared on the landing.

The place she was to make her delivery, scribbled on a card and tucked inside a fold of the newspaper wrapping, was never the same. The first time, it was just an abandoned school building with shattered windows, where she placed the bundle inside the gymnasium under a row of bleachers. The day after—judging by the array of machinery rusting in the courtyard—it was a factory of sorts, where she left the parcel behind the reception desk in a vacant office. On her way home, there had been a second stop at a theater house across from one of the yellow-star houses, where she'd been instructed to place the package underneath a chair in a middle row.

She had no way of knowing exactly what they contained. Mr. Georgy had insisted that it was for her protection, but she'd heard that in the bowels of the safe house on Vadász, which sheltered hundreds of families from the brutality of the Nazi Arrow Cross, documents were being churned on a makeshift press day and night—counterfeit marriage certificates, fake identity papers, protective international passports, which symbolized, for the few Jews in Budapest, the difference between life and death. It mattered, of course, that what she carried so serenely across town put her own life at stake, that she might indeed, as Dora had said, orphan her daughter. Yet this was her one chance to vindicate herself in a small measure from the damages of her past. Within a couple of days, hours, she would slip quietly back into her mundane existence, but for now, she could help save just one life—one life, when so many others had been lost.

This afternoon she would make her final delivery. Earlier that morning she'd signed the papers, and there was no reason to delay her return to Sopron. Things were growing more dire by the day, and there was a good chance that the trains would soon stop running altogether. She'd spoken to Dora on the phone every night but knew that she was going out of her mind with worry. It was time to go back before the noose tightened around the capital. Word was that the Russian army was just about two dozen kilometers from the old town, and she couldn't risk being trapped here away from Dora and their home, away from her baby.

As she crossed the Széchenyi Bridge, the west bank unfolded as something from a Habsburg-era fairy tale, pristine still, proud in unabashed elegance despite the cloud of smoke looming over the Pest sector on the other side of the river. Near one of the lion statues, she brushed by a group of German soldiers who, leaning on the railing, were basking in the view of the Danube, which glowed red in the setting sun. One of them stepped in her path and clicked his heels, saluting her, while his companions laughed.

"Miss, don't mind him," said a soldier, pulling her assailant away by the sleeve. "My friend here apparently can't resist a pretty face. Not that I blame him. I myself would swim across this river for a chance to speak with you."

She said nothing, just smiled as brightly and innocently as she could, waving a gloved hand somewhat flirtatiously as she walked on, knowing they were watching her. Her heart was drumming too fast, making her light-headed. Yes, tomorrow, she thought, tomorrow she would board that first train.

On the other side of the river, she took the steps to the top of the hill, stopped to rest on a bench in front of Matthias Church, where she whispered a prayer of protection, unable still to shake the frisson of fear. Sweat had gathered under her arms, yet she forced herself to continue on, drifting farther into Buda's maze of winding streets, with their majestic oaks and old-world quietness. Another right turn on Lovas út brought her not to someone's lavish residence or opulent clothing store but what appeared to be the makeshift entrance to an air-raid bunker jutting out from a hillside.

Her only instruction this time was to wait there, which she did, trying to see through the blackened windows above the sidewalk. A few minutes later, the gate opened and a dark-haired girl of about Eva's age, in what looked to be a medic's uniform, appeared, carrying a lantern. There wasn't much of an introduction as she eyed Eva.

"You are Mr. Georgy's friend, I presume? César?"

"Yes. Yes, that's me."

"Well, good, then. Follow me."

A moment later, the girl led her at a slight distance through an underground labyrinth of passageways with peeling green paint and domed ceilings topped with exposed piping. A final turn brought them through an alcove and into a large storage area lined with rows of white metal cabinets. In the corner, an iron sink was filled with towels, rags. Some, Eva could see in the dim light, were splattered with blood.

"Please wait here," the girl said, placing the lantern down and turning it off. "Use this only in case the lights go out."

Then she was gone.

Eva waited, her anxiety spiking with each passing moment. Ten minutes had come and gone, and no one had come to look for her. Had she been out of her mind to let herself be brought down here without asking what this place was? Was it possible she'd been caught in a trap? She poked her head through the archway and down the length of the corridor, trying to remember the way she came. A few minutes more, she decided, and then she would bolt. She would leave the package right on the floor, and she would run.

Before she could withdraw back inside the room, a figure appeared at the end of the tunnel, a mid-statured man coming toward her at a fast clip, his steps echoing in the silence. She took in the white coat as the person came into view, the down-cast, concentrated gaze lifting to her—and felt all the blood pool at her feet. The man also froze when he saw her. Long seconds passed as they stared at each other.

"Eduard?"

"What are you . . . Eva? What are you doing here?"

His gaze shot past her shoulder, as if looking for an ex-planation, then landed on her again. In his eyes, she saw the initial confusion fade like a cinema screen going black, and something impenetrable and cold seeped in in its place. He'd thinned since their last encounter, although it wasn't exactly a gaunt look, but one of chiseled hardness. The cords at his neck were as sinewy as sailing ropes, the temples deepened with gray. There was a weariness in the downturned corners of his mouth, which made no attempt to smile.

"What are you doing here?" he repeated, quite roughly.

"I . . . I was to deliver a package." She fished the parcel from her bag, her hands trembling as she held it out to him. "This package, here."

He took it. Stared at it for an instant, maintaining the blank expression, his lips shaping around a soundless word. Then he laughed. It came like a rumble from deep in his chest, building into a full explosion.

"You? You are our courier? Well, I have to say, you're the last person I expected to see here. For something this bold, that is. Seeing how you didn't have the courage to convey, as I believe I had the right, that you wanted nothing more to do with me."

She couldn't get the words out, struggled to form something, aware that nothing would do, that there was no explanation to offer. "I'm so sorry, Eduard," she began feebly. "You didn't deserve that; you are right, and you have every reason to be angry with me, but it was complicated. It was a very confusing time for me, and it would have been difficult to explain to you the reasons." She swallowed hard. "The reasons, I mean, why I had to leave Budapest. But I'm here now, and I'm trying to do the right thing. I'm trying . . . I'm trying to make a difference."

"Well, how wonderful that you've decided to return."

"I haven't returned. Not really. I'm only here for a few days." She was tempted to tell him that her father had died, that as of this morning, the Sopron villa was no longer hers, that so much had changed in her life, but it was absurd to think he would care. He was right. She'd exited his life like a coward. There wasn't anything at all to speak of.

"Eduard, I know there is no excuse for what I did. For whatever it's worth, I want you to know that it had nothing to do with you."

"Nothing to do with me?"

"I know you find that hard to believe, but it's true. I never meant to cause you any harm. In a way, it was to protect you."

"To protect me? To protect *me*? You shattered my heart, Eva! Do you have any idea what it was like for me? I couldn't work! For months, I couldn't even work! All I could think of is that I managed to offend you somehow so deeply that you couldn't even bother to write me a good-bye note. To leave me the way you did, without a single word, was . . . Well, whatever it was, whatever your *reasons*, they certainly were not for my protection." He drew back, composing himself as he inhaled through his nose. "Well, thank you for the delivery. Good-bye, Eva."

He turned and walked away. She watched him go through the corridor and around the corner, and then she was alone again and had to lower herself to the ground. She didn't even have the strength to cry. She just remained there on the cold, checkered tiles, leaning on the wall, hating herself.

After some time, she made her way back to the street, embarking on what would be an exhausting trek home. She had to get away now. Budapest no longer had anything to do with her life now, and she thought it almost ironic that today of all days, this last string should be severed.

God, how she missed Dora and Bianca.

She quickened her step toward the Chain Bridge, but as she crossed through Fisherman's Bastion, where she'd stopped to rest just an hour before, something disrupted her course. There was a disturbance in the air, a trembling. A hissing. She looked up at the sky, but the sky was clear. She saw only the spire of Matthias Church spearing the sky like a white medieval sword, and the usual scatter of pedestrians below in the square. Yet the sound was still there, growing, deafening in her ears.

People were running in all directions, ducking under benches, under trees and alcoves. She caught sight of a woman's red overcoat disappearing inside the church as the ground heaved underneath her feet. There was a spray of glass—she was inside it, she realized, flying through the air with the shards, twisting with them in a dance as beautiful as it was grotesque. Then the ringing stopped abruptly, as if someone had shut out the sound, and a white silence enfolded her, carrying her off as if in a dream.

18

*T*HE FACES THEMSELVES HELD NO PARTICULAR meaning. It was only the features that Aleandro focused on—the arch of a nose, an eyebrow lifted slightly higher than the other, a strand of hair like an upside-down question mark over an exceedingly high forehead. Nothing existed beyond these features. The only way he could draw them at all was to deconstruct them in this way, to pull them apart, separate them from the person to whom they belonged.

One by one, the guards came to him—or rather, he was brought to them in that same office where he first painted the commandant, and a choice, if such a thing existed here, had been offered. "If you can do something as good as this," he recalled the commandant remarking from behind the massive oak desk, brandishing the sketchbook, "I may find a reason to spare you from the firing squad. I may find a way to overlook your . . . infraction."

In truth, Aleandro would have preferred facing the wall, yet, in the moments between standing in the courtyard and this stuffy room crammed with dossiers and an oil portrait of *der Führer* hanging above the desk, something had changed in him. A reversal of sorts. Eva had come to him on the brink of death, not to usher him to it but to pull him back. It wasn't madness to see it as an omen, a sign that she was out there, still waiting for him. He'd never seen anything more clearly. And so, his choice that day had been more or less made for him. For her, and the chance to see her again, he would live.

Since then, at least a dozen more guards passed through that very same chair. Most of them sat turned in profile, smoking, as Aleandro drew them, his fingers clutching the pastel stick so forcefully that it continued to break. Occasionally, they talked to him, these faces he couldn't look upon as a whole. They told him about their families back in Munich or Hamburg, their children in Hitler's youth camps, their wives and girlfriends they hadn't seen in years and for whom the portrait would come as a welcome surprise. Once in a while came a special request: If he could fill in that slightly receding hairline or omit that scar slicing through the upper cheek, there would be a nice little reward for him at the end. If he could shave off a few years from beneath the weary eyes, he would be spared labor detail, or better yet, the cleaning of the latrines for one week.

He didn't mind cleaning the latrines, he explained time and time again. He did not want food, either, for what honesty would there be in accepting it? He wouldn't betray the men in the barracks—not for a moldy bread roll or a grayish scrape of meat they wouldn't feed to their dogs. All he wanted was to get back his sketchbook. For that alone, he would paint all of the guards ten times over, he would clean the latrines every day, he would work in the quarries until his palms bled. Most times he was laughed at, shoved out of the way, but one day, one day, the miracle he prayed for materialized.

Something was tossed to the floor.

"Here you go, maestro," said one of the older guards, a man with a leathery, mottled face and bloodshot eyes, which regarded him with some detached curiosity. "This is what you've been asking for, isn't it? Well, consider this an early advance. For what, I'm not sure. But surely there will be something. There always is."

Aleandro fell at the foot of the chair on which the guard sat and picked up the sketchbook. Holding it to his chest, he turned away, gathered the oil pastels in a tin box, and handed the man his portrait.

"My God, she seems quite above your station, doesn't she?" There was an indifferent shrug as the guard swiped his coat from the back of the chair, narrowly missing Aleandro's face. "Well, we all fall for the wrong woman, don't we? God knows my choices haven't been all that different. But my one piece of advice for you is that you get yourself together." He laughed as he made his way to the door. "If I were in your place, I would try to forget her. It's not like you'll ever see her again."

All Aleandro could do was nod numbly. After the guard left, he crouched on the floor, muttering a prayer of thanks to the patch of sky in the window, where a gray column of smoke billowed above the distant scattering of cypress trees.

For many nights after, he held the sketchbook in his hands, sinking into dreams of her. Every detail had become a source of concentration, a source of sleeplessness: The tiny specks of gold in the depth of her blue pupils. The sprinkle of freckles on her tanned shoulders, like stardust flicked from a hand. The silver ball in her earlobe catching a glint of sun as she pushed back her hair and tucked a daisy behind her ear. These simple details were most important to him: from these details he could reconstruct the larger ones. He regretted drawing them in only charcoal, wished he had just once captured Eva in color.

In the morning, he placed the sketchbook underneath the mattress, got on with whatever was required of him, no longer caring what he had become. No longer caring that he was no more than a puppet on a string that the guards would keep alive as long as his hands kept producing.

And so, days passed, months, soon nearly half a year. At some point he no longer saw himself as human, but as a force floating outside of a body, which he regarded with increasing detachment. Flesh set apart only by a sea of armbands: red for Communists, purple for Jehovah's Witnesses, the yellow star for the Jews. Black for vagrants, criminals. Brown for people like him. They were all just flesh, sleepwalking on the periphery of life.

———

One afternoon in late October, a new prisoner was shoved into his barrack—a small-framed man with a pronounced Adam's apple and skin as translucent as a day-old corpse's. As soon as the guards left, the man went down to his knees, then collapsed to the floor in stages, as if releasing a long-held breath. To have been brought here, to this barrack occupied mostly by labor prisoners, seemed a mistake, for someone drenched in sweat and weak as he was would have been taken straight to the infirmary, or worse, to the brick building in the back of the camp from which no one returned.

The others didn't notice him: clustered in groups, they talked quietly among themselves while others sat on their bunks with vacant looks, dreaming of food. It was Aleandro who scooped the man up in his arms and carried him to the back, where he laid him in a crevice between the bunks and the wall. From his canteen, he poured water on his sleeve and swiped it across the man's fevered temples.

"Köszönöm."

"What did you say?" Gently, Aleandro shook his shoulder, then again, a little more forcefully. "What did you say?" He was nearly sure that he heard it correctly. *Thank you.* "Tell me, are you Hungarian? Are you from Hungary?"

Hoping to revive him, Aleandro lifted the man's head and poured some water into his mouth, but only some nonsensical, feeble ramblings came in response. For the rest of the night, all he could do was to keep vigil, rocking him gently as he might have one of his brothers, dribbling more water into his mouth as his frail body thrashed and shivered. "Stay awake, stay with me," he kept whispering, something that seemed meant not just for him but for his brothers as well, and all the others he'd seen die, far from home, alone, broken. After some time, Aleandro lay down next to him and draped his coat over them both. Warmth was perhaps the only small comfort that he could offer.

At dawn, when Aleandro's eyes flickered open, the man was no longer beside him. Disoriented, he staggered to his feet, and in the silence of the barrack, his heart plunged.

"Damn it! Damn, Aleandro!" he shouted to himself. Then, in the semidarkness, he spotted a mound on one of the empty bunks and flew like mad over the planks.

The man lay there with his knees drawn to his chest, facing the wall, and at first Aleandro hesitated to touch him, afraid that when he did there would be no movement, only the definitive stillness of a lifeless body. But the man did stir ever so slightly, and when Aleandro rolled him onto his back he was met not by a blank stare but by one so lucid, so present, that it jolted him away.

"I thought you were dead," murmured Aleandro in Hungarian, overcome with such sharp relief that his throat ached with tears. "I didn't think you would live to see the sun come up this morning. I was almost certain of it. But here you are, alive."

The man motioned for Aleandro to come closer. He smelled rank, and his cheeks were hollowed, as if the flesh had been scraped with a scalpel from the bones sustaining them, but his smile was utterly serene and untroubled as a full moon on a clear night.

"I nearly was dead," he whispered in Aleandro's ear. "It's a small miracle. A miracle indeed, my dear friend, that last night you didn't drown me with all that water."

His name was Rudolf. Rudolf Luben, born and raised in Budapest, the eldest child of a Romanian Jewish mother and a

French father whose ill-fated move to Hungary before the war had landed him in this unfortunate circumstance. He had inherited his mother's petite stature, but certainly not her fiery temper. No, Rudolf was a man who measured his words as well as his actions, a man who used his intellect as a weapon. An educated man. That much was clear to Aleandro from the way Rudolf spoke, using eloquent words he barely understood, yet somehow managing to make more sense than anyone ever had in all of his twenty-four years. And his eyes: there was a warmth in his whiskey-colored eyes, a glimmering light that seemed to belong to a madman at first, but now he viewed it as something entirely different. Rudolf seemed to float over all this horror as if he were observing it from above, and learning.

"So, tell me, Aleandro," Rudolf said in the following weeks, challenging Aleandro to see beyond their grim reality. "What of all this bothers you most? Is it the baseness, the humiliation we must endure, or the fact that such cruelty is inherent in human nature?"

"Both, I suppose. What about you?"

"Well, certainly I don't enjoy not knowing when my last day will come, but too much focus on the self leads to nothing constructive. Because when all a man thinks about is his own survival, he becomes no better than an animal. Fear can turn you into that, you know."

Until now, Aleandro had numbed himself in order to survive, but since meeting Rudolf, his humanity began to reawaken a little more each day in the hardened terrain of his soul.

"The body is just a vessel. It is the mind that can't be destroyed," Rudolf would remind him as the two stood in the courtyard at roll call before dawn with rain pouring down on them. "I want you to memorize these words, Aleandro, to say them as often as you can. I want you to repeat them in your dreams! Let's say it together now! Come on, let's say it now!"

Some mornings they were marched together through the main gates to a merry tune played by the camp orchestra, taken to the outskirts of the camp. Together they carried sandbags, broke concrete, dug ditches and tunnels. More often than not they had to use their bare hands, as tools were scarcely made available and sometimes held back on purpose by the guards. More than once they were harnessed to a massive roller, forced to push it across gravel roads, and they chanted Rudolf's words, sang them in defiance of their pain.

Aleandro could have easily used whatever influence he had with the guards to get out of this harshest form of labor, but he feared that Rudolf, not fully recovered, would collapse. Many stronger than him died every day, and he felt fiercely protective of the man. He had never begged for anything, but he did beg for Rudolf's life. On his knees he pleaded, and bargained, and offered anything at all that would be deemed as a payment. Only after accepting to produce a glorifying landscape of the camp and the surrounding grounds was Rudolf given all of two weeks to recuperate and prove himself fit for labor.

To the guards' surprise and unrelenting mocking, Aleandro began accepting the extra food rations he'd earlier turned down, although he never consumed them on the spot. Rather, he found a way to smuggle them inside of his coat, which had once belonged to a guard, and hand them to Rudolf outside of the bunker at night, while the others slept. To him, it was no longer a betrayal. None of it was a betrayal if he could save just this one man.

"Do you ever make mistakes in your portraits?" Rudolf asked one such night, taking a small, spotted apple from Aleandro's hand and polishing it fervently with his sleeve. "Do you, for instance, ever find yourself having to start over, to begin the whole thing from scratch on a clean sheet of paper?"

The question took Aleandro aback. "Why do you ask?"

"I'm just curious. Your pastels must run out much too often, do they not?"

"Well, truth is I try not to make mistakes. Mistakes in a place like this can be costly, you know that."

"That's just it. Only by making mistakes can you create something that truly counts, something of value." As Aleandro tried to make sense of his words, Rudolf chewed with relish the last bit of the apple, ate the core, too, giving a great groan of appreciation as he licked the juice off his fingers. "All that discarded paper bearing your errors could be put to a different use. They could reveal a . . . different reality. Do you see what I am saying?"

He did not, not right away. It took him a few long minutes to understand that all that squandered paper was indeed a precious commodity, that he could use it to document what unfolded inside the camp. A moment longer, he vacillated. The idea was so outlandish. He would no doubt be shot right on the spot. If a breach of this kind was discovered, he would be dragged across the roll-call square, and the wall under the watchtower would be the last thing his eyes would fix on. But, then again, hadn't he seen how cheap life was in a place like this, how easily crushed? And this, as Rudolf had said, was the one thing worth gambling one's miserable life on.

"So, Aleandro, are we in agreement, then? The great camp

portraitist must embrace his privileges and stop wasting his time with a scrawny little Jew. There are more crucial things to occupy him, yes?"

"I don't know about this, Rudolf. I just don't know. Those guards, they are beasts; they will work you into the ground and I cannot let them do that to you, I will not let them . . ." Aleandro kept rambling, but Rudolf gave him a hearty pat on the back and went inside the barrack, whistling serenely under his breath.

———

The first time Aleandro stuffed the scraps of paper and broken pastels in his pocket after a session with one of the guards, his knees shook with fear as he made his way across the campsite. Yet as the treasures under his mattress grew next to his sketchbook, he felt no fear any longer. He was alive, truly alive, in a way he'd never been before. He rose eager to see light budding in the narrow strip of glass across the barrack. While the others slept, he would take out his supplies, then draw in the near-dark, in the latrines, in any moment of solitude when the prisoners were out of the barrack. His agile hands moved with precision, each stroke redeeming him, each finished piece leaving him exhausted yet utterly exhilarated.

Alone, on the screen of his imagination, his drawings of the camp were held in the hands of men in free lands, their eyes filling with knowledge, with truth, with *his* truth. If even one of his drawings could find their way to the other side of the barbed-wire wall, he would die a content death.

———

Sometimes after midnight, he and Rudolf would talk freely in Hungarian, but never about their lives from before. It had become a defense mechanism, a way to preserve. Here and now was all that mattered. Their joint reality grounded them to each other, and to depart from it, to revisit the past, seemed a minefield of its own.

That changed one night in late November. In the depth of a cold night, as the wind whipped so fiercely around the barrack that it threatened to pull it from its pivots, Aleandro finally extracted his sketchbook from under his mattress. As Rudolf flipped through the pages, Aleandro began to tell him about the woman in the portraits.

It was the first time he'd said her name since the fire. *Eva, Eva.* Her name was a destination across a vast sea he navigated without a compass, but saying her name out loud dispelled the fantasy of what he might still be to her. Yet he kept going anyway, knowing he couldn't stop. Knowing he had to reach the end of the story, or he would never tell it again.

It was for her that he'd been keeping himself alive, he explained, for her that he'd accepted to do portraits for the guards and garlands in the margins of letters, and copy illustrations from photographs of people who did not know him and wished him dead. "Is it foolish?" he kept asking, breaking up the account. "Is it foolish to think it possible?" Foolish to think they could simply resume. The fire and the loss of his brothers had been punishment enough for the simple transgression of loving Eva.

He didn't want to speak of his brothers now, drained of vigor; he couldn't speak any further. Instead, he closed his eyes, needing, wanting, to shut out Rudolf's sad, inquisitive stare.

"It's all right," Rudolf said. "It's all right. It might help ease your burden if you tell me. It might even bring you some peace. So let it out, Aleandro. Get it off your chest. What happened with your brothers after the fire?"

"We were taken by the SS guards, just on the other side of the border, in Austria," resumed Aleandro after a long silence. "We were on a train for days. It was dark, and there was no air, and my little brother kept asking for water. The stench in that wagon was too much to bear; there was only a common bucket in the corner, and we all had to relieve ourselves, even the women, all of us, in plain view of everyone. We were brought to a forest. I remember, Rudolf, those beautiful lean trees that reached to the sun, as if one still existed. We were forced to sleep there among those trees, in the open air, in mud, in the swarm of worms. Whips came down on our backs; it seemed the beatings kept coming for no reason. No reason. After a couple of weeks, they began selecting the men, separating them from the women and children. By then, there was no need to separate me from my brothers. Lukas . . . he was always fragile, he'd hardly been conscious since we were let off the train, and Tamás and Attia, too, had fallen ill with dysentery. They just all lay there, staring up at that dreadful sky beyond the peaks of the trees.

"The next day they came and took them, and I kept screaming until they beat me unconscious. Someone told me a few days later that anyone who couldn't stand was tossed in a ditch at the edge of the forest. With the other bodies." Aleandro began weeping, raking his hand through his tangled curls as if to expel the horror of those visions. "And that, Rudolf, was the last time I saw my brothers. But above all, what I can't forgive myself for, what torments me more than anything else, is that the fire, that awful fire had been set *for me*. It was because of my foolishness that we were forced to flee Sopron, because of my foolishness that my brothers died."

"The most terrible thing we will ever endure as humans, Aleandro, is losing those we love," said Rudolf after a long contemplation, "but you must see that you are not to blame for the fire, nor are you to blame for your brothers' fates. You, just like me, just like everyone else in this godforsaken place, are the victims. Although, do you see? By doing what you're doing now, you are seeing that they haven't died in vain. You are honoring your brothers, and you are honoring Eva and what she meant to you. And that, my friend, is your comfort. It is your strength."

In the darkness and the silence that fell upon them, Aleandro nodded and smiled. It was his first smile in more than a year.

19

Budapest
Winter 1944

THE AIR—COLD, DRY, IMBUED WITH something medicinal—raised goose bumps on Eva's skin. An electric white bulb dangling overhead kept winking in and out. She tried to anchor her eyes on it to keep the room from spinning, but couldn't. She couldn't even lift her hand to her temple, there, where it felt as if a blade sliced through the bone of her skull and into the pulp of her overwrought brain.

Something cool and moist landed on her forehead, and as it came away, a smearing of blood like a swipe of watercolor flashed in her vision, dark pink more than red. She shivered beneath a scratchy blanket, then another was placed on top, bringing the sensation of being bathed in warm water. She blinked, tilted her head, forcing her eyes to take in the surroundings: a sea of beds. She was in a sea of beds and dark green uniforms, bandaged limbs, festering wounds, naked torsos. She was in a sea of moans and curses and cries, and the smell of blood and sweat was too much to bear.

When she opened her eyes again, a person was there, bent in concentration over some part of her, her left forearm, she thought. The face lifted and came into view, and Eva saw it was a woman's. Above the mask, deep brown eyes stared back at her. She seemed vaguely familiar. Why?

"Don't try to talk," the woman said, her voice clipped, her mask sliding down her longish chin to expose a beauty mark in the corner of her wide, pale lips. The voice, curiously, stirred recognition.

It was the woman she'd met earlier at the entrance of the bunker. Her dark locks had been chopped crudely, unevenly, to her chin, but it did not deter from her femininity, rather it accentuated the lines of her chiseled, heart-shaped face. With the efficiency of a warden, she was busying herself with a fluid bag next to the bed, pulling it off the pole, checking the connecting tube. There was something Eva meant to ask her but couldn't keep her eyes open, and her thoughts scattered from her, spinning into a tangled web.

The next time she woke, it was in a full frenzy. No fog covering her eyes now, and the dull ache in her temple had mellowed, but it was as though her heart, remembering something that her brain could not, insisted that she get herself moving. The girl was no longer at her side but was tending to someone across the aisle, bending her slender figure over the bed to tuck the sheet under the mattress. Noticing Eva trying to get out of bed, she was back at her side in an instant.

"I have to go, miss, can you help me?" Eva used every ounce of strength to hold herself upright in the bed. "I have to go. There's a train I must catch tonight. In the morning, at the very latest."

"Eva. It's Eva, right?" The voice held the same authoritarian note, but her eyes were kind and tolerant, reminding Eva of the Sisters of Mercy from her primary schooling days. "Please try to relax," she said, as Eva swung her legs off the bed. "You are in no position to go anywhere. I'm afraid that if you don't sit down, you are likely to faint. Please do us both a favor. Lie down," she insisted.

She did as she was told and leaned against the raised pillow. The woman was right. A weakness was spreading through her, and she felt light-headed again.

"Which hospital am I in?"

"Don't you remember? You delivered a package here. I met you at the door, brought you inside. As you were leaving, you were caught in a skirmish by the bridge. You suffered a head wound, and a pretty nasty one at that. Plus, some lacerations on your arm. You are very fortunate, considering the strength of the blast. You could have easily been killed."

"Well, I do feel much better now. And I have to go . . . Tamara," Eva added, struggling to read the name tag pinned to the white apron. "I have a train to get to tonight."

"Eva, even if I could let you walk out of here, which I won't, I'm afraid there won't be a train for you to catch."

Eva stared at her in disbelief, wondering if she'd heard her correctly. She couldn't be kept here against her will. "Tamara, look," she began again. "I appreciate your concern. But I have responsibilities at home. In Sopron. Responsibilities that cannot wait. Not for something as simple as a tiny head wound, a few scratches. I'm perfectly fine now. Surely your energy would be better spent elsewhere."

"I understand. But there's no point in trying to catch a train, because the fact is, there are no trains departing Budapest at the moment."

"That can't be true. I checked the schedule just this afternoon, before coming here. They are running as usual, and I intend to be on one."

"This afternoon?" Tamara regarded her, one shapely, raised eyebrow forming a crease in an otherwise perfectly smooth forehead. She shook her head. "Let us start again. My dear, you've been here for three weeks."

The shelling targeted Castle Hill, where the Nazis had concentrated their forces and fortified the hillside with cannons and artillery posts. Fortunately, it had not hit the Royal Palace but had created a gaping hole in the middle of Castle District, where Eva was. Ever since the bombings had intensified, the underground hospital nestled under the hillside had become overrun. Aboveground, in a city that was a battlefield on both sides of the river, the air sirens sounded day and night, forcing the vast majority of Budapest citizens to live in their basements. The city had begun to starve, all hope that Budapest would be declared an open city dashed. Hitler would not relinquish the Pearl of the Danube to the encircling Russian army at any cost, and was willing to fight for it to the last man.

"So, Eva," Tamara concluded as she updated her on these grim events, "you are safest here. The passages I walked you through, if you remember, connect to Saint John's Hospital aboveground, and we are still able to get supplies and food, not to mention that we are in a safe place that's practically bombproof. Some of the patients are begging to have their families stay here, too. Believe me, if you saw what is out there, you would be begging to stay as well. To consider walking out right now would be sheer madness."

It was then that everything poured out of Eva like water gushing through a fissured dam. She confessed to this girl whom she barely knew and wasn't sure at all if she could trust the one thing she hadn't been able to tell a soul. She had a child, a baby, just seven months old. A dear friend was taking care of her in her absence, a most beloved friend who was mourning her perhaps in this very moment, thinking her dead. It didn't matter in the moment if Tamara kept her confidence or if she didn't. All that mattered was that she had to reach Dora somehow, to let her know that she was alive.

"A telegram. I have to send a telegram. Please, Tamara, I must get word to my friend that I'm all right. I would be indebted to you for the rest of my life. I will do anything to repay you. Anything at all. Just ask."

"I will see what I can do, Eva. Just promise you won't do something so foolish as trying to get out of here, or Budapest, for that matter. It's entirely surrounded by Stalin's men. The roads to Vienna have been seized anyway; you wouldn't be able to make it to Sopron. Not outside of a casket."

Another week passed before Tamara told her that a medic who had gone to the Pest side for penicillin managed to send the telegram to the address that Eva had given, with only three words: *I am safe.*

There was no time to feel relieved or thank Tamara or wonder if the telegram had reached Dora. Every hour of the day, every minute, brought a new crisis. More stretchers arrived, hundreds, thousands, overflowing the hallways and corridors. Some of the beds were pushed together so that the wounded could be stacked lengthwise to maximize the available space. As Eva ambled through the rows, she found it impossible to distinguish the soldiers from the civilians, the Germans from the Hungarians, the adolescents from the men. Those who didn't last the night were taken outside and left in the bomb trenches or on the sidewalk in front of the hospital entrance. The ground had frozen, making burials an impossibility, so they were just left there, where a layer of snow could preserve them for the time being. No one had any idea how much longer it would continue, when the nightmare would end.

The whole time, Eva rarely saw Eduard. Once in a while, he passed through the ward, wan and exhausted, a shadow of a man drifting through the landscape of ruin. He checked on the severely wounded, shouted a few orders, doled out a few words of comfort, held a few hands, checked charts, then he would leave. He looked like a shelling victim himself, his fatigues covered perpetually in blood, his hair mashed with dirt and sweat, his eyeglasses fissured. One day, as he was tending to a soldier in a nearby bed, she noticed a deep cut on his right hand, spanning from his fourth finger down to his thumb. It had been stitched crudely and looked to be infected, the wound shining an angry purple beyond the tiny metal teeth.

"Eduard, you should have that tended to, disinfected. It may have to be restitched," she shot in his direction. It was the first words she'd spoken to him since that initial encounter, and he turned to look at her but said nothing. Only showed a tiny, sad smile. Then a new deluge of stretchers poured into the ward and he disappeared in the swell of activity.

"Please let me help," Eva implored Tamara the following week. She would go mad here if she didn't do something, and the truth was, the wound on the side of her head was nearly healed. The headaches and fainting spells still came and went, but that alone didn't warrant her taking up a bed, or lolling around the ward like an invalid when so many others suffered far greater afflictions. "I'm really just fine, and I've been studying for the past couple of years to become a nurse," she explained as Tamara changed her dressing, swiping iodine at the wound at her hairline, which, despite herself, made her wince. "I don't have any formal training, but I can wash bandages, I can clean bedpans, I can do anything. Whatever you need."

She saw in Tamara's eyes what the answer would be, but Eduard had appeared at her side with an air of agitation, interrupting the exchange.

"Ready?" he addressed Tamara, not glancing in Eva's direction, as had become his habit. "Let's do it now. I heard another transport is being brought in right now, and we will need all the blood we can get. Have you asked the rest of the staff if they can contribute?"

"I have," Tamara replied solemnly. "I did so myself, just this morning." Then, as an afterthought, flashing an eyebrow toward Eva: "Doctor Kovaks, my friend here says that she wants to help, but perhaps you can explain to her that this is no place for a civilian to do anything but recover."

"Let her," Eduard said, surprising both women. "She's right. She does have some medical knowledge, as far as I recall. Certainly enough to do what she's offering. And we do need the help. Desperately."

"Thank you," Eva muttered as he turned his back to her and walked to a chair. Plopping himself in it, stretching out his legs, he rolled up his sleeve, his arm extending to the fisted, injured hand, his face turned inward, focused. Then Tamara was right there beside him, kneeling at his feet as a worshipping saint, applying a tourniquet before inserting a needle into his vein. The blood flowed, plentiful and bright red, through the thin plastic tube, and Eva had to look away from the intimacy of the scene.

"Enough," Tamara said after several vials were filled. "That's plenty."

"No, not enough. Don't stop."

"Doctor, please."

"I'm fine, Tamara. Keep it going. I'm all right."

But he was not fine, for he'd turned white as a sheet, and as Tamara glanced up at him and said now, tilting her lovely lips to his ear in a voice so tender that Eva's blood rose to her cheeks, "Eduard, please," that she realized what had evaded her all this time. It wasn't just admiration Tamara felt for Eduard. And it was because of him that Tamara had insisted that she stay in the bunker.

20

J N MID-JANUARY, AT THE END of the sixth week since
Eva's arrival at the Hospital in the Rock, word trickled
in that in Pest, the Russians were battling the Germans
and Hungarians street to street, house to house. People were
succumbing to eating dead horses to keep themselves from
complete starvation. In here, the supplies had run out altogether, and the sanitary conditions were growing direr by the
day. Saint John's Hospital had been badly damaged and evacuated, most of the victims brought here, exceeding the capacity
tenfold. It had become a common sight to see blood smeared
on walls, to see the bedpans unemptied, abuzz with flies. The
stench of decay was unbearable; the screams were relentless.
Bandages were stripped off the dead and reused, and Eva spent
most of her days washing them in a sink.

Eduard had still only spoken to her just a few words, but

sometimes she would look up from her grim tasks and see him watching her. Once, she held his gaze and did not drop it away, forcing him to see her, to really see her. She was surprised to see a tiny nod of acknowledgment, as if to say, *You are doing a good job.* Then Tamara was back at his side, as she seemed to be constantly, bringing him charts to sign, X-rays to look at, insisting that he get something to eat, that he needed to get a few hours of rest.

Eva herself never slept more than three, four hours a night, waiting for a stretcher to become vacant, ate whatever could be scrounged from the kitchen after the patients had received their rations—a hunk of hard bread mostly, and water she prayed was not contaminated. The only time she went above-ground for some fresh air was to help bring in the stretchers. She and the other nurses would huddle by the gate and lis-ten to the ambulance sirens shriek closer and closer, the boom of cannon fire and bursts of machine guns at the riverbank drowning them out momentarily. She became numb to even the most horrific wounds—missing limbs, third-degree burns, faces disfigured by the grazing of bullets.

All in all, it kept her own terror at bay: terror that she may never see Dora or Bianca again, that they might not have survived, that she herself may not live long enough to get back to them. Terror that she would have to live the rest of her life mourning, mourning them, her mother, Aleandro, stumbling through endless, vacant days with only memories to sustain her.

One afternoon, when a new load of patients was carried inside, Eva was called into the operating theater to attend on a surgery. There were several doctors in the hospital whom she'd assisted from time to time, doctors who did not know about her lack of training and more often than not settled on the first nurse or Red Cross volunteer available. She expected the usual set of tasks, comprising mostly holding a hand or a floodlight, or swiping the surgery site with alcohol. But this time, the surgeon in full fatigues waved to her from the sink to come join him, and when she walked over, she was shocked to see that it was Eduard.

"Wash," he instructed. "All the way to the elbow. For twenty seconds. Then glove up."

"Yes, of course," she said, flustered by his directness. "What do you need me to do?"

"You have small hands."

"I'm sorry?"

"Your hands. They are small, I remember. And for what I need, delicate hands and slim fingers are vital. It's why I called for you."

"Thank you," she said. "I can help." Eduard motioned to the sink with his chin, hands held up in the air.

"Wash now."

Minutes later, they stood at the operating table where a soldier lay unconscious, his chest stripped bare to reveal a bullet hole, right above the heart. A medic dosed the patient with iodine, and a scalpel was passed into Eduard's hand. A measuring look passed from him to her across the table, which she met with a steady gaze. Then it began quickly, without much fanfare, the room falling into full silence.

There was a cut. Long, precise, along the length of the boy's torso. Yes, the soldier was just a boy. Eduard worked alone as he opened the incision using retractors, stretching the layers of muscles with utter calmness, humming softly under his breath. An array of other instruments passed into his hand, and after a few more maneuvers, his eyes flashed up to her, intent, blazing. Eva's breath cut a bit short. He'd looked at her that precise way once, the night he'd proposed to her. As if they were embarking on an unknown journey.

"You ready?"

She nodded. She still didn't know her role in all this, but she was ready for whatever it was that he needed. Her heart was in a full run, a current threading under her skin.

"Good. Now come here, Eva. Right next to me."

She did. She came close enough to see, to really see the incision site, and there, underneath the skin and muscle, was the boy's heart. Beating. Miraculously beating.

There was no time for her to fully absorb this as Eduard took her hand. "Your finger," he instructed further. "Give me your forefinger." He then brought it down to the boy's chest and guided it deeply into the incision, into the soft pulp of muscle and flesh. A sound came from her throat. The pulsating rhythm intensified under her touch. Her finger was resting on a man's heart!

"Now, Eva." Eduard's voice grounded her. "There is a shell fragment in here, and I need you to find it for me. Can you do that? Find it. Feel for it. It should be close to the surface, and tiny, like a seed of rice. Concentrate."

She did. She poured all of her focus and will into it, and found it—a slight, sharp rising underneath the heart wall, and she gave an affirming nod.

"Good. That's good. Now hold it in place. Do not let it slip away." Then, without further warning, his scalpel came down again, carving a hairline in the dark pink, pulsing organ right where her finger was.

Blood poured out, an awful lot of it, and she couldn't help but back onto a wall. Yet it was all right, for she was no longer needed; her job was finished. Eduard extracted the piece of shrapnel, then immediately begin stitching, unaware that she was no longer beside him, the others taking over for her as she stared down at the splatters of blood on her blue uniform, trying to catch her breath.

The whole thing had taken no more than five minutes, but she was flushed, and her own heart drummed wildly. She'd helped save a life! She and Eduard saved a life together; she'd helped him mend a wounded heart. He'd trusted that she could do it. But it wasn't just pride, or wonderment, or even the rush of adrenaline, that kept her awake half that night.

Seeing Eduard work stirred something inside her deeply dormant.

———

Early the next morning, Eva was with Tamara, extracting antibiotic ampules and bandages from one of the cabinets in the storage area. They were silent at first—Eva still caught in the events of the day prior, yet as she closed the cabinet door, Tamara turned to her quite abruptly.

"What was it like? Yesterday, in the surgery, what was it like?"

"It was . . . it was incredible. To see a beating heart, it was magical. Rather shocking, but magical."

"No, what I mean is what was it like working with him?"

"Well, you know. You do it all the time. He's . . . precise, confident. He doesn't hesitate. He's solid."

Tamara surprised her with a laugh. "Solid? Good God, Eva, do you realize that procedure has only ever been performed a couple of times before? Only a couple of times. By an American army surgeon who no doubt had far better equipment than we do down here. So I guess you could say that makes Doctor Kovaks . . . solid." She gave another tiny scoff. "Is that how you think of him?"

Now she felt embarrassed, provincial. How was she supposed to know that? It wasn't like she'd been briefed beforehand. She'd been called in and she'd done what she'd been asked. But she blushed when she thought of how to answer Tamara. How did she think of him? With utmost respect, of course, but something had shifted in her feelings for him. It wasn't a definable thing, but more a slight stirring, a feather brushing on her heavy heart. If anything, it reminded her of how she felt when she met him the night of the party and knew right away that he would always treat her as an equal, that he saw in her the possibilities that no one else had. This, however, she couldn't confide in Tamara. She knew nothing of their past.

"Well, I'm grateful, of course," Eva tried redirecting. "Grateful for the opportunity that Ed—I mean, Doctor Kovaks gave me yesterday." At least this part was true.

"Yes. *Eduard*," Tamara said, emphasizing the name, "clearly holds you in quite high regard. Because he's never called in another nurse to assist on a surgery like that. I suppose you should be grateful. If that's all that you really feel."

Heat pounded in Eva's face. "Look, Tamara," she began

again before Tamara could fire any further probing questions. "If I've somehow given you the impression that I'm trying to take your place in all this, I want you to know that's not the case. I'm merely trying to help."

"Help. Is that the only thing?"

"Yes . . . help. As I told you before, it keeps me from thinking that when I walk out of this shelter, someday, there will be nothing out there for me. That all that has been good in my life might no longer exist. So yes, helping, keeping busy, it's really a gift."

"This war." Tamara breathed out sharply as she turned and collected some freshly washed towels drying on a pipe over the sink. "We may never go back to the lives we once had, but what I do know is that life will go on. In whatever capacity, we still have it within us to rebuild. Sometimes the bigger tragedy is not seeing what we already have, what is still here, within our reach." She said this in a very sad sort of way, walked toward the door, then stopped halfway, looking down at her full hands. "Perhaps you might want to open your eyes, Eva. Because what you still have is far more than dust."

Then she was gone, leaving Eva there to ponder the meaning of her words, until another siren sounded, and the shelter door burst open, bringing in a new wave of wounded, and she was in motion again.

———

Several days later, Eva and some of the nurses went outside to wait for the ambulances, only to find the city eerily quiet. No bombs now, no sirens, nothing but a deadly silence stretched into the crisp, sunny sky. A truck of Soviet soldiers rumbled by, waving flags, cheering, passing around a bottle of vodka. One of them shot his rifle into the air, but it was only a shot of cheerful jubilation.

The stark change must have been noticed down in the bunker, too, for within minutes, the entire staff and all the patients who could walk poured out through the gate, stumbling blindly to the end of the street on crutches and sustaining shoulders, afraid to go any farther. It was decided that a couple of medics would walk over to Castle Hill to check out the situation. An hour later, they returned with news: the battle for Budapest that had shaken the earth for nearly two months was over. The German army and their Arrow Cross accomplices had been crushed, and the few who had escaped were trapped in buildings, surrounded by the Russian soldiers with little choice but to surrender. The Soviets held the city.

Through the frenzy that erupted, the cheers, the cries, Eva struggled to find Eduard. There was no sign of him anywhere, and she panicked that they would part again without a single word. At the very least, she wanted to thank him, to wish him happiness, but then realized that likely he'd already gone and that perhaps it was for the better, for it wouldn't change much between them. That perhaps having her assist in the surgery had been his good-bye, his way of parting with her on his terms.

Still, she tried the bunker one last time. No Eduard, but Tamara was there, feeding soup to a young boy whose left eye had been covered in gauze.

"I was just telling József here," Tamara said, not taking her tender gaze away from the boy, "that he should not be afraid.

He is safe here, and he can stay as long as he needs. And afterward, the Red Cross will help him find his parents. I will see to it myself. In the meantime, we will take good care of him here. Isn't that right, Eva?"

Tenderness rushed through her. Eva sat down on the bed behind Tamara and set her chin on her shoulder, inhaling her smell of slight perspiration and something woodsy. Tamara was one big contradiction: tough as much as warm, tending to the boy with the same devotion Eva had experienced personally, even though she'd once been the fiancée of the man Tamara loved. For this woman certainly loved Eduard, but Eva wasn't feeling jealous—more a coursing, dull regret.

"Before I go, I want you to know, Tamara, that I'll never forget what you've done for me. For that telegram you sent on my behalf. For taking care of me while I recovered. You are one of a kind. And a wonderful nurse."

"Go on," Tamara said in her unsentimental way. "Go on, get out of here. Get back to your daughter, to your friend. Be careful, though—it will not be safe out there for a while, if I had to guess. The reputation of the Red Army precedes itself. God help us for what is still in store now that they've got Hungary under their boot. I can't help feeling that we've escaped the clutches of one monster only to land in another's. Well, at least there will be a reprieve. For now."

"I will be careful. And you, Tamara? What will you do now?"

"No different from what I did before. I will take a long bath. I will sleep. I will reconnect with those from my past who have been fortunate to survive. I will cry for the others. Then, in time, I will return to this, to my nursing job."

Eva couldn't help smiling. "Perhaps, Tamara, at some point, we might get in touch? Maybe we can get to know each other better. Under different circumstances."

"I don't think that would be wise," Tamara said, maintaining her unreadable expression. "Under different circumstances, as you say, we would have been good friends. But I'm afraid you would always remind me of a loss of my own." She shook her head. "Don't look at me like that. I'm not blaming you, Eva. We all cause one another's losses without meaning to; it's the way of humankind."

There was no time to argue with her—or point out otherwise, or to come right out and say that the path to Eduard was open, for hers had closed long ago—because Tamara had resumed feeding soup to the boy. Setting the bowl aside, she began singing him a melody, and the boy reclined against the pillow, his features softening into a deep sleep.

From across the ward, Eva glanced in her direction one last time. "I wish you luck with all your dreams," she shouted out, then she turned and left, wondering how it was that she and Tamara understood each other so well and yet so very little.

———

It took Eva nearly six hours to reach the Pest side of the river and make her way on foot toward her home on Andrássy, praying that she would find it in one piece. All seven bridges spanning the Danube had been blown up by the Germans in a last attempt to hold Buda, and she'd had to wait on the riverbank amid a mass of people to find room on one of the fisherman boats carting civilians across.

Part of her wished she hadn't left the shelter so soon. If at all possible, the chaos out here was even worse than what she witnessed inside the cave. Families stood on the bank amid bundles of clothing, hugging shell-shocked children, weeping. On the other side of the river, navigated with much difficulty among patches of ice, she walked through the charred streets riddled with burning cars, scraps of metal, piles of concrete. Some of the buildings had been stripped of their facades, exposing interiors of lives interrupted—dining tables strewn with plates, toys scattered on rugs. In a square, just four blocks from her own home on Andrássy, what looked to be a dozen dead German soldiers had been piled near the statue of Franz Liszt. Liszt looked down on them as if in judgment, his large hands splayed on the bronze chair shattered by bullets. Soviet tanks rumbled by like a swarm of ants, the soldiers singing victorious songs in a city of ruins.

At the time, she had no way of knowing that while she'd been sheltering in the hospital, forty thousand civilians lost their lives in those ruins, that another thirty-five hundred men, women, and children had been shot on the banks of the Danube and dumped into the freezing water by the Arrow Cross militia. That within days their bloated bodies would begin clogging the riverbank, slowing the construction of pontoon bridges. She would have no way of knowing that Igor Georgy had been among them, or that every person inside the building on Vadász utca where she'd collected the packages was marched only seven days later to that same spot where the river would be stained red for years to come.

Looking back on this, she would be glad that in that moment, she did not know any of these things. It would have been impossible for her to draw one more breath from the smoke-filled sky, to take another step into a world such as this. All she knew then was that to see her daughter again she would have to traverse this land of apocalypse, and so she kept her eyes downcast, willing her feet to move.

21

*E*VA NEARLY FAINTED WITH RELIEF AT the sight of her home standing—marred by bullets, yes, but standing— and the Venus statues welcomed her solemnly through the entrance, unlocked, to her surprise. The phone line was dead. None of the three families on the lower level had answered their doors—not even when she pounded them with her fists—and then came nighttime, another night she would endure without knowing if Dora and her baby were safe.

There was no electricity in the apartment, no heat, and all of the windows were either fractured or shattered. She tried every light switch, every furnace, then luckily in the kitchen she found a couple of utility candles and matches. She lit one, then ambled back through the vastness of the flat littered with glass and crumbled plaster, never having needed a shot of brandy more. The liquor cabinet was empty, but at least an old pack of Gauloises was there, in a gap underneath the glassware shelf where she'd made a habit of stashing them. Numb from cold, she extracted the matches from the filmy wrapper and sparked one, smoked it standing in the middle of what she realized now had been a looting. Above the mantel, in place of the Vermeer oil portrait that had been in her mother's family for two generations, there was only a lightened patch in the layer of soot, and on the sofa table, the bronze centurion statuette had been replaced by an empty gin bottle next to an overstuffed ashtray.

She locked the door twice, shuddering once more at the unnerving quietness of the hallways, and made her way to the bathroom, where she placed the candle on the ledge of the tub. The water spurted ice-cold and smelling of rust, killing any desire she might have had for a bath. Instead, she took her last shriveled cigarette to her room and smoked it in the window seat from which once, on a night like this, she used to watch the Champs-Élysées of Budapest come alive in an array of colorful umbrellas and fancy frocks, moving in a cluster of unsuspecting cheerfulness in the direction of the Operaház. Exhausted, she crawled onto her bed and fell asleep with her shoes and coat on.

It was midday, perhaps early afternoon, when she woke with a searing headache, a queasiness swelling in the pit of her stomach. In the dressing mirror across the room, when she scooted herself up against the headboard, the face of a stranger looked back at her. The sharp, feral eyes, the plastered hair, the ghoulish twisted mouth couldn't have belonged to her. She forced herself out of bed, went back into the hallway to see if the phone was working. This time she screamed, banged the useless receiver on the edge of the hallway table, not giving a damn that she was damaging a hundred-year-old antique. Then a sharp knock at the door cut through her frustration, and she let the receiver drop.

"Who's there?"

The rush of sudden adrenaline should have sent her reeling but instead she inched closer, splayed her hands on the bloodred, lacquered door. "Whoever you are, leave now! I have a gun and I swear I will use it. In three seconds, I will shoot it right through this door."

"Eva. Eva, let me in."

She leaned against the surface. Pressing her cheek to it, she listened for the voice again.

"Eva, please. It's all right. Please open up."

Shakily, she unlatched the bolt and pulled the door open to see the man standing before her. A faint chorus of voices trickled in and broke the heavy stillness between her and Eduard.

"How did you know I was here?" Eva said when Eduard stepped inside and looked around gravely at the state of the place, then anchored his steel-blue gaze on her again.

"I didn't. I took a chance."

He was wearing a thin coat too flimsy for the weather, one she remembered vaguely from the spring prior, and in his hand, there was a brown paper bag from which he lifted a bottle of wine with a faded, silver label. "From before the siege," he explained. "Well, it seems I got here just in time. Apparently, we could both do with a drink right now."

A few minutes later, Eduard made a fire with a few splinters of wood found in the hearth basket while she did her best to pull herself together, scouring for a clean dress inside her armoire, running a brush uselessly through the tangle of her hair, then eventually pulling it into a ponytail. The wine was slightly turned, but it hardly mattered. She was just happy to sit there with him, to feel, even if it was to pretend, that her life was the same as it had been two years ago. Just to pretend.

"I heard about your father and wanted to say how sorry I am for your loss," Eduard said from the opposite end of the sofa, his eyes intent on the wine, which he swirled in his glass. There was a formality in him, which seemed displaced given their time in the hospital, and Eva thought soberly that he wouldn't stay long. "I came here to tell you that, because I behaved rather . . . gruffly in the past few weeks. It was just such a shock to see you, and I needed time to process it, if I have to be honest."

"Thank you, Eduard, that's very kind. But my father and I . . . we had differences at the very end. We were never really close in the first place, as you know, although yes, losing a parent is never easy, is it? But you don't owe me an apology of any kind. If anyone should apologize, it is me. You were right when you said that I treated you unfairly."

"*Abhorrently*, I think would be a better word," he retorted. There was a trace of humor in his voice although none of it rose to his eyes, which remained pinned on the glass. A faint flush permeated his face. It had not occurred to her that he might be nervous as well, and a warmth inundated her.

"Do you think you could ever forgive me, Eduard? Do you think now, at the end of this awful road, there is a chance that we might still be friends? Because I would like that. I would like it very much."

"I've already forgiven you, Eva. How could I not, after all that I saw you do in that hospital? I saw the goodness that has always been in you, the goodness and determination and courage that enchanted me when we first met. And I thought, because at least that still existed, maybe now, as you say, after all that we've been through, you might finally be able to confide in me what you couldn't before. If it is friendship that you want, Eva, I'm here to give it. But some things must be settled before that. I'd like to trust you again."

"Oh, Eduard, does it really matter? Does any of it matter now?"

"It will always matter to me, Eva. You see, despite everything, it seems that I still care for you deeply. And yes, I do need to know. For my own peace, I do."

She measured his expression as he refilled her glass, recalling Tamara's words. *What you still have is far more than dust.* Yet he wasn't hers to have any longer; she'd forgone that right long ago.

"Tamara has said nothing to you? In all our time in the bunker?"

"No, nothing pertaining to us. None that I recall."

"Tamara loves you, you know. She loves you, Eduard. And she would make you very happy." They were beyond pretenses now, and she was rather glad for it.

"I know," he acknowledged, resigned. "And not long ago, I thought perhaps I could love her, too." He searched Eva's face, his eyes gleaming with renewed energy. "You see, Eva, unfortunately for me, it seems that nothing can change my feelings for you. Not her, not even this godforsaken war."

Eva bit her lip and looked into the embers in the fireplace as they petered out, leaving the room in its usual coldness. How easily it could have been once to marry him, to have this man at her side, this man she did not deserve nor love in the same way she'd loved Aleandro. How very awful, she thought, that the heart should so stubbornly attach to phantoms while everything real and true should subside under its tyranny.

But she had seen him through Tamara's eyes, and she couldn't pretend now that the words he'd spoken meant nothing to her. After a moment, she concluded that she would do it. She owed him that much. And bravely, she said:

"Let's take a walk. Let's see if we can find a bench in City Park, a place from our past that might still exist. Then I will tell you, Eduard. If you are willing to listen, I will tell you. Even though I fear you'll despise me after the fact."

"I could never despise you, Eva. No matter what stands between us, the one thing I promise you now is that I could never despise you."

———

There had not been a bench—not one that hadn't been fully submerged in grime and ash—and they stopped on a bridge overlooking the pond. Eva kept her gaze on the glassy water as she spoke, unable to look at what might be in Eduard's eyes, aware of this last bit of anguish that she was inflicting. His hands gripped the stone railing so tightly that his knuckles turned white, but otherwise he betrayed nothing. She knew there would be no friendship at the end, that there would be no concessions, no way to move forward into a future of any sort in which her betrayal would be a constant guest, yet she wanted the best for Eduard and did not intend to keep him hostage in his feelings for her. And so she held nothing back. She told him everything there was to tell, even about Bianca, and when she opened her eyes, she did not expect him to still be there.

But he was. Motionless still, his face bent down toward the water, where an empty, flattened tin can floated underneath the bridge. "Did you love him?"

"Truly, I don't know. I thought I did. Or perhaps it was just the freedom that he represented that I loved. Perhaps it blinded me."

"And you didn't think that you would have that with me." It wasn't a question but a statement accompanied by a reaffirming nod. "And is it over now, Eva?"

She looked at him, at how stoic he was as he asked her these questions. The graciousness in Eduard's heart made her ashamed, ashamed that while she had spoken the truth, there was one thing that she could not admit, would not admit even to herself: yes, she had loved him. She loved him still; she would always love Aleandro. But it was as though a chamber of her heart had detached from that love and was now reaching for what was here, still possible after this terrible war, precisely as Tamara had said.

"It was over before I even knew I was to have her. Perhaps that's why I think of her as singularly mine. So yes. Yes, that chapter of my life is fully closed now. It's been for some time."

It startled her, the small cry from Eduard's lips. He moved away from her, walked to the other end of the bridge, where he tilted his face to the flock of birds flying in formation through a gloomy early February sky, departing to warmer lands. And when he came back to her and reached for her hand, she felt herself detach even further from the impetuous girl she had once been and step fully into a life in which she became a woman. Into a life devoid of any ghosts.

22

Dachau

Spring 1945

ORE PRISONERS WERE BROUGHT TO DACHAU by
the thousands, crammed in airless boxcars from
other camps, which had been evacuated as the Allies rolled steadily toward Berlin, or marched on foot through
freezing snow. In Aleandro's barrack, two or three prisoners
shared a bed now or slept taking turns. They slept on the
ground, slept standing up, slept in the latrines, which were
overflowing with excrement. The first days of warmer weather
had not brought any relief from the typhus fever that had
spread through the camp since December, and all around him,
men dropped in their walks like marionettes cut from their
strings. He saw their bodies being tossed into the ravines at the
edge of the campsite and other prisoners shoveling dirt over
them, no more than corpses themselves, their eyes pinned on
nothing present, only the afterlife. He saw children stoking the

crematorium fires, and the stench of death clung to his skin, to his clothes, to the back of his skull.

To draw such inhumanity seemed inhumane in itself, an aberration of life, and soon his drawings, which had been dwindling for weeks, stopped altogether. Now he counted his days just like the others, wondering if he was condemned to this pit of hell for all of eternity.

Then one day, he sensed a change in the air. The sharp odor of burning paper drifted over the campsite that entire day and continued well into the night. There was something about the guards, too, who seemed agitated, ill at ease, moving about the camp. As Aleandro ambled about the grounds the next afternoon, he caught sight of three guards he knew well, hauling stacks of files from the gatehouse and tossing them into a large metal bin, dousing them in kerosene. A few minutes later, the commandant emerged with another stack under his arm, which he threw not in the bin but in the back of a jeep. He got in the front seat, yelling something in German to the driver. The jeep then sped away through the gates, leaving Aleandro in a swirl of dust.

Back inside the barrack, Aleandro sat on the edge of Rudolf's bed and gently shook his shoulder. "Something is going on. The guards are burning documents. Rudolf, what do you think it means?"

When Rudolf turned to him, his face beaded with sweat, Aleandro was struck all at once by the stench wafting from his body as much as the realization that Rudolf—his Rudolf, who'd been his pillar, whose optimism had pulled him from the edge of his own abyss—was crying.

"I shat myself, Aleandro. I shat myself. Please go away from me."

"Rudolf, it's all right, it's nothing. We'll get you cleaned up. I'll help you, come now," Aleandro said, but Rudolf didn't budge. For three days now, Rudolf's fever had been rising. His breath came in shallow gasps and that ghastly pallor had become more than alarming—it had become a new horror that Aleandro would not acknowledge, refused to acknowledge. Rudolf's life was his last string to anything human. He could not, would not, accept the loss of Rudolf.

"You do not have typhus, Rudolf. Do you hear me? You do not. It's just a stomach virus. You must believe me. That's all it is."

There was no reply.

"You are strong, Rudolf. You are strong, and you will get better. You must, because without you, I don't think I can make it. Do you hear me? I don't think that I can."

Still silence.

"Fight with me, Rudolf, fight!" Aleandro shouted now. "Goddamn you, get up to your feet! Stand up now!" But Rudolf just regarded him with a blank stare he might give to a stranger on the street asking for directions. Then he launched serenely into an old Hungarian folk song, his eyes too radiant in the light of the ghastly moon.

———

That night, Aleandro bid his good-byes, knowing that in the morning the guards would come and haul Rudolf away. There would be no way to stop it now, nothing at all he could do to delay it; there would only be an empty void where Rudolf had lain, an empty void in Aleandro's heart, which could not withstand the loss of another brother, another love.

"I love you, Rudolf," he whispered, holding his limp, waxy hand in his, brushing it endlessly with his fingers. "You've given me a reason to keep living, you've given me a purpose, and I will always love you." Then, because there was no more to say, he lay down on his own cot and wept.

To his surprise, in the morning and as the hours wore on, the guards had not shown at all. He went outside, desperate for some air, and found that there were in fact no guards in sight. Not near their barrack, at any rate, or anywhere in his immediate line of vision.

He stumbled through the barracks, noticing a pile of discarded prisoner uniforms. He picked one up, staring at the tiny, limp shape, at the gaping holes in the armpits, realizing it belonged to a child. Belonged. So many men and children had perished while he'd managed to live, and Rudolf would now die, too. His uniform would be stripped from his body, it would join the ragged piles scattered among the grounds, and no one other than Aleandro would even remember his name by week's end. No one would remember this man who had been his brother in this place where no brotherhood, no humanity, existed.

It was perhaps this realization that shattered whatever composure he still possessed. A blinding rage pulsed through him, paralyzing his senses, making his legs give out like snapped twigs. He heard himself howling. Howling like an animal, his eyes closed against that indifferent blue sky, his hands balled into fists, drawing blood from his palms. Another wail came, then another, and he scrunched his eyes, bracing for the bullet that would pierce his chest, make everything go black. Maybe in this very moment, he and Rudolf would take their last breaths together. What a relief it would be.

Yet, just as on his first day here, the bullet didn't come, and when all of his strength had left him, he lay down flat on the ground with his arms splayed out, as if on a cross. He was no longer there. He was in a field of flowers, he was dancing around a fire, he was lost in the sound of his fiddle. A cool spring air enfolded him, the moist grass tickling his bare skin. That sun, so bright, so bright. *Perhaps this is how death comes*, he thought then, not in darkness but in a funnel of light.

Then something pulled him back, jolted him, forced him upright and to his feet. A roar coming from the courtyard, and another from the barracks, joining together, building. Voices everywhere, shouts, cries, banging on pipes, prisoners running past him, the sound of gunfire.

And then the most astonishing thing, a thing he could not comprehend at first, a thing that he thought was a mere concoction of his failing mind until he rose to his feet and turned in a full circle: the sound of laughter, of singing. And someone shouting from the direction of the camp gates:

"We are free! We are free!"

23

I T TOOK RUDOLF NEARLY THREE WEEKS to recover after the liberation, three long weeks of plasma transfusions and interminable nights in an old prison barrack that had been converted by the U.S. Army into a hospital ward. Aleandro never left his side during this time. Deloused now and vaccinated, his head shaven, and wearing some civilian clothing doled out from the back of a relief truck, Aleandro stood guard against the Four Horsemen much as Rudolf had stood guard for him once.

Every day, hundreds still died, unable to recover from the ravages of illness or months of starvation, despite the medics' relentless efforts to save anyone who could still be saved, and bodies were lined up outside of the ward to await the burials, which could not be carried out quickly enough. But not the man next to him. For Rudolf, Aleandro would beat back death with his own fists.

Finally, when Rudolf opened his eyes and looked at him with that clear, penetrating gaze, Aleandro felt that he, too, had reopened his eyes, that he, too, took his first renewed breath, that he, too, had been reborn in a world in which change might be possible. And he wept, clutching Rudolf's hands in his. Together they wept for all that was lost to them, they wept for all that they had seen and would never forget, they wept for their lost mates. But mostly, they wept with gratitude. And so it would seem they had been among the lucky ones.

Slowly, as the color in Rudolf's cheeks deepened and he was able to hold down solids, they began taking walks around the old campground. It seemed more or less a replica of its former state, soot-covered still from the constant crematorium fires, but now American flags flew on the guard towers, and the army officers regarded them not with hatred but rather solemn reverence, which unsettled them and made them, without meaning to, glance over their shoulders.

Rudolf asked him about the liberation, when they stopped to sit outside the camp. Aleandro recounted the night the American soldiers stormed the camp gates and scaled the walls, and how the prisoners ran toward them, falling at their feet, begging to be rescued. He told him about the American commander putting a pistol to the forehead of that SS capo and pulling the trigger, the others following suit, machine-gunning the remaining SS guards who hadn't already fled, there in the courtyard where they used to carry out their own executions. And of the boxcars that were found at the edge of the camp containing the bodies of thousands of men, women, and children in various stages of decomposition.

"Have you ever seen a soldier cry, Rudolf? A man in uniform sobbing in his hands? Neither had I. Neither had I. But on that day, when the Americans stormed the gates and came in over the wall, when they stood in the midst of what you and I had come to regard as everyday life, I did see such a thing. Many of them were weeping, Rudolf, sobbing like little children."

"So it really is over," said Rudolf in a bewildered whisper. "This is not just a pause in the war. The Allies have really won."

"It is over indeed. But in our hearts, will it ever be?"

"No," said Rudolf, his own voice breaking. "But I don't suppose that a thing like this should be relegated to memory. What of your drawings?" he said after a silence. "Do you have them still?"

"I do. And I still have my sketchbook. For whatever they might be worth now."

"More than enough," said Rudolf, and his eyes drifted back toward the milky-blue sky, reaching over to pat Aleandro's hand as his father had done once after a good violin play.

———

Slowly, they inched back toward what might be some sense of normality. By then, the recovered prisoners were being transferred in stages to displacement camps in Austria, and Aleandro and Rudolf found themselves among a diminishing population of survivors lingering with the army staff. In the canteen where the prisoners had once served the SS guards, American soldiers doled soup from steaming metal pots—real soup, filled with bits of carrots and rice—and the conversations echoed freely of things that came from a different world, from other families who had endured losses of their own an ocean away.

Rudolf, fluent in English, had befriended a sturdy American rabbi with a healthy complexion and earnest brown eyes who had arrived at Dachau the day after the liberation to minister to the survivors and was compiling ledgers of names to distribute beyond Germany's borders. He had also offered to send letters on the prisoners' behalf to families or to friends from before the war—a fact that Rudolf delivered back to Aleandro in practically one breath, with great jubilation.

"You should write to Eva! I know that you want to write to her, so why not do it now? Don't you want to know if she is still out there waiting for you?" He kept shaking Aleandro's shoulder in a way that jarred him. Lately, Aleandro was so tired that all he wanted to do was sleep. But there was no escaping Rudolf now, who had gripped his hands and refused to release them. "You've always told me that you lived to see her again. If I were you, I wouldn't waste another day. Not when so many have been wasted."

"I'm not sure." Aleandro swallowed, a heat crawling up his neck. "I'm not sure that I can do that yet. It's been so long, so very long. What if she doesn't answer? What if my letter doesn't find her at all? What if she doesn't want to hear from me? I don't know if I could take it, Rudolf. Maybe some other time, maybe later, maybe . . ."

In the silence, Rudolf regarded him. "You, Aleandro? Will you really give up so easily? Is it pain that you fear? Is it disappointment? Because if that's what it is, I will stand right by your side come hell or high water. But don't you want to know what is still out there for you? Besides, sooner or later, this camp will be dissolved and you will have to figure out where life will take you now, how it will resume. So you might as well start right now."

"Resume? What a strange concept that sounds."

"Yes, yes, Aleandro, resume. Resume life, of which there is still plenty. So, what will you do, maestro? Will you take this next step with me? Because, you see, heartbreak is quite ordinary. There are worse things in life to fear."

The shadow of a grin rose to Aleandro's lips. "You sound just like her. She once said something to me, something very similar."

"That is a sign. You do believe in signs, don't you? So come, Aleandro, let's go see this rabbi friend of mine. You will like him. You will like him a lot."

It took Aleandro three whole days to draft his letter. More than a dozen sheets he ripped up, and it was only when the administrative sergeant in the Red Cross office told him there would be no further paper for him that he settled on five measly lines. What to say? What to say after all this time? He felt ridiculous conveying that he was alive, that he never forgot her, that he hoped she managed well enough when he knew that no one had managed at all in the inferno that had engulfed an entire continent. The words sounded shallow and removed from his own ears, blocky simple sentences that a child might write, and in the end, he handed his letter to Rudolf in disgust. He wondered if the address he pulled from his dusty memory would be sufficient.

"Ah, there it is! Courage, my friend! Courage." Rudolf beamed, brandishing an envelope of his own and waving it in the air. "Caution to the wind! That's what life is made of! This is not a time for regrets, it is a time for living!"

"Thank you, Rudolf," Aleandro uttered after Rudolf dashed off to deliver the letters into the hands of his friend.

Alone, after Rudolf left, he sat on the edge of his bed, his hands dangling futilely between his knees, trying to imagine what his life could still be beyond these walls.

———

In late July, ten weeks after the liberation, Rudolf received the long-awaited reply and wept reading it, lifting Aleandro off his feet even though Aleandro towered over him by a whole head. Rudolf would go to America. His cousin, his only surviving relative and best childhood friend, would sponsor him to come to New York, and that night, they sang some Hungarian songs and danced in the barrack stripped of beds where they once shared their deepest secrets.

"New York, Rudolf!" Aleandro kept saying, shaking his head in disbelief. "I can't believe it. You will live in the city of skyscrapers! You will stroll through Central Park, you will . . . you will wear a proper suit! You will take it by storm. I'm quite sure of it. How wonderful, Rudolf, how wonderful this is."

"We should not lose faith," said Rudolf, who could read Aleandro like a book. "Your letter will come, too. I know it in my heart, Aleandro. Just be patient. And I'm not going anywhere in the meantime. I will stay here and wait with you. However long it takes, I will wait with you."

It seemed almost fated that the next day, the chaplain delivered Aleandro's envelope while he and Rudolf were eating supper in the canteen. He ripped it open in one swift move but couldn't bring himself to read it. He was shaking like a leaf, and it was only when Rudolf unfolded it and placed it on the table in front of him, slamming his hand down on it, that Aleandro let his eyes travel over the lines. And read it again as he held it up against the light.

Dear Aleandro,

To say that news of your survival was met, at least on my part, with absolute joy would be an understatement. I cannot imagine what life has been for you in these two long years since you and Eva, believing perhaps rather innocently in a world in which you could be together, were forced to part. But as you said so eloquently in your own letter, war is war, and victims are not only to be found on the battleground.

I know what my dear Eva felt for you. She whispered it in my ear through some very tough moments of her own, moments when I thought that her singular happiness rested solely on your return.

I assume you already know who I am, but in case you do not, let me say that I have cared for Eva and have loved her ever since she was a child. And as much as my heart is filled with compassion for you, Aleandro, it is Eva's best interests that I must protect now. Simply put, she is happy. Happy now, at last, after so many losses of her own, eager to reconstruct a life that had almost slipped through her fingers. And so I ask you not to disturb that happiness won at

great personal cost. Nothing has been fair in this terrible
world and much has been sacrificed for those we love with no
more than a wish that they should live now in peace. And so
I ask you, Aleandro, I beg you for one final sacrifice. Do not
write to her again.

Yours,
Dora

It was Rudolf's turn to keep vigil over Aleandro that night.
Rudolf made no effort to stop his weeping, until he freed one
of his hands from Aleandro's grasp and rested it upon his head
like a priest offering a blessing, or, in this case, a prayer.

"Aleandro, come with me to New York."

"How can I, Rudolf? How could I come with you, even if
I wanted to?"

"Well, that's just it. You can. I didn't tell you this earlier—I
didn't because I knew you would object or think me mad—
but, well . . . I took it upon myself to tell my cousin about
you, about all that you've done for me, and she agreed that if
you, too, should find yourself without a home, she would be
happy to take you under her wing, to sponsor you as she has
me. Only if you should desire it, that is."

"What? Do you mean, to come with you? To come with
you to America?"

Rudolf nodded. "Yes, Aleandro. So come with me! Come
with me to that city of skyscrapers; come and walk with me

in Central Park! Let's see where this new path will lead us. Because I know that your best days, despite what you might think right now, are still ahead of you. Don't say anything yet—just sleep on it, Aleandro."

It took Aleandro only half the night to figure out that Rudolf was right. Rudolf was the only person he had now, the only person he could trust in the world. Their journey was not over, it could never be over, and there was nothing for him in Hungary anymore. Not without his brothers and not without the possibility of her.

He should have been desolate, but in the course of the night a bubble of hope rose up in him again, a full wave now for what might still be within his grasp. And so he delivered his answer without delay the next morning as he and Rudolf took their usual stroll under a starkly clear sky.

"The thing is, Rudolf, maybe in America, just maybe, I might still be able to apply myself, to see if I can do something meaningful, something of which she might take notice. To become not the penniless fiddler that she remembers, but someone whom she might admire someday. Don't say anything, because I know what you are thinking. I know that you think I should forget her now. But we all need our reasons, do we not? Much as we have in the past. We all need reasons to move forward, even if those reasons are illusions. So, for that alone, Rudolf, I will come with you. I will come with you, my brother, and with God's good grace, we will become better men."

Rudolf tilted his face to the passing clouds, and when his eyes set back on Aleandro, that mischievous light, that light that had become Aleandro's sustainment, was there again. A whole galaxy was contained within it, an infinite blank page upon which love and loss and victory could still be rewritten.

He, too, would rewrite his own blank page, and he would find his way back to her again. He believed it then, believed it with the same intensity he once felt when, in the light of a bonfire under a star-studded sky, they were falling in love.

Part III

RESTORATIONS

24

New York
Summer 1955

THE SHRILL OF THE ALARM BORE through Aleandro's skull like a pickaxe. Pulling a pillow over his ear with one hand, groping for the clock on the nightstand with the other, he managed to crack open an eye, and sat up with great effort. Last night he'd forgotten to draw the curtains, and his room was flooded with light.

He groaned as he got out of bed and staggered to the window to yank the curtains shut. Rubbing his temples, he sat on the windowsill. His head felt as if it would split open like an overripe melon, and the recollection of yesterday night began to seep in.

"Urgh." He groaned again, this time into his hands. The wall to the right of his massive oak bed was stained with red wine, rivulets trailing down to a pile of shards that had been one of his best wine goblets. Lord, it looked like a murder scene. *Well*, he thought, *lesson to be learned here*. That was the last time he would break things off with a woman—even though he thought he'd done it so gently, so reasonably—in his own apartment, much less in his bedroom. He checked his watch. Eleven fifteen. The cleanup effort would have to wait if he were to do anything at all with this day. Hoping Estella hadn't sprinkled some shards in her furious wake, he made his way barefoot to the shower and flicked on the silvery knobs.

An hour later, jostled in the back of a checkered cab, which navigated through the quiet Sunday of the Upper West Side toward the livelier downtown, Aleandro finally felt a little bit better, but now a terrible remorse filtered through in place of his nausea. He shouldn't have had so much to drink at dinner, shouldn't have brought her to his apartment, shouldn't have, especially, gone to his room to lie down for a bit, only to open his eyes and find her sitting at the foot of his bed, in a negligée, sipping her wine seductively. The timing, oh Lord, the timing had been terrible. He would have to call her, try to make some reparations, but damn it, it wasn't like he hadn't been honest with her from the get-go. He'd been honest with all of them.

Sooner or later, he explained on each occasion as earnestly as he could, they would tire of his schedule, his frequent absences, his moods, his bouts of isolation. Sooner or later, he would let them down because the truth was (this part he didn't particularly convey but used it more for his own justification) his heart was simply unavailable. His art was the only thing that moved him, the only thing that made him feel alive. Love was never part of the bargain. And yet more often than not it ended much the same way.

At the corner of East Second Street and First Avenue, he

took a much-welcome breath through the window, feeling the knot in his stomach loosen a little as he tapped on the glass:

"This is good. You can leave me here, my good man."

He counted a few wrinkled bills from the pocket of last night's pants, thanking God there was enough to pay for the fare, then crawled out of the seat with his sketch paper and tin case, heading to the usual spot, where he hoped to take advantage of a few hours of the spectacular sunlight.

On his short trek, trash bins were lined up curbside and in gangways, overflowing, ready for Monday morning's pickup, and he inhaled deeply, inhaled the scent of tossed leftovers and rotten flowers and cigarette butts with satisfaction. In the posh West Side neighborhood where he'd moved three years prior, there were never any trash bins—not for long, at any rate— and, as much as he knew it wasn't normal, he missed this smell. Then again, he'd long stopped believing that anything about him was normal.

Setting down his supplies, he sat on his old stoop at the base of a dilapidated walk-up across from the small cemetery. Ah, but how good it felt to be home! This building with a fire escape zigzagging four floors of grime-crusted windows, where he and Rudolf had spent their first five years in New York, would always be home. Five years of scrounging pennies and eating only slightly better than they had in those last days of the camp, making do with whatever Rita, Rudolf's cousin, could spare from her own meager means. Even after they came into some money, real money, after they'd paid Rita back every penny, after he managed to sell his first Dachau piece with Rudolf's help and secured an exhibit in a small gallery on Fifty-Seventh, after they began dining in the restaurants where they used to wash dishes, Aleandro refused to move. Perhaps, he thought now in retrospect, they might have never moved at all and would be living here still had Rudolf not met Marlena. But Aleandro couldn't get in the way of first love, not he of all people, and so it was decided that it was time.

Rudolf installed himself in Marlena's loft five blocks away, and he, in the first apartment that had been shown to him. After collecting his keys, he stood on the terrace overlooking Straus Park, stunned at the view as much as the realization that Rudolf would not be here to share it with him.

But he couldn't concentrate in that apartment, despite the large sunny room that was his studio, despite the tranquility of the oak-lined street. A piece of himself had remained right here on this stoop, where he and Rudolf would share a beer in the sweltering New York summer nights, counting their tips.

Now, as he did each time, he scanned the street for some activity that would spark his inspiration. This time, it was a gaggle of kids running in the middle of the street through the spray from a busted fire hydrant, dodging the trickle of intermittent cars. Digging out his supplies from the case, he began with a rough sketch of the neighborhood boys, deepening the shadows and accentuating contours as he went along with his oil pastels, which were, after dabbling in other mediums, still his favorite. A second later he disappeared inside his work, humming a melody.

"Are you Aleandro Szabó?"

He looked up, slightly annoyed by the interruption. The only downside to coming to work here was that the entire neighborhood evidently knew him, and people would creep up on him unexpectedly, startling him, disrupting his momentum. But this time, it was just a young girl with pig-tails and a beret, licking the glaze from an enormous sugar pretzel.

"I guess so," he said, smiling.

"Are you making a painting of the cemetery?"

He shook his head. The cemetery was the one thing he would never paint, that he had no desire to paint. It was life that was his sole interest. Only life now.

"Would you like to see? Here, come sit." He scooted himself over to make room for her, and the girl sat.

"Would you like a bite of my pretzel?"

"No, thank you. That's very kind."

"Well," she began when he resumed drawing, "my mommy says that your pictures of the war camp are disturbing. She saw them at the gallery over on Madison, and she said it made her want to cry. And art is not supposed to make you want to cry. Art is supposed to make you feel happy."

"Is that what she says? Well, please give her my apologies."

"Don't worry. She's not upset with you." She leaned in closer as if sharing a secret. "She says you're handsome. But I'm not allowed to repeat that in front of my daddy."

"I'll tell you what," Aleandro said. "If you hang around just a bit longer until I can finish this, you can take it home with you. To give to her. With my compliments." He took one of the charcoal pencils from his supply case and scribbled at the bottom of the unfinished piece: *There is beauty in tears.* Then he signed his name underneath and went back to the finishing touches.

———

It was nearly dark by the time he headed home, close to eight o'clock if he had to guess. Time had slipped away from him after the little girl left and he'd begun a new piece. A young woman this time, who had appeared on a stoop of her own three buildings down in bare feet and hair in curlers, caught his eye. She smoked a cigarette, tapping the ash with a long, bloodred-varnished fingernail, her expression nondescript, bored. She looked in his direction for a few seconds, then, to his surprise as much as relief, she finished her cigarette, ignoring him before going back up the steps and slamming the door shut. He hadn't finished the drawing, not so much because it was hard to see now, but because the act of drawing her stirred him with restlessness, rousing the memory of drawing a different face, a different woman of that same age. It was his own fault, he should have known better; he'd waltzed right into his own trap. And as he walked up Second Avenue passing groups of early evening enthusiasts, he suddenly had no desire to flag a cab, no desire to be back in his empty apartment, where he would regress back into that tunnel of daydreams that would lead him to empty another bottle of whiskey. Instead, he headed back the way he'd come, in the direction of the Bowery Hotel.

Rudolf and Marlena were home. Their lights were on, and he went up the short flight of stairs to their loft, but just then, the door swung open, and people spilled out onto the landing, and he scrambled quickly down the steps and began walking away. Behind him, he heard Marlena's voice in the swirl of laugher. He kept walking quickly, until at the end of the block he heard steps behind him and his name being called out.

"Aleandro! Hey! Wait! Hey, my friend! What are you doing

here? I thought that might be you. Marlena thought she saw you just now."

Rudolf looked as he always did when wearing a shirt and tie—like an overgrown child eager to get out of his Sunday church clothes. His suspenders hung down over his trousers, his tie slightly askew, as he beamed with the glow of wine and company cheer. Rudolf seemed incapable of aging, had lost none of that youthful mischievousness, while he, despite being just thirty-five, felt as though he'd already stepped firmly into his middle age. Or maybe it was just that he felt old, tired. God, he felt so very tired.

"Ah, don't worry about it, I was going to drop in to say hello, but you have people over, so I didn't want to intrude."

"Intrude? Hell, if we knew you were coming, we would have delayed dinner. Why don't you come up now? I'm sure we can pull together a plate for you. Marlena made her legendary spaghetti and meatballs, and I know you can't say no to that."

"Thank you, Rudolf. That's all right. But tell Marlena thank you. I will see you guys next week, right?"

"Aleandro, don't be silly. Come on, now. You know you don't need an invitation. Our home is your home, for God's sake. Let's go."

He went up, only because he couldn't say no to Rudolf. Marlena, huge in her seventh month of pregnancy, her reddish hair and porcelain skin glowing in a way that matched Rudolf's, bustled around him with astounding energy, introducing him to her friends, who, despite her casual, easy demeanor, seemed to withdraw within themselves as though he were a principal walking into an unruly classroom. In the end, he ate his pasta in the kitchen while Rudolf sat on a chair across from him, sipping a glass of white wine and watching him with the usual concern.

"What's going on with you, Aleandro? What's new?"

"New? You mean in all the five days that you haven't seen me?"

"No, I mean with you in general. You look like hell. You look . . . I don't know. Out of sorts."

"I'm just hungover, Rudolf. I drank too much last night, and I did something . . . well, from what I can recall of it, a pretty awful thing. Don't ask. I'm not proud of it. And today, you know, I was out on our stoop and this little girl sat next to me and told me that my paintings were disturbing. And, let's face it, they are disturbing. They have nothing to do with today's world or New York; they are just the concoctions of a man on the edge of madness. Why does anyone want to see all that misery? Why should I now, ten years later, insist on inflicting that on everyone? It's all rubbish."

Rudolf shot up from the table, disappeared for a moment, and returned with a newspaper in hand.

"No, sit down, Aleandro. Don't you dare move. I want you to sit there and listen while I read this to you. Then you can go if you want. Because this just came out in today's paper while you were nursing your hangover and feeling sorry for yourself."

As Aleandro Szabó emerged with no formal training or pedigree in New York's competitive art scene, many questioned more than one gallery's willingness to sponsor his reproductions of one of the grimmest episodes in modern history. Yet Szabó's works of the Nazi concentration camp at Dachau have not only sold in record numbers, they have deeply stirred the public and critics alike. Rendering in heartbreaking detail what the Hungarian-born artist witnessed in his year of captivity, Szabó spares nothing, forgives nothing. Ultimately, what hits one squarely in the chest when observing his works is not the horror of what has come to be known as the Holocaust but his moving depiction of the quest to survive, the beauty and fragility of life, and the perseverance of the human spirit.

John Gott, for the New York Times *Art Review*

"So no, not rubbish, Aleandro," Rudolf said, slamming down the paper, "not rubbish! And I never want to hear you say that again. We've worked too hard and for too long to get here, and I will not let you turn around now and throw it all away. Now go home and clean up. Sleep and have a good breakfast, and stay off the booze, goddamn it. Because in two nights, we have a new opening. And you, my dear friend, have got to rise to the occasion."

He did go home. And poured himself a Jack Daniel's while he took out the portrait of the girl on the stoop, determined to finish it. But now the eyes no longer seemed right; the mouth was not set at the right angles. And he, pushing the paper under a lamp, began to reconstruct the eyes, elongate them, tilt them up just slightly at the outer corners, to make them wider, more direct, less indifferent, yes, more direct. Then he moved to the chin, which was also not right—it was too wide, too soft—and the pencil then moved to the hairline, which he lowered from the exceedingly high forehead and diffused with a gold pastel, rubbing the paint with his finger until it burned. He held it up against the lamp, tossing the shade aside; then, realizing what he had done—again, for the hundredth time—he poured himself a new drink and crumpled the unintentional likeness of Eva into his fist and tossed it out of the window. He watched it float down to the street, land in a gutter, where a bicycle rode over it, dragging it into the darkness.

25

*B*IANCA! BIANCA! PLEASE OPEN THE DOOR, darling. Don't do this now. We are late—more than late—we may not make it in time for your own recital. Darling, you cannot miss your own recital. Think of all the people who are coming to see you play."

"I don't give a fart."

Eva closed her eyes, breathed out, letting her forehead drop against the door. Her daughter was exasperating her. Exasperating her as she loved doing, especially in moments such as this, when she needed her to cooperate the most.

"Bianca," Eva began again. "You've been practicing for months. This is your chance to shine. You've worked so hard for this, darling. Come on, now."

"I don't want to play for those bureaucratic pigs. I won't! So go away, Mama. Just go away."

Another long breath came through Eva's gritted teeth. The "bureaucratic pigs" was in fact a new development. The husband of Bianca's violin teacher worked for some ministry or another, and at the last minute, invited half a dozen colleagues to see the fruit of his wife's relentless efforts. Eva herself was not exactly thrilled about it, but God, who taught this child to speak this way? It was unbecoming for a girl of twelve. And knowing Bianca's tendency to blurt in public whatever came to mind, it was downright dangerous.

Perhaps it was her own fault. She and Eduard had never done a good job of hiding their late-night banter about what was happening in Budapest, what had been happening since Bianca was a baby. But Soviet occupation or not, she couldn't allow her daughter to put them all in danger. Nor could she allow Bianca to throw away years of hard work—years during which the violin was the only thing that kept her interest and grounded her in a calmness she was otherwise incapable of displaying.

"Bianca!" Eva rapped on the door, trying now to reason with her. "You know your father is leaving work early to come see you play, and he may already be there. I left work early, too, if you'll recall, young lady, to help you get ready. You can't do this now."

"It's not about you! Must everything be about you?" The door opened just a crack. "If you and Papa don't mind working for a Bolshevik-run hospital, that's your business. But I will not play for some fat, smelly, vodka-swilling Russian swine. I will not."

"Bianca, please, dear God! You can't say stuff like this!"

"Then don't make me go."

The door slammed in Eva's face.

Eva sat in the kitchen, sparking a cigarette as she watched Dora frost the post-recital cake, creating a swirling pattern with a butcher knife and sprinkling it with some colored sugar granules. Buying regular sugar alone in Budapest these days had become a near impossibility, and yet, somehow, Dora always managed.

"I can't get her to budge, Dora. This girl is going to put me in an early grave," Eva said, getting up to run what remained of her cigarette under a stream of water at the sink. "Maybe you could . . . well, could you go see if you can make some progress? Because otherwise, there won't be much need to finish this gorgeous dessert you've worked so hard on all day."

Dora gave her a questioning look. "I'm happy to do it, Eva, of course. But I thought we decided that you would be sterner with her, that you wouldn't rely on me as much with . . . well, with the disciplinary part. You are her mother. I can't fill in those gaps forever."

Eva sat back in her chair, feeling the usual defeat. She tugged on Dora's hand. "You are the only person who can reason with her. So please, Dora, please. Will you go talk to her? Besides, you know well enough that you are her mother just as much as I am."

It was all true. Eva could still recall those early days after the war, when Dora had come to Budapest with Bianca, not on a train but in the Red Cross car that Eduard had sent for them. How she'd cried seeing them, alive, in one piece, how they couldn't let go of each other for hours, for days. They'd set up home in Budapest, in the apartment on Andrássy, which Eva and Dora had repaired with their own two hands while Bianca toddled around their ankles, still somewhat stunned that they'd survived, that they still had each other, that there was yet another chance for life, for hope and happiness. Although not quite entirely as before.

Eduard became a constant presence in their lives, often dropping by for dinner, bearing gifts from the hospital for Bianca, sometimes no more than an old stethoscope that no longer worked. And on the day when he bounced Bianca on his knees and she reached up to his face with her tiny fingers, regarding him for a long moment before she began to giggle, Eva knew that her life could be complete again.

They'd married on a Sunday the year following. In the courthouse, Eva stood across from him in a simple blue dress, with Bianca whimpering in Dora's arms in the first pew. She wept. She wept not only out of gratitude for this new beginning, but also because she'd never wanted this life more. And she entered into that new life minutes later, into the honey light of an October afternoon as Eduard scooped her up in his arms and shouted to the stream of pedestrians below the courthouse steps: "This is my wife, ladies and gentlemen! My wife!"

That recollection still made Eva smile. A decade passed, a decade during which they'd worked together side by side, embracing work that they both loved, easing into a life that had not been simple for either of them but was in many ways exactly the way Eva had envisioned before that fateful summer in Sopron. But then again, for years, she would get startled out of sleep with a sensation so searing, so hollowing, that she couldn't breathe. She'd sit up in bed and try to force air into her lungs, gasping, until Eduard would wake and put his arms around her.

"It's just the war. That goddamn war. You are here now. You are all right."

She would fall back onto her pillow, into the crook of his arm, nodding, a tear sliding down her cheek. It was not the war. It had nothing to do with the war. But this she could never tell Eduard. And she never did. And by then, it seemed already that she could no longer reach Bianca, who, despite being just a tiny bundle, regarded her suspiciously, as if reading her deepest thoughts, as if reading right through any lingering thread of deception that constituted her feelings for Aleandro. And more often as time wore on, it was Dora to whom Bianca turned, Dora whom she joined in the kitchen for a late-night lemonade, Dora who filled in the spaces Eva never could while she plunged deeper into her work.

Now, Eva followed Dora toward Bianca's room as was the usual routine. The other woman pounded on the door.

"Bianca. It's me. I want to talk to you, sweetheart. I've made this beautiful cake for you, chocolate, which I know is your favorite, and I'd hate to throw it away. Which I will if you don't open this door in ten seconds and do what your mother says. Besides, you know well enough that if you don't play tonight, someone else will just take your place on that stage. Now, do you really want to have that happen? Just think of someone else sitting in that chair, taking your accolades, and you here locked in this room with no cake. Now, please, darling, don't make this difficult."

Instantly, the door opened, Bianca standing on the threshold in her pink taffeta dress, her lips rouged with a lipstick she must have lifted from Eva's dressing table, her eyes lined in heavy kohl.

"Here I am!" she shouted, splaying her arms out in an exaggerated way that conveyed she was complying under duress. "Well, let's not keep our captive audience waiting!" Then she pushed past them both, grabbed her violin case from the corner of the living room next to her note stand, and continued toward the front door. "You coming, Mama?"

———

They had walked in ten minutes late, greeted at the recital hall entrance by Bianca's violin teacher, who had whisked them backstage.

"I'm sorry," Eva apologized again. "I couldn't leave work early enough, we had an emergency at the hospital, and the tram was late, and . . ."

"No time for that." The grim Mrs. Ivanov practically shoved Bianca toward the stage. "Go. Go now and take your place." Then, after Bianca made her way to her chair with her violin at the front, the teacher turned to Eva with repressed fury. "If you are not capable of taking this seriously, Mrs. Kovaks, I would appreciate it if you wouldn't insist on wasting my time. Need I remind you again that I used to play with the Moscow symphony? I have a line of students eager for my tutelage." Before Eva could open her mouth to reply, Mrs. Ivanov turned on her heels and marched down the side steps, head high and smiling tightly to her front-row guests.

In the fifth row, where Eva took her own seat next to Eduard, she felt as though she could finally breathe again. "Don't ask, darling," she whispered, kissing his cheek. "Don't even ask. She was in rare form today."

"I was late myself, just got here about five minutes ago," Eduard confessed. "The surgery ran late, and there wasn't a thing I could do about it. Surely Mrs. Ivanov noticed my tardiness, too. Surely we will be expelled without delay from her fervent clientele list."

Eva couldn't help chuckling under her breath, then looped her arm through his as the lights dimmed and the curtain rose.

The conductor, bowing deeply with a special little nod for Mrs. Ivanov, led the orchestra into the opening stanzas. First the flutes came in, then the cellos, with their mournful sound, all soon fading in unison for the entry of Bianca, who, seated to the right of the conductor, was not looking at the notes, nor at the strings, but rather at her magenta fingernails. But she didn't miss her entry: she came in like a fighter plane diving for its target, making Eva's breath come to a halt. A small whimper came from her lips, and she shot up straight in her chair, pierced with a memory of a different violin, a different player who attacked the strings the same way. She couldn't breathe, was nearly on her feet now, blood in her face, but there was nowhere to go—not without attracting attention to herself— and so she reclined back in her seat, smiling proudly to the surrounding faces.

Then, when it all seemed to blend harmoniously into the second movement of Jean-Baptiste Accolay's No. 1 in A Minor, Bianca stopped. Stopped playing, causing a confusion in the orchestra, which tapered into silence. There was only silence in the audience, too; not a sound came, not a single cough. Eva saw the smile rising up to her daughter's face, the devilish grin that spelled trouble, as Bianca tilted her chin up defiantly and launched into a solo piece of her own.

———

Afterward, as Eva and Eduard scooted out of their seats, silent, averting eye contact, hoping they could find Bianca quickly and slip away unseen, a heavyset man wearing a thick leather coat and shapka hat ambled up the aisle toward them, nearly blocking their path.

"Doctor Kovaks?"

"Yes," Eduard said, searching Eva's face, seemingly for some information.

"Well, nice to meet you. I'm Ana Ivanov's husband."

Eduard paled a little, clearing his throat. "Yes, well, we are indebted to Ana for all her efforts. As you can see, she's done quite a good job with our daughter. And her . . . vocation for the violin."

He laughed. "Well, yes, I have to admit she's rather good. Above average, I would say. But a girl like that, well, Doctor, surely you must know that you've got your hands full with her. You should keep an eye on her, Eduard. May I call you Eduard?"

"By all means. And yes, she can be rather spirited. She has ideas of her own."

"Indeed. But it does make one wonder where those ideas come from. What precisely she hears in that apartment of yours on Andrássy." He shrugged a shoulder, smiling broadly. "Just a curiosity, that's all. Well, I won't keep you further. Have a pleasant evening, Mrs. Kovaks, Eduard. It's been lovely chatting."

Back home, there was no desire for celebration. Bianca stormed straight to her room, ignoring the cake that Dora had set on the dining table alongside their best china while Eduard took off his coat and tie and poured drinks for himself and Eva. Dora had also retired to her room, resting from her usual late-night palpitations for which Eduard had been prescribing her pills, and the two of them sat now in silence by the fire, sipping their much-needed drinks.

"Well, I can't say that I'm exactly furious," Eduard said, swirling his glass. "I mean, what she did was reckless, foolish, but I can't say that I blame her entirely." He held up his finger, catching Eva's look. "I myself wish I wouldn't be forced to attend to those Russian clowns who take what they want when they want, who eat caviar and drink our best wines when the rest of the country is struggling to make it from one day to the next."

"Dear God, you sound just like her."

"Like what?"

"You know." She lowered her voice, running a hand over the side of her hair, which she had pulled earlier into a hasty chignon. "A revolutionary. You must stop. We must all stop even whispering about it in her presence. She's just a child; she doesn't understand the implications."

"I agree. But you know, Eva, it did give me just a little satisfaction. Under different circumstances I would say that she made me a proud father tonight."

"The girl could murder and you'd still find a way to be

proud of her. Ever since she was a baby you've indulged her too much."

It was in those early days of their marriage, when Bianca was still a toddler, that Eva had considered having another child. Even though she did not exactly burn with desire for another pregnancy, what did seem necessary to her was to complete the circle of their family by giving Eduard a daughter or a son of his own. Yet, as the years passed and they were unsuccessful, there seemed less and less reason for it. Eduard was utterly smitten with Bianca and the other way around. They laughed at each other's private jokes, completed each other's sentences, Bianca always eager to tag along with Eduard wherever he went. All of her affection seemed reserved either for him or for Dora, who—unlike Eduard, who couldn't scold her, and Eva, who scolded her with no effect—could get the girl in line with no more than three sentences. It had saddened Eva for a while that often she felt like a weekend guest in her own home, then she came to accept it as another strange twist in her strange life. It was simply the way they were, and after a while she abandoned the idea of another child altogether. Their family, imperfect as it might have been, was complete.

"What do you think is going to happen?" Eva resumed now, frowning into her glass. "I didn't like the look of that man one bit, much less the way he spoke to us. It worries me, Eduard. What should we do?"

"We do nothing. We go to work as usual and keep our heads low, try not to invite any further attention. Bianca goes to school, even though I think it might be wise to cut off her lessons with Ana for a while. It's a pity. That girl could shred the strings right off a Stradivarius if she wanted to."

"Hmm," Eva mumbled, unable to return Eduard's smile, her heart turning in a leap at those words just as it had earlier in the recital hall. Lightly, she patted Eduard's chest and departed to their room, eager to change out of her best formal dress.

Later, she tried to sleep, but she couldn't. She couldn't sleep because seeing her daughter play like that had opened the door to buried ghosts—to those summer days with Aleandro and his brothers, which she'd tried so hard to erase from her consciousness. And also because she wasn't able to shake the feeling that, heads low or not, they'd just walked into the eye of an invisible storm.

26

New York
Autumn 1956

LEANDRO HAD TOSSED AND TURNED LAST night in
his bed, unable to get a wink of sleep. Having to
wear a tux alone caused anguish enough, and he
couldn't even bring himself to think about how he'd handle
the press without breaking out in a cold sweat. It was the first
time Aleandro would have to attend an event on his own, to
answer questions usually relegated to Rudolf. Questions about
his painting technique (apparently, he'd started a trend using
pastels in the same way that the Impressionists used small, visible brushstrokes to render shape and light), questions about
Dachau, questions about his upcoming work, which, above
all, left him tongue-tied and blathering like an idiot. Only Rudolf was able to rescue him from some insistent benefactor
with expert timeliness just before his unease bubbled into a
full anxiety bout. But tonight, Aleandro would have to muddle

through the whole dreadful thing without his indispensable manager. Tonight, he was on his own.

Two days prior, Marlena had departed for New Jersey to attend to her mother's health, and Rudolf was immersed in caring for their young son. Not that Rudolf loved anything more than doting on that child—constantly singing and cooing in his ear as he fed or dressed him—whether Marlena was at home or not. Aleandro himself had to admit that Hans, as they named him, was the most beautiful baby boy that he'd ever seen. The shock of red hair that he'd inherited from his mother and the eyes, which were a replica of Rudolf's, left Aleandro choked with a nameless emotion. It wasn't exactly love, not like what he'd felt for his brothers, but each time Aleandro touched Hans's soft curls, each time Marlena and Rudolf left him in his arms to prepare a bottle or speak alone in the kitchen for a few minutes, Aleandro found himself tearing up.

"It is not too late for you, Aleandro. Despite what you say, it is not too late," said Rudolf at the door the last time, pulling Aleandro into a bear hug and not letting go. "Remember? I told you that once. It's been more than ten years, Aleandro. Maybe it's time. Because life won't stop and life requires one to be present. You can't keep living in the past, Aleandro, not when you have so much to live for."

Aleandro had laughed, patting his back in an offhanded way: "Tough teaching an old dog new tricks, my friend. Well, enjoy your little cocoon of bliss. I'll be back Wednesday."

But for some reason he couldn't bring himself to go over on Wednesday, and the week went by in a flash, and now it was

Saturday and the uptown gallery was teeming with people even prior to his arrival, a half hour before the show.

There was the usual handshaking, the autographing of glossy reproductions, the photographs taken with eager patrons, followed by the three-line opening speech, during which his hand quivered holding the scrap of paper. No more than twenty minutes into the reception, he found himself scanning the mass of suits and evening gowns for an escape route, dying to free himself from his constricting bow tie. A clear path to the restrooms finally opened up, and he was making his way there, when he was intercepted by an amply bosomed, silver-haired woman wearing a black sequin dress.

"Ah, Mr. Szabó. I've been dying to meet you, but I couldn't get anyone around here to introduce us properly. I'm a big fan of your work. Marta Adami."

She had a distantly familiar accent, and she shook his hand so forcefully that it jolted him out of his anxious haze.

"Ms. Adami. Thank you so much. But I was just stepping out. Could we talk a bit later?"

"Not leaving already, surely?"

"No, just taking a break."

"Well, I'll just walk with you for a moment. I assure you I make a good escort, and I'm dying for a word with you."

Aleandro eyed her suspiciously. Was she flirting with him? Dear God, he was used to getting quite a bit of it, but he'd never had a woman of this age approach him this brazenly. She had to be at least seventy, even though the pixie cut and twinkling, lively eyes suggested a spirit that defied the years.

"My dear Mr. Szabó," she resumed in her husky voice, as

if reading his thoughts, switching to his utter surprise to Hungarian. "Charming as you may be, I assure you that I'm too old to have anything but honest intentions."

He laughed delightedly, intrigued. "Well, in that case, please, right this way. I could never refuse a fellow countryman . . . uh, I mean, woman."

They sat in the entry hall on a banquette near the window, where traffic lights passed in an endless stream, sipping champagne that had come around on a serving tray. Marta explained she was not just an admirer of his paintings but also the wife of the Hungarian ambassador to the United States.

"Truly?" Aleandro was astounded. "Gosh, I'm so sorry, Madam Adami, I had no idea. I hope you didn't find me rude just now. Sometimes I find all this overwhelming."

"I'm sure it is overwhelming. A success like yours—a rapid success, as it was—must not be easy to handle. When was it that you first exhibited at that gallery on Fifty-Seventh? Two, three years ago?"

"Four," Aleandro said. "But you know it? You've seen it?"

She gave him a complicit sort of smile, which again seemed to belong to a younger woman, signaling for two more flutes and handing one to Aleandro. "My husband and I have seen your work several times. In fact, he regrets a great deal that he couldn't be here tonight, but I suppose you could say that he sent me as his emissary."

"Emissary? Emissary to what?"

"Mr. Szabó, when was the last time you saw Budapest?"

At the mention of Budapest, his fingers tightened around the glass. "I actually never have. I'm from Sopron. I never got the chance to visit the capital, to my greatest regret. As much as I would have wanted to . . . once. But, impossible now, right? The Soviet Bloc countries are inaccessible to Americans, to everyone in the West. They have been, am I right, since the end of the war?"

He didn't want to tell her that he knew better than anyone the impossibility of returning there. For years he'd looked for a loophole, an opening of any kind that would allow him passage through the Iron Curtain, to no avail. At some point he'd relegated himself to the idea that Eva as much as Hungary were no more within his reach than they'd been during the days of the war.

"Well, there are exceptions," Madam Adami said.

"I don't understand. What kind of exceptions?"

Marta drained her champagne slowly, seeming to relish the suspense. Then she gingerly patted the corner of her mouth with a napkin, careful not to disturb the bright peach lipstick. "Have you heard, Mr. Szabó, of the Hungarian National Gallery?"

Aleandro shook his head, still not grasping where she was going with this.

"Well, it's not actually scheduled to open until late this year, but the timing might just be perfect. Its purpose, Aleandro—if I may call you Aleandro— is to showcase exclusively the works of Hungarian artists, including ones living in the West, and I think your works of Dachau would be ideal for the opening."

"Well, thank you, really, thank you very much. I'm truly flattered. But even if I wanted to take part in it, it would be impossible for me to get into Hungary." He cleared his throat. "Not just because of obvious restraints, but because in Hungary, I'm afraid I'm considered a deserter. Because I came here to New York, instead of returning after the war."

Marta shrugged, undeterred, smiling widely at some passing patrons. "All infractions can be forgiven for the right reasons,

Aleandro. The Soviets, I'm sure, would be quite pleased to display the brutal atrocities of their infamous former foe. And, if you are truly interested, Aleandro, I think you'll find that my husband and I can facilitate greatly in that regard. Here." She snapped open her clutch and took from it a pearly white card. "Take my number. Think about it. Come visit us sometime. Even if it is just to take in the view of the big park." She leaned in, giving his arm a squeeze with her bejeweled hand. "It's worth it, I promise."

Then she set her glass down and departed graciously like a black swan over the marble terrain, leaving Aleandro there in a cloud of bewildered agitation, pondering her offer.

It seemed a dream, another fantasy he'd concocted for himself, and he rubbed his moist palms on his trousers as if to awaken himself from it. But this was no fantasy. This was real. He could go to Budapest! Budapest, where Eva watched the sun rise every day, where she lived and breathed—Eva, whom he hadn't thought he'd ever see again in this divided world. An exhibition of this prestige would surely be announced in the papers; it would draw an audience, and maybe it would reach her ears. And maybe, just maybe, she would come.

It was perhaps just a foolish notion, but already he was caught in a frisson of euphoria, his heart galloping ahead of any reason. *Rudolf was wrong*, he thought then. *You see, Rudolf, you can re-create the past if you hold on to it dearly enough. You can, because the universe is timeless; it always pulls you back where you belong.*

With a broad smile on his face, he waltzed back into the exhibit a changed man, no longer anxious but glowing with the renewal of a long-dormant dream. In short, a man on the cusp of something he'd long forgotten how to feel. A happy man.

27

IN THE SOFT LIGHT OF THE October afternoon, Eva sat across from her daughter and watched her pick at her food. It was supposed to be a special afternoon together, one for which Eva had switched her daytime shift at the hospital, yet Bianca didn't seem even slightly enthusiastic.

"Don't you like it?" Eva encouraged. "It's clafoutis. It's what I thought you liked. That's why I brought you here."

"It's fine," Bianca said, letting the fork clink down on her plate. "It's three o'clock. I should be getting home. I have to practice my violin."

"Oh. But I thought we were going to see a picture show after this. Remember?"

Bianca shot her a pained look. "I've changed my mind. I think I just want to go home."

"Bianca, look, I'm trying here. I know you're disappointed

about having to drop your lessons for a while, but believe me, it's for the better, for now. Besides, it will give us a chance to spend a little more time together, and you know how much I've wanted this, for so long."

"Yes, I know."

"So we have that chance now. Besides," she joked, "don't tell me that you really prefer Ana Ivanov's company over mine."

Another look. "Ana is brilliant."

For weeks now, Eva had been trying to pull Bianca out of her funk, to no avail. It was as though a light had gone out in her eyes ever since she and Eduard announced that she would have to take a break from working with Ana. They'd tried a couple of other tutors, conservatory students who were either only marginally more skilled than Bianca or found themselves intimidated into quitting by week's end. Bianca seemed intent on returning to the good graces of Ana Ivanov at any cost. Russian pig of a husband or not, Ana, as she'd said, was brilliant.

"All right, well, if you're not hungry, then slide the beautiful pie over here. I'll finish it, and then we'll go see the picture show as we planned, young lady. It's not debatable."

"Whatever," said Bianca. "I guess I'll have to practice later tonight. Hopefully the neighbors won't mind."

They went to a small theater house on Buda for an old black-and-white Charlie Chaplin comedy, but as Eva expected, Bianca hardly cracked a smile through the whole thing. As they streamed out of the theater two hours later, Eva couldn't help feeling irritated. Not only had she changed her work schedule to spend more time with Bianca, but money was tight for indulgences such as restaurant outings and picture shows. She wished Bianca could make an effort to at least meet her halfway.

"You know, Bianca, sooner or later you've got to talk to me. I'm a good listener, I really am, but I can't crawl inside your head. I want us to be closer, but you've got to help me. You've got to talk to me."

She shot a look to Bianca, but Bianca wasn't listening. Not exactly tuning her out, but intent on something else, something across the river as they turned from the winding lanes onto the passageway to Margit Bridge.

"Look."

On Pest, from the depth of the buildings, there was a flash of brightness. A quick burst, flaming and disappearing.

"What on earth," said Eva, then from behind them came a swell of joyful jubilation. A stream of pedestrians moved in their direction toward the bridge with arms linked, some singing, waving small Hungarian flags.

"Sir, what's happening?" Eva asked, catching the arm of a man as he passed by. "What's going on in Pest?"

"We're joining the students!" The man beamed at Eva. "We're going over to support the students in Parliament Square. Didn't you hear about the demonstration?"

She did. She had heard about it leaving the hospital earlier, around one o'clock. Some university students had organized a protest in support of Poland, which had, just three days earlier, announced its intention to withdraw from the Warsaw Pact. At the time she thought it would last no more than an hour before they would be forced to disperse.

"Come with us. Join us!" said the man, handing Eva and Bianca tricolor ribbons to pin to their coats, and Eva had no time to answer or consider, for Bianca was already dashing ahead as if heading into battle, and Eva had to hurry to not lose sight of her.

On the other side of the bridge, more people, not just students, but men and women and children in the thousands were marching on the banks of the Danube. She held on tightly to Bianca's hand, and they were carried along with the crowd, passing intersections where trolleys lay abandoned on their tracks. Traffic, Eva realized, had stopped almost completely. Only a thin trickle of cars managed to get through. People were waving and cheering from balconies, pouring streamers over the crowd, chanting *Ruszkik haza. Ruszkik haza. Russians, go home.* A boy was cutting the sickle-and-hammer emblem from the Hungarian flag with a Swiss Army knife. Then he waved the flag in the air, and another roar erupted, and Eva and Bianca, too, cheered and began chanting the slogans as Eva's heart pounded in a way it hadn't since her courier days of the siege: *Russians, go home. Russians, go home.*

She looked down at her daughter and saw her smile.

It took twice the time to reach their home on Andrássy, where she'd practically had to drag Bianca away from the crowd as it continued on toward Heroes' Square, where some had whispered in the crowd that they planned to topple Stalin's statue.

"You want to go home now? Are you serious? Mama, you can be such a coward!" Bianca protested as Eva pulled her through the entrance of their building and held her hand firmly, going up the steps. Bianca's cheeks were burning, and her eyes shone brightly with an almost manic quality that alarmed Eva. Truth was that she, too, was emboldened, intoxicated with the energy of the crowd, with the prospect of freedom, but it was getting dark, and she was fearful that things would boil out of control. Above all, she was fearful Bianca would slip away from her in the frenzy.

"What about your violin?" she tried reasoning. "Didn't you say you wanted to practice?"

"The violin? Now? Oh, Mama! Don't you see what this is? This is a revolution! Who cares about playing violin in the middle of a revolution?"

Even as Eva unlocked the front door, fixing Bianca with a stern look, she couldn't deny the truth: despite what her daughter thought of her, they had much more in common than she would ever know.

———

Thankfully, Eduard was already home from the hospital, listening to the radio in the living room, still in his coat and surgeon's garb. He shot up from the sofa when he saw them, and Bianca flew into his arms. "Papa! You're here! Oh, I'm so happy you're home early!"

He held her closely, caressing her dark head, even though his eyes were on Eva. "Oh, Eva, come here," he said, then pulled her into their hug. He kissed her cheek, smoothed a strand of hair away from her face. "Eva, I was worried. Where have you two been?"

"At a boring picture show," Bianca explained, her face still buried in Eduard's coat. "Can you believe what's happening, Papa? Isn't it wonderful? And to think we missed half of the excitement watching some clown trip over his feet!"

For once Eva didn't mind the jab, didn't mind at all because Eduard was here, and they were all together, on the cusp of something monumental. Dora then rushed in from the kitchen, dinner forgotten, and they all stood in their living room, embracing and smiling with tears.

"Ruszkik haza," repeated Eva in Eduard's ear, and he pulled her closer and kissed her cheek again.

The day's events were indeed monumental, unfolding with such speed that they couldn't adjust their minds to it as they took in the evolving news on Radio Free Europe. By eight o'clock, the peaceful demonstration had mushroomed into a full revolt, and violence erupted throughout the city. The AVO, the Hungarian Secret Police, had fired at the crowd in front of the radio station where protestors had gathered.

Then, by morning, after a sleepless night during which Eva and Eduard watched the activity on Andrássy from their window, the Soviet tanks arrived. People began throwing Molotov cocktails at the convoys, raising weapons of their own. Within hours, the casualties climbed up.

Eduard, despite Eva's protests, went to the hospital early morning, and Eva stayed behind to help Dora keep an eye on Bianca, who was in her room, banging things around.

"Well, if I'm to be held hostage," she said, poking her head through the door, "then I might as well rearrange my room. This, for example," she said, holding in her palm a crystal rabbit that had belonged to Eva as a child, "this might as well be the Kovaks family mascot! Well, it's taking up too much room." Then she hurled it across the floor.

Something snapped in Eva. She rushed to Bianca's door and dragged her out by the hand. "Come here. Come here, Bianca." She pulled her into her own room, past Dora's stunned look, where, from her armoire, she extracted her nursing uniform from the Hospital in the Rock, packed in an old leather hatbox. It was still covered in blood—she'd never washed it all these years, not only because she didn't think she'd ever use it again, but because it was a reminder of that time.

"This was my nurse's uniform in the war," she said, removing the bloodstained item from the box and shaking it in front of Bianca. "Look at it. This is what I wore every day. I've seen people die. I held their hands as they died. I saw children younger than you brought in with wounds that would make your blood curdle. I helped your father once extract a bullet from a man's heart. So do me a favor, Bianca. Do not ever refer to me as a coward." She had to pause for a breath. "Now if you really want to help me and your father, pipe down. And stay inside."

Bianca was silent. She was silent, and for the first time in her life, she did something Eva thought she'd never do. She took her mother's hand in hers and brought it to her cheek. Then she swiveled on her heels and exited the room.

Still holding her soiled uniform, Eva raised it to her chin, inhaling its stale, musty scent. It seemed a lifetime ago when she'd worn it yet she was deluged suddenly with vivid memories of that time in the bunker—and how amid all that suffering and danger and uncertainty about her own future, she'd found her true strength. It had shaped her into who she was today. She had once been part of something larger than ordinary life, and she'd fought to make a difference in a troubled world.

And that was precisely when the idea came to her.

———

At eight o'clock, when Eduard got home, Eva drew him a bath and sat on the ledge next to him, listening to accounts of what had been happening all day in the streets. Saint John's, where both Eva and Eduard worked, was overflowing; ambulances shrieked endlessly around intersections and squares, around burning buildings, unable to attend to the wounded quickly enough. As they carried the stretchers toward the Red Cross cars, some of the medics had been shot at by rooftop snipers or Soviet soldiers who roamed the city with rifles pointed through the open roofs of their trucks. There was no shelter anywhere for the freedom fighters, Eduard confessed grimly, no way to protect them, to come to their aid.

"But there can be," Eva said, handing him a bar of soap from the sink. "There can be, if we put our heads together."

"How?" Eduard said in a defeated voice, staring blankly at the leaky faucet.

"Well, I was just thinking today. Just thinking, mind you, that as chief surgeon at Saint John's, you have certain privileges. Power. People respect you. People would follow your lead. They would band around you no matter the risk. And because of that, Eduard, I thought . . . why not reopen the Hospital in the Rock? Not officially, you know. But you can arrange to have supplies smuggled through the underground passages, just like during the war. And you can get others to join in the efforts clandestinely. No one has to know. That hospital hasn't been used in eleven years, and no one would know."

It took Eduard only a minute to ponder this proposition. "Eva, you might just be the wisest person I've ever met." Reaching for a towel, he crawled out of the tub, splashing Eva with a few droplets as he dried his head. "This is brilliant. You are brilliant!"

"Well, not as brilliant as Ana Ivanov." Eva laughed, but the comment was lost on Eduard, who, grabbing his robe from the back of the door, was already headed to his study, leaving behind a trail of wet steps.

A second later, he was on the phone, making one call after another, his voice revived, buoyant, and Eva listened with a renewed energy of her own. She and Eduard were at their best in times of crisis. Crisis, survival, bound them. And they would do it again.

28

OR TEN DAYS AND NIGHTS, AS the clashing continued, thousands of freedom fighters—some wounded, some simply seeking a place to rest—poured into the Hospital in the Rock. Eva took a leave from her regular job in the maternity ward on account of her daughter's health, the only thing she could think of to justify the absence, and she and the others worked in the cave around the clock, much as they had in the days of the siege. To Eva, it was like stepping back in time. Everything was eerily similar: the wounded, the lack of space, the relentless efforts of the medics, even Tamara. Tamara, whom Eva had only seen a handful of times in the past decade at some colleague's dinner party or another. Tamara, who had changed so little, still lithe and quick on her feet, still scanning the evolving situations with the acuity of a hawk. Still looking at Eduard, she realized with a sudden shock, the same way, and he at her with a casual ease, which made her wonder if perhaps Tamara had remained a part of his life all these years, and whether he had kept this from her.

But just as before, there was no time to dwell on personal matters, for graver things were taking place aboveground.

Just a few short weeks since Eva and Bianca had marched in the demonstration, the Soviets amassed a full army that waited at the Romanian border to quell the uprising. One rainy morning in early November, all hope that Hungary would wrench itself from Soviet control was dashed. The Russian armada crushed the revolution with unusual brutality in a matter of hours, setting an example for the rest of the Eastern European countries under their control. By sundown it was all over.

In the stunned despair that blanketed the city, Eva and Eduard cried leaving the hospital that day. They cried as many others did in the streets for the twenty-five hundred people who had lost their lives for a dream of freedom that would not be.

"It was not for nothing," Eva tried consoling Eduard. "At least we did our part. And I'm so proud of you, Eduard. I'm so proud of you for your courage."

Eduard would not be comforted. "The West," he said. "The West stood by and did nothing. They did not send help; they turned their eyes the other way." A sheen of drizzle had gathered onto his red scarf and the shoulders of his overworn coat, into the stubble of his unshaven cheeks. She reached up and swiped the wetness from his brow, but he seemed utterly unaware. "We are alone, Eva. This illusion, that we are still part of the larger world, has died today." He paused, swallowing hard. "Well, at least we still have our family. We have each other. And whatever comes now, we will have to endure."

"Yes," Eva agreed, "we will endure." And she couldn't help being reminded of what Tamara had said to her once, in the last days of the siege. They couldn't bend fate to their will, but they would endure. They had no other choice.

That night, their family indeed felt as though there was nothing beyond the small universe they shared. As they embraced Bianca and Dora, who'd spent most of those days in the basement shelter of their apartment while Eduard and Eva toiled in the hospital, not a tear was spared. But in those tears, there was love; there was a future. Wherever this next path would lead, whatever chapter would open, they were not alone.

"It was not for nothing," Eva repeated to Eduard later that night, resting her head on his chest in their bed.

Eduard was already asleep, so she shifted her head onto her own pillow. But in the darkness, she wondered. She wondered how true those words really were.

No more than a week later, there was an early-morning knock. Eduard was still sleeping, still exhausted from the work at the hospital, and Eva went to answer the door. It was Tamara.

"Tamara. Hello! Is everything all right?" Eva was less surprised to see her here at half past seven than by the way she looked. Her dark cropped hair was lank and plastered behind her ears, her eyes deeply shadowed. From underneath the coat, the edge of a flannel slip peeked out, and Eva wondered if she'd somehow left the house forgetting to change.

Eva herself hadn't taken much time with her appearance since the return from the hospital, for she, too, was preoccupied with other things. Bianca seemed withdrawn, frightened from the gunfire, and refused to sleep alone in the dark. Most nights she either curled into bed with Dora, or dozed on the sofa between her and Eduard. Eva loved this new closeness, though she'd be lying if she said Bianca's sudden neediness didn't concern her a little.

"Is he here?" Tamara's gaze shot past Eva as she walked inside without so much as an invitation, taking in the sofa strewn with blankets and the coffee table where they'd left their tea mugs the night before. "Please say that he is."

"Yes, he's still sleeping; they all are," Eva replied, filled now with annoyance. The casual exchange between Tamara and Eduard in the hospital was still on her mind, and she'd been waiting for the right time to bring it up with Eduard. And now this early-morning intrusion. Turning away from Tamara, she tied her robe and brushed the hair out of her face. "So what's happening, Tamara? What is it that you want?"

"I must speak to him. I must speak to you both. Please, Eva, go wake him. Go now."

"Can't this wait? As I said, he's still sleeping. Perhaps you might like some coffee. It will give us a chance to talk."

"Eva, please."

Trying her best not to lose her temper, Eva turned and marched into the bedroom. She shook Eduard, who was snoring softly, his head buried under the blanket.

"Eduard, Tamara's here."

He groaned, turned the other way.

"Eduard, it seems important. What do you want me to do?"

Another groan. Finally, he sat up at the edge of the bed with his hands planted on his thighs. "Can't you tell her to come back later? Tell her I've a headache and cannot get out of bed. Then come back and get in here with me for a couple more hours. Dear Lord, it's not even light out."

Eva did not have the chance to agree wholeheartedly, nor to take comfort in the fact that Eduard seemed not in the least interested in Tamara's presence, for a moment later, Eduard threw the covers off and slipped his feet into his moccasin slippers. "Well, if she's here, we might as well find out what it's about. Maybe it's to do with the hospital." Then he grabbed his robe and shuffled toward the door as Eva followed suit, hoping that the exchange with Tamara would not ruin her day.

"They know, Eduard. The Secret Police know," Tamara said, her face pale and stern in the weak light by the kitchen window where they'd retreated to speak. Tamara had insisted that they turn on the radio to drown out their conversation from any neighbors who might overhear, and now Eva's irritation was replaced by an acute pang of panic. "They've already questioned several of the medics who were in the hospital with us, and they know somehow that you arranged to have supplies smuggled from Saint John's. They are trying to get others to sign confessions. It hasn't happened yet, because, Eduard, you are loved, truly loved by so many, but they will continue to harass and press until they get what they want. Do you understand what I'm saying?" Her eyes shifted directly to him, grazing past Eva. "Do you understand what this means for you?"

"How could the Secret Police possibly know such a thing?" Eva chimed in, trying to take in all that Tamara was saying. Grabbing a glass from the cupboard, she filled it with water from the sink and took a gulp, aware that her hand was shaking. "The medics are loyal to Eduard; they would never cave, certainly not this quickly. So how could they possibly know about the smuggled supplies? No, it's just not possible. It's not possible to charge him with anything without proof."

Tamara shot her a look, her brown eyes zoning in on her in a challenging way that went through Eva like cold water. "Well, Eva, somehow they do know. I don't know *how* exactly. But the fact is: once they confirm that Eduard was at the center of it, that he organized the whole thing, he will be declared a revolutionary. It may be just days, hours perhaps, before they come to arrest him. It's why I'm here."

It connected then. Everything connected in a formidable clash, and it left Eva light-headed, grabbing for the back of the chair in which Eduard sat glumly, staring at the floor: The vision of Eduard on the phone, recruiting the medics. Ana's caved, humiliated face at the end of the recital. The unpleasantness with her husband as they were leaving.

It does make one wonder where those ideas come from. What precisely she hears in that apartment of yours.

"Oh my God," she cried out in the silence. "Oh God, Eduard." She fixed her eyes on Eduard, who looked up at her, ashen.

Yes, they did have proof. And they would come for him. Tamara was right. It was only a matter of time.

29

*T*HE GALLERY OPENING DID NOT TAKE place, as it turned out, for another year. One year during which Aleandro checked his mail daily, checked his messages hourly, and did his best to refrain from calling Marta more than once a week. An uprising for independence that had begun as a peaceful protest had shaken Budapest the past November, Marta explained gravely, and the city had sustained significant damage. Thousands of people had been wounded, killed, or arrested by the Hungarian Secret Police for doing nothing more than coming to the aid of the freedom fighters. At the moment, no one in Hungary was in the mood for art. The capital was once more rebuilding itself from the ashes.

"But the good news, Aleandro," Marta said. "The good news is that you are one of the few Western artists who've been granted entry into the country. Now it would seem, more than ever, just as I told you before, your art is pertinent there. So it is no longer a matter of *if*, but *when*. Just be patient."

It had not occurred to Aleandro in all the long months of waiting that Eva might have been harmed. He refused to believe it. All that mattered now was getting there, to seize this small chance that would never be offered to him again.

And when at last Marta announced that the opening was just a month away, Aleandro fell on his knees and shouted like a madman in his apartment, and made a new portrait of Eva, two, three, five, ten—drew them for five days and nights with the same fervor he'd drawn his Dachau pieces. Everything seemed possible again. And at some point, because it could no longer be postponed, he decided that it was time to tell Rudolf.

———

Marlena's mother's house in New Brunswick looked exactly like every single one in the three-mile stretch he'd traversed from the train station: a tiny cottage with an overgrown, unfenced yard, strewn with Hula-Hoops and plastic tricycles. Marlena and Rudolf were spending two weeks here with Hans, and Aleandro had waited so long to break the news that he'd had no choice but to leave the island and venture into this suburban oasis, which to Aleandro might as well have been a safari.

He wore a suit that not only seemed completely out of place but was also impossible to endure in the relentless late-September heat. By the time he reached his destination, his tie had come off, and he was carrying his coat on his arm, praying that someone would answer before he was forced to unbutton all the buttons on his overstarched Egyptian-cotton shirt.

On the third ring, which croaked like a morning rooster, Marlena's mother appeared in the doorway, her reddish curly hair shorter than Marlena's, sporting a maroon, grease-splattered apron that read: *Beware the cook.*

"Aleandro!" she shrieked. "What a surprise! Well, come on in, darling, let's get you out of this heat!"

"Hello, Sandra." Aleandro kissed her hand, scanning the tiny parlor with its walls plastered with wood carvings bearing more sayings that made little sense to him: *Home is where you make it* and *Not all those who wander are lost.*

"Ah, but you just missed them!" sang Sandra excitedly, closing the door behind them. "They've taken Hans to the weekend fair downtown, and I don't expect they'll be back until dark. But please make yourself comfortable. Surely, you'd enjoy an ice-cold lemonade."

Despite himself, Aleandro could not exactly disagree.

A few minutes later, he felt a bit refreshed and settled into the same conversation he'd had with Sandra the last time she came to the city for a visit—mostly about Hans and how quickly he was growing up, some about the latest "perfect girl" she had for him.

"You know, my bridge partner's daughter is an artist herself."

Aleandro held back a comment, relishing the last few sips of lemonade and popping an ice cube into his mouth.

Sandra continued, "Well, not an artist like you, not quite the same way, but she designs wedding cakes for La Neige Bakery in the city. And she's tall and slim like you, Aleandro, an—"

"Thank you, Sandra, that's really very kind, maybe some other time. Because, you see, I will be traveling for a little bit now. In fact, that's why I came today. To tell Rudolf."

"Ohhh, anyplace exciting?"

"Hungary. I'm going back to the old country. Although I'm not sure how exciting it is at the moment. I'm going for work. It's unavoidable."

"Yes, I've heard about all that's been happening there. The capital is in a cold war."

"Yes, something like that. Which is why I didn't tell Rudolf earlier. I knew that he'd object. And he would be right, Sandra, he would be right to object, because it is a bit . . . imprudent to go there now. But I must." Then, catching himself in his monologue, which he'd rehearsed in his head for Rudolf, he frowned. "Sandra, would you happen to have a pen and paper? I think I'll leave a note for Rudolf, if it's okay. I have to get back to the city to pack tonight."

"Of course." A moment later, Sandra appeared with a huge yellow pad and a ballpoint pen bearing the address of a bank. "Well, I'll leave you to it." She hovered around for a few moments, then, discouraged by the lack of attention, she ambled to the kitchen to finish her baking.

My dearest Rudolf,

By the time you find this note, I will be on a plane to Budapest. I know you steam with fury reading this first line, that you will think it a betrayal that I have not shared it with you sooner when everything in our lives has been shared to such minute detail. Perhaps it's better this way. I know that you would try to talk me out of it, that you would enumerate a thousand reasons for which this is foolish, even dangerous, and I would be hard-pressed to argue with you otherwise.

My reasons haven't changed. They are the same as they were in our last days in the camp, when I looked to America with such hope for a new and meaningful beginning. Part of that dream has been fulfilled thanks to you, yet I fear that it hasn't made me the better man I'd envisioned becoming then. So I'm going. I'm going back to see if, after all this time, there is still a chance for me to start living in the full sense, to become that man you can be proud of in every way. Kiss Hans and Marlena for me. You guys are my family. I love you, my brother.

Yours,
Aleandro

Content with his letter, he asked Sandra for an envelope, sealed it, tapped it on his knee, and placed it on the coffee table. Then he bid her good-bye and walked back onto the street with its scalding pavement, and farther to the train that would take him back to New York, and farther still to the plane that would bring him to where he hoped to find what he'd lost.

30

FOR DAYS ALEANDRO HUNG AROUND THE much-publicized Budapest exhibit. The rooms were crowded to capacity: patrons coming and going, the press, the dignitaries, the minister of culture posing with him endlessly, caterers offering him food and drinks, none of which he could manage to get down. His nerves were tied up like a bundle of wires, every movement around the room startling him, making him jolt. Would she come? He didn't know. He didn't even know if she would pay attention to any arts and culture news when the country was in such turmoil, and now his rationale seemed as flimsy as a tower of building blocks, a creation of child's play. Still, he'd had no choice but to come. There was nothing that he expected, nothing that he hoped for, just a moment to set his eyes on her again.

More than once, he thought he'd spotted her, each time

his heart kicking against his rib cage, only to be plunged into a new well of bleakness. Now all he could do was drift through the crowd, smiling here and there for the cameras, shaking hands absentmindedly, his eyes searching.

A young girl accompanied by an elderly woman in a fur coat, which seemed decisively out of place in Soviet Budapest, handed him a small bouquet of daisies. They were wrapped in paper and a bit wilted, but he was touched as much as thankful, for now, if Eva did come, he would have something to give her. He thought with dismay that he should have brought her a small gift, but what? What could he have possibly brought her? What was in his heart could not be expressed with gifts, and perhaps she would think it trite. Eventually, he handed the bouquet to one of the staffers to place in water and resumed strolling through the exhibit.

Soft music played in the background. It soothed him, just a little, and to distract himself from his nervousness, he focused his attention on the people examining his paintings. It was always strange for him to see his paintings through the eyes of others, and usually, in such moments he felt vulnerable, but now he didn't quite mind it. An elderly man in a drab suit was patting at his eyes with a handkerchief, running it over his temples. Noisily, he blew his nose in it, and Aleandro felt propelled to reach out. When he touched his shoulder, the man startled, and, recognizing Aleandro, a radiance came into his face.

"I, too, was in the camps," he explained, tucking the handkerchief in his pocket. "In Belsen. Oh, Mr. Szabó, this work . . ." He was choked with emotion, and they stood there together, looking at the painting of a young boy, no different in age than his brothers might have been then. Naked from the waist down, he was squatting over a hole in the ground, and the tip of a bayonet was pointed directly at his shaved head. The guard holding it was not in the picture, for the focus of the painting was the boy's eyes. In them, there was no terror or defeat, but rather something steely, indestructible. As if gazing right past them, into the future. As if knowing that a future beyond this would exist.

Aleandro put his arm around the man's shoulders. Even under the suit, they were sharp, thin. He knew people in this country had been struggling, that they were hungry, that they'd had to manage with rationed electricity, that since the revolution everyone lived in terror of arrest or persecution. And here was this man, weeping at his paintings.

Perhaps coming here was the best thing he'd ever done. Whether he saw Eva again or not, it was still the best thing he'd done.

He began to say something, but a movement caught his attention, and he turned away from the painting. There she was. He reached up to rub his eyes as if to convince himself she was real. No, this time he was not mistaken. He stood there watching her drift through the sea of people, and he placed his hand again on the man's shoulder, this time to steady himself. He heard the stranger ask if he was all right, but he was already moving in her direction.

She was just as beautiful as he remembered, as he'd envisioned a thousand times. No longer a girl but a woman, with a whisper of maturity in her delicate features, caution in her movements. Her face. The same face he'd painted in the days of his youth, those same luminous eyes that had haunted him for over a decade. She was wearing a dark trench coat, something loose and too big for her frame, with a yellow scarf with pink roses tied over her hair.

Another step. He felt like he was walking through water. She had not seen him yet, and she drew her head scarf away. The curls tumbled from underneath—darker, the color of bitter cherries—had she dyed her hair? Her hand drew to her throat as she inched toward the row of glossy black frames on one of the walls.

Another swell of people came from behind her, and she disappeared from him. Panicked, he pushed through, offering apologies, and there she was again, whitewashed in the multitude of miniature spotlights illuminating the walls. At the disturbance, she turned, and there they were, staring directly at each other, their words silent, trapped in their throats.

Aleandro.

Eva.

The room and everything in it dissolved. The Eva of his Sopron days, and of his Dachau days, his Eva, his eternal Eva, was standing before him, not in his imagination, but in flesh and blood. Stupidly, he realized how, in all the times he'd envisioned this moment, he never thought of what he would say to her.

"Aleandro." She spoke his name. It was suddenly real.

"Eva. I'm so happy to see you." His words, lost in the crowd, barely reached his own ears. "I prayed you would come."

She smiled, her cheeks red. She turned back toward the paintings, perhaps to hide her fluster. "I read about your exhibit in the paper, and I just had to see it for myself. Oh, Aleandro, you did it! You've made your dream come true. You don't know what an amazing thing you've accomplished, and how happy I am for you."

Her back was still turned throughout the entire delivery, and he wanted to see her face, wanted to have her speak to him directly, but she wouldn't turn to him. So he stepped beside her and brushed her hand with his. The silk of her glove snagged slightly on his calloused skin, and she gave a tiny chuckle, her hand sliding past.

"I really couldn't believe that was your picture in the paper," she went on in a voice just a little more than a whisper. "I kept staring at it, thinking that I was dreaming. All this time, I thought you were . . . Well, I'm just so sorry for all of it, for all that you've had to go through. It's unimaginable you've lived to see such things." Finally, she faced him, and he was shocked to see that her eyes were brimming with tears. "And your brothers. Is it true, Aleandro? Is it true what I read?"

"It's true," he said, and now his own eyes burned, for he knew how much she'd cared for them. Knew that while for him the pain had dulled over the years, she was acutely in its grip, and in that moment, he thought he'd never loved a person more.

"Your paintings, Aleandro." Her hand lifted, brushing the air separating them from the works as if to touch them from a distance. "They are astonishing. It's like you've painted them from inside the canvas. They are laced with such honesty, such feeling . . ." She caught herself and stopped. "Well, I really should go. But I just wanted to tell you how much they've moved me."

Yet she didn't budge, and they couldn't look away from each other, and it was as though all the years were erased between them, and they were sitting on the grass again holding hands, they were dancing around the fire, they were what they should have been before the war.

"Please don't go, Eva," he found himself pleading. "Please stay awhile longer." Only three sentences he'd spoken to her, and already he was begging her to stay. He couldn't imagine her walking out.

"I don't want to keep you."

"Keep me? Keep me? It's for you that I'm here, Eva."

Shaking her head, she looked away from him into the vastness of the room. "Why? Why would you say this to me after all this time?"

"Don't you know?"

Through her tears, a vague smile came. It was enough to make her bend.

***

They ended up grabbing a late-night bite after the exhibit just a few short blocks away, at the lavish if slightly dated Hotel Gellért, where Aleandro was staying. The restaurant was already closed, yet Aleandro had managed to get the *maître d'hôtel* to reset a table for them next to the terrace, with its glow of lampposts and lush canopy of rose vines. There was some wine, some fancy eclairs scrounged up from the kitchen, which Eva devoured with such fervor that it nearly broke Aleandro's heart. She hadn't had many sweets in the past year, she explained, drawing back self-consciously. It had been a very tough year, more so perhaps than in all the years since the war.

"Tell me everything. Tell me about your life," he asked.

"My life? Oh. Well, it hasn't been quite like yours. But it's been a good life. I became a nurse. I love my work. It isn't glamorous, and most days you could say that it's almost mundane. But there have been moments . . . moments when it did feel . . . glorious. Moments when I thought I could make a significant change."

"Yes, I remember how much becoming a nurse meant to you. You used to carry those big biology books with you wherever you went. You'd bring them down by the pond, and while I was drawing, you'd recite to me all the muscle groups. The town children, I remember, would run around afterward, making rhymes with those words they'd overheard. They called them spells. Do you remember that?"

She shook her head, not smiling as he'd hoped, looking into the light of the garden. "Oh, Aleandro, your brothers. I'm sorry, maybe I shouldn't bring it up, but . . . I had no idea. I cried for days . . . They were so lovely. I just don't know this world anymore. To endure so much loss, it just seems so very cruel."

"It's all right, Eva. I don't mind speaking of them. Especially not with you. I know how fond you were of them, Lukas above all." He had to pause, startled by the intensity of his stirred grief, and had to swallow a sip of wine against the forming tears. "For whatever it's worth, they still live inside me. They always have. They live through my art. Not just the camp paintings but what I draw today. I try to look at life through their eyes, through their innocence, and capture it as they might see it. And in a way we are still together. As long as I keep painting, they are never far from me."

If anything this only seemed to deepen her sadness. Her

hand traveled up to her cheek, rested there, her eyes still on the garden and the potted white roses abutting the window. When it came away, he noticed that her fingernails had left faint crescent marks on her skin.

"Ah, let's talk about happier things," he quickly said.

Her eyes returned, and she smiled. Finally, she smiled. "Yes. Happier things. Tell me about New York."

"New York. What shall I tell you about New York?"

"Everything," she said, echoing his earlier words, and he refilled their wineglasses, thinking where to start.

Over the next twenty minutes or so, it was he who did most of the talking as he recounted the brutal fourteen-day trip over the ocean amid a sea of refugees, and his first impressions of that daunting, incandescent city he now called home. He told her about his early days with Rudolf, and that first exhibit where his art had been called raw and honest, revolutionary, and how in the short year that followed, he went from bussing rat-infested kitchens to dodging camera flashes. Of how he still painted on the doorstep of his first building in New York, because it was for him (and always would be) a bridge to his past.

Some things he left out. He didn't speak, for instance, about how in every woman he'd dated he'd searched for her— the sound of a voice, a gesture, a likeness of her tiny stature, and how his hands, roughed by paint and turpentine, had touched many bodies but had truly only ever touched hers. Nor did he speak of his drawings of them, in which he tried to re-create her semblance, women he ended up withdrawing from because they weren't her. They could never *be* her.

Such things he couldn't speak of, so he stuck with the larger themes, but spoken or not, these thoughts were there between them, and without meaning to, he reached across the table and brushed his fingers over hers. Touched the golden band on her ring finger, which had consumed him the entire evening. Her hand flattened under his on the lavender tablecloth.

"You married." He didn't want to ask so abruptly, but now the words were out there, searching for an answer. "You married Eduard?"

She didn't say anything, just nodded her head.

"And you have children?"

Again, she wavered. "Yes. A daughter. We have a daughter."

And there it was, the hammer on his heart that he'd been almost expecting. Of course. Just like that letter had said— that letter that he was burning to mention and couldn't bring himself to mention—her life had gone on, she'd married, had a child, while he'd been living like a phantom caught between two planes, waiting for this moment—to sit with her again, to talk to her, to look into her eyes. But it was too late now not to delve forward, and so, closing his eyes, he asked:

"And are you happy, Eva?"

"I was. We were, for a long time. Eduard and I . . . Oh, it's difficult to explain. There have been some recent developments, some . . . unpleasantness in our lives. It's not something that I can talk about. As I said earlier, it's been a difficult year."

A new wave of pain pulsed through his chest, for in these unspoken difficulties, a life had been built, moments had been lived, changes had been traversed. A life. She had lived a life without him, and now it seemed impossible to mention anything at all about the letter, and whether, in all this time, he still existed for her in some small chamber of her heart. Instead, he braced himself for whatever his next words would invite, interlacing his hands on the tabletop to keep them from trembling.

"Please tell me about your family."

She toyed distractedly with the golden links of her watch. "Oh, what does it matter now?"

"Because it matters to me. And it always will. Also, because more than anything, I want to listen."

Her expression shifted; she looked at him in a new way, a thankful way, and for an instant, he thought she would open up. But there was a brisk cough from one of the staffers hovering near the kitchen, and she straightened in her seat and shot a glance at the small dial on her watch.

"Oh, it's late, Aleandro. They're trying to close up, and I really should have been home long ago."

"Can I see you again, Eva? My plane leaves tomorrow, but I can rearrange my flight for another day. Maybe we can finish this conversation tomorrow. You know, this is my first time here. Maybe you can show me around, and we can talk a bit more. Just say that you'll see me again."

"Aleandro." She was already out of her seat, collecting her coat, which she held in a jumbled bundle. "You know that I would love that. I really would. But what would it add in the end? We are not what we once were. Please try to understand."

"Then why did you come? Why are you here, Eva?"

She took an abrupt step back from the table, pulling her coat and purse closer to her chest. "Perhaps I shouldn't have come." She shook her head. "But things between us were left unfinished, and I thought . . . I thought this was our only chance to make peace with that chapter in our lives. And it's been wonderful seeing you, Aleandro. More than you will ever know."

She might as well have thrown kerosene in his face saying those words. No, they were not what they once were. She was gone, still here for another moment but already gone from him, as she'd been all these years. All he could do was stand from his seat numbly and lift her hand to his lips.

"Let's not say good-bye," he heard her say as he stared down at her hand. "I'm just going to go now. And we will not say good-bye."

But it was good-bye. He watched her turn and walk through the length of the restaurant and through the main hotel lobby, and his heart twisted inside his chest like a dying bird.

31

AT HALF PAST TEN, EVA SLIPPED quietly into the apartment and took off her shoes at the door. She'd walked all the way from Hotel Gellért, not minding that, since the uprising, it wasn't safe for a woman to be alone on the streets past sundown. She needed the walk, needed to get her emotions in check, but it hadn't really helped. In her bedroom, she peeled off her skirt and shirt, ambled into the bathroom in her slip and bare feet, and splashed some cold water on her face. Splashed it again, dipping her head under the faucet, letting it cool her fevered skin.

His beauty had stolen her breath. She'd been staggered by it because it was not only intact, but enhanced by the passing of years, the majestic, stark lines of his face, the expensive suit, those black piercing eyes made even more stunning by the soft lines beneath them. And to hear him speak to her the way he did! To lay himself open to her as though no time had passed, to look at her that way still—it had fissured every brick and barricade she'd erected between them in the time since.

She curled into a ball on her bed. Pulled a pillow into the crook of her body and pressed it into her stomach. She ran her fingers over the other pillow nearby, forcing her thoughts to Eduard. Eduard, who was her husband. Eduard, who'd been her husband through occupation and poverty and revolution. Yet her existence with him had been mostly one of quiet contentment—they knew each other well and loved each other, but it was a calm sort of love, the kind displayed by older couples with forehead kisses or a squeeze of a hand over a dinner table.

With Aleandro tonight, she'd felt every atom in her body come out of its inertia as if a part of her had been dead in all the years that he'd been gone. This sensation overwhelmed her. Pushing the pillow into her face, she cried silently.

It was impossible that she would get any sleep, and after an hour of tossing, she went into Dora's room and shook her shoulder gently, but Dora didn't move, so she slipped in next to her, nestling her forehead against her damp, papery temple, taking comfort in her scent of cold cream and camphor. After a few minutes, Dora woke, and in the darkness Eva felt her warm palm on her cheek, brushing it gently.

"Another tough night, darling? What time is it? Do you want to talk?"

"No. I don't want to talk. Just want to lie here next to you."

"Darling, you can't lose hope. Right? You know that you can't. Bianca needs you to be strong. And you are strong. You've always been strong, Eva. A solution will emerge, you will see. It will come soon."

"I saw him, Dora."

"You saw him?" Dora shifted and scooted herself up against the headboard. "What do you mean, you saw him?"

"Not Eduard. That would have been impossible, right? I saw . . . I saw Aleandro. I went to the exhibit."

"Dear Lord, Eva."

It sounded like a reaffirmation of her foolishness, a condemnation that Eva could only meet with a desperate need to be closer to Dora. She moved up right next to her, buried her face in her shoulder. "I couldn't help it, Dora. I just couldn't help it. I didn't intend to stay; all I wanted was just to have a glance at him, and then I would go. But then he saw me, somehow, and, well, we talked for a little while, and it was . . . it was the same as before."

"Dear Lord," Dora repeated. "Sometimes, Eva, I think you are your own worst enemy. And how much did you tell him? Please tell me that you did not speak about your family's situation. That above all, you didn't mention anything about Bianca."

"I only mentioned that I had a daughter, that's all."

"And what of Eduard?"

"Only a bit. There wasn't much time, and besides, I thought it best if he didn't know."

"Well, that was wise," Dora said with an undeniable tinge of sarcasm. "Because, absence or not, Eva, you do still have a husband."

"You don't need to remind me!" Eva scooted away to the edge of the bed away from Dora, swung her feet onto the floor. "I am well aware of my obligations, and my seeing Aleandro changes nothing. It's just something that I had to do. For my own peace, I had to do it, and now it's done with."

"I'm sorry, darling. Please forgive me." Dora's hand now was in her hair, her fingers threading firmly through its length, and Eva reclined back against the pillow, relishing in this small comfort.

"I just don't understand, Dora," she resumed, pulled back into her thoughts. "All these years he's been living in New York, and in this whole time, there was not one word from him. Not one word. I know it's not easy to get correspondence from the West, but surely he might have found a way, if for no other reason than to let me know he was alive. And you know what's strange? When he first came up to me, when he approached me in the gallery hall, he said that I was the reason he came to Budapest. At first, I thought he was just saying it in jest, but he looked quite serious. Why would he say that, Dora? Was it out of guilt? Was it to torment me?"

"I don't think it was to torment you, Eva," Dora said pensively, her fingers still in Eva's hair. "Although, yes, maybe out of a small sense of guilt. For whatever it's worth, I think perhaps he, too, grappled with some demons of his own, wondering perhaps all these years if he should have been more persistent."

"Persistent? Persistent with what?"

The hand came to an abrupt halt. She felt Dora slide away from her and from the bed, saw her move across the room where she sat in a rocking chair by the window. "Oh, it's nothing. Really, don't mind me. It's really nothing, darling."

"Never mind what? What's nothing, Dora?" In the darkness, the creak of the chair as Dora's heavy frame rocked against it was like the ticking of a clock, a building to something that severed Eva's breath. And then the words came:

"He did write. Once."

"What? Are you making this up? To make me feel better?"

"No, it's true. He did."

"You are making this up. I never received any letter from him." .

"No, you did not receive any letter. You did not, because it was me who opened it first. Oh, Eva, I don't—" Dora's voice fractured, dropped into the space between them. "What I did was wrong, I know, but it was right after the war, and you and Eduard were just beginning to spend time together again. It seemed there would be a chance at happiness for you, and the timing . . . the timing was terrible. I knew that if you read that letter, everything would change again, that you would once again forgo Eduard, that you would give up everything for even a small chance to be with Aleandro. And what was he going to offer you? What? He'd just survived a concentration camp, and his own life was no doubt in far worse shape than yours. I couldn't let you throw everything away, not when it looked to me that your life could finally have some stability."

The sound that came from Eva's lips was more of a gurgling than a cry. "So you withheld his letter from me? And kept it a secret all these years?"

"Don't you see, I had no choice! I witnessed firsthand what this infatuation of yours, this reckless love, did to you. I was there, remember? I was there when you seemed no more than a corpse as you expected that baby, when you would go down to the gypsy camp and stare at it for hours on end. So when the letter came, when I realized who it was from, when I opened it and read it, I knew it could never reach your hands. And afterward, time took its course and you were happy again. You were happy and content, and that meant everything to me. It was all that I ever wanted for you. It was for your own good, Eva. What I did was out of love for you."

In the reverberating silence Eva grasped that it was true, all of it, but Dora's words still hurt, still angered her.

"And you thought that was justification enough?" Eva was on her feet now, her back pressed firmly against a wall. "How could you do that to me? He is the father of *my* child, Dora! Have you forgotten that? How could you take that decision away from me?"

"Eva, stop it! Keep your voice down before you wake Bianca! Have you lost all your senses?" Dora's shadow moved across the room, and Eva felt the firmness of her hands on her shoulders, and she twisted her face away because she couldn't stand to look into Dora's eyes.

"So what did you do with the letter? You just discarded it, hoping it would be the last one? Were there others?"

"No, Eva. There weren't others. Because I wrote him back. I wrote to him when he was still in the camp. I told him that you were happy. That you had moved on."

She laughed. She threw her head back and laughed. She understood now, yet it came to her like a sheath of ice, seeping into her bones. That's why he'd gone to New York after the war. He'd gone because he'd lost his brothers, and he thought he'd lost her, too. He'd gone because there was no reason to return.

"I loved him, Dora," she said without any vigor. "I loved him. And if you'd made a different decision, everything might have turned out differently." Then she peeled herself from the wall and walked past Dora across the flat and into her own room.

For a whole ten minutes, she ignored Dora's desperate

knocks as she sat on her bed, her hands between her knees. Aleandro would leave in the morning, and she would never see him again, and he would not know this one simple truth.

She stood. Her hands and legs felt as though they'd been encased in lead, but she slipped into a fresh dress and brushed out her damp hair, and tied her scarf at the chin so she wouldn't catch a chill. From the stool at her dressing table, she grabbed her trenchcoat, shot herself a look in the mirror as she buttoned it, questioning. Was it too late to tell him? Did it matter at all after all this time? She didn't know. But she had to tell him. Too many things unsaid stood between them, and she couldn't let him leave without knowing at least this much.

She pushed open the door. She did not look at Dora as she walked past her and her insistent words, did not falter as she walked through the front door, too, back into Andrássy, with its array of broken windows and bullet-splattered walls matching the state of her heart. She walked firmly toward the Liberty Bridge and Gellért Hill, where she prayed that she could still find Aleandro. At least this decision belonged to her. Foolish, reckless as it may be, it belonged to her.

32

JUST BEFORE THE KNOCK AT THE door came at half past midnight, Aleandro was sitting on a pale silk sofa facing the river view, cradling the sketchbook of Eva's portraits in his hands. Still in the same clothes, drink at his side, doing precisely what he'd grown accustomed to doing back in New York. Mourning her. Mourning her again with her so fresh in his mind, with the vision of her profile against the garden light and the way it caught the tiny gold curls at her temple, with the faint scent of her floral perfume still in his nostrils. Well, he'd done it to himself with his own two hands. Perhaps he deserved this.

With effort, he stood from the sofa and went to the one suitcase he'd managed to pack, unzipped it, and placed the sketchbook inside a hidden compartment. He would leave in the morning. There was no reason to remain in Budapest a day longer. No reason at all, because now he had confirmation that everything between them was finished long ago. A daughter with Eduard. Eduard, whom she wouldn't discuss with him; Eduard, who was part of her real world, not the fantasy he'd built inside his head. Perhaps now, at least, he would be set free. Perhaps all this self-inflicted misery had not been for nothing.

He zipped the suitcase, then went to the desk and picked up the telephone. It had been days since he'd spoken to Rudolf, and he burned with the desire now to hear his voice, but as he began dialing, he realized that it was just past three in the afternoon in New York. Rudolf would likely not be home, so he disconnected the call. He switched to the reception desk, wanting to at least arrange for a car to the airport, but there was no answer; he would have to call back in a few hours. Then, because there was nothing more for him to do, and because he felt slightly drunk and more than a little depressed, he began making his way to the bedroom, kicking off his shoes on the way, fumbling with the knot in his tie. And that's precisely when the knock came.

A bellboy, he thought at first, getting the wrong room number. He ignored it and continued on, yanking off his tie and tossing it on the floor as he went farther into the bedroom. Another knock followed, and then another, and, with a flare of annoyance, he made his way to the door. Then, as he opened it, disbelief. A wash of happiness, then again, disbelief.

He thought at first his eyes were failing him, that he had fallen back into one of his reveries, that he was once more seeing her face as he had a habit of doing in a perfect stranger.

But it was her. It was Eva exactly as he'd last seen her, two hours earlier.

"I'm sorry," he heard her say. "I'm sorry to come up unannounced. There was no one at the reception desk, no one at all for more than twenty minutes, and the guest ledger was open on the counter, so I couldn't help looking up your name. I hope I'm not intruding, but you said that you were leaving tomorrow, and I couldn't take the chance that I would miss you." There was a pause. "I had to come speak to you."

Wordlessly, he opened the door wider, and Eva stepped into the vastness of the suite with its tall ceilings and lights too bright, its rosewood furniture from a distant era. "You are not intruding at all," he said, rushing to remove his discarded shoes from the center of the rug, even though it seemed like the most senseless thing in the moment. It was hard to think. All he wanted was to drop down to her feet and weep.

She pivoted toward him, tried smiling as she drew off her head scarf and bunched it into her fist. "I only came because there is something that I needed to tell you. Something that I didn't know myself until after I left the restaurant. May I sit?"

Not waiting for his answer, she pulled out the chair at the writing desk and sat. Her hand came up over the glossy wooden surface, traveled to the vase of lilies, touched the white petals, and rested there, as if enraptured by the delicate white trumpets. But even in profile, he could see her face was etched in anguish. The scarf had slipped to the ground, yet she seemed entirely unaware of it.

"I didn't know, Aleandro," she began at last. "I had no idea that you wrote to me after the war. I never got your letter.

Whatever reply you received, whatever it said, it was not sent with my knowledge."

The words didn't crystallize right away. They hung in the air, hovering above Eva and Aleandro, refusing to sink. He'd heard her well enough, but it was as though the words had been meant for someone else. As if they'd landed in the wrong room, between the wrong people.

"But how could that be? That letter. You mean . . . I thought it was you who asked your friend—Dora, is it?—to write it on your behalf. She sounded very close to you; she sounded . . . she sounded as if she was speaking on your behalf. As if she was conveying your wish."

From across the room, their eyes met fleetingly, and her beautiful mouth twisted. "My wish? My wish, Aleandro? Don't you think I would have at least wanted to know what you'd been through, what you'd survived?" She shook her head, drawing her bottom lip between her teeth. "No, that was not my wish. And I couldn't let you leave Budapest without knowing. I don't know why, but it was important to me that you know this. That's why I came back."

He stumbled to the sofa and sank into it, not bothering to remove the newspaper or magazine underneath him. Head in his hands, he forced himself to think, to reach for anything logical. "But it made sense! Everything that was in that reply made sense! After my time in the camp, I had even less to offer you than I did before that fire. I had nothing. For your own happiness, I had to release any hope of you."

"She had no right," he heard Eva say distantly. "She had no right to keep your letter from me. All this time, I assumed that after the fire, everything changed, and my God, I spent so many weeks, months, praying that you were still alive. I didn't know that you were alive until I read about the gallery opening in the paper." She paused, drew in a sharp breath. "She had no right to keep that simple knowledge from me."

"Oh, Eva." He felt like crying as he said her name. His love, his Eva, his muse—he couldn't stand to see her like this, and it no longer mattered what he felt. It no longer mattered that his own heart was breaking anew. His heart would always break for her, and he had to ask the one question that could still pull them back, that would reconstruct the reality they'd both known.

"And would you have made a different decision, Eva? If you had read that letter, would it have changed anything at all?"

For a few moments she didn't say anything, then she lifted her chin and looked straight into his eyes. "It would have changed everything."

Her words undid him, and he came to her and took her hand and placed her palm flat against his chest, at his thrashing heart. She pulled back from him, as if her hand had been burned, and stood from the chair, clutching the backrest before she turned and began for the door. And he couldn't let her go, couldn't let her go now any more than he could stop what had been set in motion. At the door, he reached for her, crushed her to him.

Then there were no more words, no space for them. There was only their arms, legs, and lips, his palms curving around her shoulders and her waist and the sharp bones at her neck, and her voice breaking in his ear, *Aleandro, oh God.* At some point they'd moved farther into the room, but he registered none of it now. Nothing existed but her in his arms, and him kissing her, kissing her cheeks and eyes and the hollow at her throat.

If this was right or wrong, he didn't give a damn. For the first time in his life he didn't care what he was taking from another, didn't care what damage he was causing. A recklessness poured through his veins, and with it the sharp stab of jealousy, something that felt oddly like poison, like hatred. Hatred, yes, if that's what it was, for the man who'd put that golden ring on her finger, for the life she had lived without him. When he undressed her, it was a bit roughly, but she didn't resist, and for a moment, it filled him with a dizzying sense of power. But then something happened, something broke apart inside him, and he slid down to his knees. He was weeping, his cheek pressed against the silkiness of her stomach, weeping for all the years stolen from them, which he could never take back.

It was she who broke away from his grasp and reached for his hand. And led him into the other room, where she peeled away the bedspread. When they fell back against the sheets, there was no moon and no sun anymore. There was no world beyond this. There was only here and now, and the two of them crashing like waves, all of eternity distilled yet made whole in this one single moment.

———

Aleandro did not expect that she would still be there in the morning. Yet she was, her golden hair fanned out on the burgundy silk of the pillow, her eyes pinned to the ceiling, her thin arm still bearing the gold watch folded across her breast, hand at her throat. God, she would never stop taking his breath away. He watched her a bit longer, not shifting a muscle, not daring to breathe, drinking in the near transparency of her skin, the large areolas surprisingly dark, and the beauty mark in the crevice between her breasts. If he blinked, he feared that she would disappear. He willed himself not to blink.

"You are exquisite," he said after a few minutes, and she startled and turned her face to him, blushing a little. "I could live ten lives and never get enough of looking at you."

Drawing the sheets around her, she sat up, bashful, turning herself from him. "What time is it?"

She did not check her watch, forgetting perhaps that she was wearing it, remaining still, as though she was the subject of a painting. Then when she shifted, it was to move away from him. He felt the void of her as she went to the window and pulled the drapes open a little, letting in a strip of sunlight. "I should go," she said, not turning from the window, running her fingers over the silk panels. Her head dipped forward, and her hand moved away from the curtains and to her forehead. He thought she might be crying, and he felt the burn in his own throat, because he knew that she would leave. That in a moment she would dress and exit this room and his life once more, return to her family, and there wasn't a thing he could do to stop her.

"Come back to me," he said nonetheless and she turned. To his utter, utter surprise, she walked back to the bed and lay across it, resting her head on his chest. They stayed like that, each with their thoughts, each with their fears, each with the recollection of the night before. With so many recollections of a simpler time.

He didn't know how much time passed. Only that the strip of light in the window had rounded at some point, that his plane had left long ago, that his stomach churned with hunger, that she was still here in his bed. They made love again, slower this time, in a way they had not before, as if there was no reason to hurry, then dozed off in each other's arms. When he woke, she was no longer beside him. She was on the phone in the other room, her voice steady, calm, escalating only a little at the end. He couldn't hear what she was saying, didn't want to know what she was saying, but afterward, when she emerged again in the doorway, naked under his suit blazer, his heart ached and he couldn't help asking:

"You must go, yes? Back to him?"

She nodded solemnly.

"Does he know where you are?" He couldn't help sounding a bit hopeful.

"No. It wasn't him that I spoke with. It was Dora. She still lives with us—she takes care of my daughter—and I had to let her know that I'm all right."

"And what will you tell him when you do speak to him?" Still hopefulness in his voice, but now, sharpness.

For a long moment, she looked at him, then she walked across the room and sat at the foot of the bed where his discarded clothing lay in a pile, and scrunched the edge of the bedspread in her hands. "This, us, it has nothing to do with Eduard. This is just ours."

"Nothing to do with him? Don't you think, Eva, that perhaps he might be wondering at this very moment where you are? Where you've been all night?" His tone was no longer mild; it was curt, rough, last night's jealousy stripping away all of his remaining possession. And so his worst fear was not unfounded. Everything was just as in Sopron, only now, more serious. She was married to Eduard now, and he was perhaps no more than a diversion, a slip of consciousness she would blame on nostalgia. A trip down memory lane.

"Well, I'm sure you've already come up with how to explain me away."

Now she was the one to appear wounded. "Is that what you think of me? That I could so easily betray him with you, then make up a lie? How little do you know me?"

He threw off the covers and got out of bed but couldn't go to her, as much as he wanted to. He couldn't look at her now and kept his back turned, hands on his hips. "You're talking in riddles. Perhaps you don't think I understand all of this, but I can see clearly enough, Eva. You mean to keep this a secret."

"That's not true."

"Do not toy with me, Eva. I don't deserve that. The least I deserve is the truth."

She came up behind him then, and put her arms around him. Her floral scent was there again, that scent that he would never be able to expunge from his jacket or his pores, and he wanted to die.

"I never meant for this to happen. I never did. And the reason why I couldn't speak about Eduard in the restaurant last night, the reason why I can't tell him about us now, is not at all what you think. It's complicated, and it will complicate everything between us if I tell you."

"So let it."

He heard her intake of breath and felt her cheek pressing into his back, not with desire now, but seeking solace. "Aleandro . . . the truth is: I haven't seen my husband since just after the revolution. For nearly a year now, I haven't seen him."

33

*A*FTER RECOUNTING HER TRIALS, STARTING WITH her and Bianca getting caught in the demonstrations and ending with Tamara's unexpected appearance at their door, Eva could go no further. The entire time, she'd spoken facing the window, unable to look at Aleandro and his intense gaze, and now she dipped her aching head against the cool glass.

"We had no idea," she resumed after a few minutes, sliding into the chair beneath the window and pulling her knees to her chest. "We had no idea, you see, that we were being surveilled, that they'd tapped our phones, that they'd been watching Eduard for a while. That they were watching and waiting for an opportunity to ruin him, to ruin us, yet it all came to us clearly in that moment. To be tagged as a revolutionary . . . I don't have to tell you what that means in this country.

"Luckily," she went on after a pause, "Tamara and several of the other medics had already arranged passage into Austria at Pamhagen while the borders were still open, and he went with them that very same night. In all the chaos that ensued, there was a good chance that they could make it through. Tens of thousands had fled already in those early days after the revolution, but then the Soviets were sealing the borders quickly and there wasn't much time. No time, I mean, for us to figure out a better way to go with him as a family. My daughter was still shaken from the days of battle, and Dora's health had been fragile for quite some time. It was inconceivable that we could bring her, and I couldn't leave Dora any more than I could put my daughter through the danger of a border crossing, through more trauma. So he went without us. It was nearly impossible to convince him to go, but in the end, he did it. Truly there was no other choice. If he'd stayed, I don't think he would be alive today."

It was a long while before Aleandro could speak. "Dear God, Eva, and have you had any word from him since? Anything at all? Do you know where he is now? And are you safe? Are you safe here, in Budapest?"

"All I know is that he's in Austria, in Vienna. And yes, I believe that I am safe. It is not me that they want, not while I might still lead them to him." Her fingers brushed over the dark green brocade, tracing the swirls of carved wood on the chair. "I get word from time to time through other people's families, through Tamara's sister. I hear that he is trying everything to get us out of Hungary, to arrange for us and Bianca to join him under safer circumstances, but I fear that might be impossible. It could take years, or possibly never. And then there is her, Tamara. All that I know is that she is there with him. She is there with him in Vienna, and I don't know what to think from one day to the next."

Now they were both silent, and Eva could only guess what he was thinking: Eduard now gone, and him here, here with her, the window that had opened for him as much as it had for Tamara. The uncanny reversal of circumstances. It was almost impossible to believe.

"Aleandro, I could never blame Eduard for anything, no matter how it turns out. He always fought for the right thing, even if it meant putting himself in harm's way. In the end, all I want for him is happiness, with or without me. He has been a good husband to me all these years; he's given me more than you know."

"And you love him. Do you love him just as you did before?" His voice, weak, desperate, reached for the last bit of truth.

All she had, all that she could give, was the truth.

"I always cared deeply for Eduard, even before I met you, but it was always different with him than it was with you. It's hard to explain, and perhaps there isn't really a way to phrase it. We built a home together, we raised a child, we shared our work, a whole life. But, for whatever it's worth, I wanted you to know before you left for New York that I've been on my own for a year. Perhaps it's no excuse for my being here, but at least now you know."

A long silence followed.

"I can't go back to New York," he said.

"What? You can't be serious. What do you mean?"

"I cannot go back to New York without you. How can I leave you here now?"

"Aleandro. You don't know what you're saying."

"But I do. I know exactly what I'm saying. You were married to me, too—once, in heart."

It was so poetic that it might have been a verse in a book. Him, her, Eduard. They were tied together in a vortex of fate that would never release them. Forever she would be caught between these two men, with the wheels of history, which took one away, then the other, tearing up the boundaries of her heart and her life. How messy love was, when it should have been simple, beautiful. How much damage it left in its wake.

"Go home, Aleandro. Go home and live your life. You will always have my love, but there are responsibilities here that I can't walk away from."

"I want my life to be with you."

She had to close her eyes but couldn't block out his words, nor the questions that surfaced without invitation. Could she go with him? Could she leave Dora? Yes, she was quite angry with Dora, but could she really leave her behind? Dora was her soul mother; she had been there for her through thick and thin, she'd given her a home, she'd helped raise her daughter. And Bianca. Could she tell her the truth about Aleandro? She would no doubt resent her, and Eva had only just begun to bridge the distance between them.

And Eduard. It would crush him. If he ever came back to find them gone, it would crush him. He would think their whole life a hoax.

"I have a daughter," she said with renewed resolution. "A daughter who loves him, whom he loves. A daughter who's probably looking out the window right now for him to come up the road with suitcase in hand. I can't take that away from him. Nor from her."

"I, too, could learn to love your daughter, given the chance," he went on, undeterred. "All I ask for is the simple chance. Everything I've accomplished in this life, Eva, everything that I've done, I've dreamed of sharing with you someday. I stayed alive in that camp for you. All I ask is for the simple chance. So please say yes, Eva. Please."

Her hand traveled to her mouth to suppress a cry. *Your daughter, my daughter, our daughter.* Eduard's daughter above all, above all. Bianca, whose name she couldn't say, for if she did, she feared that she would reveal the one thing that would unravel them all.

"It's impossible."

"It is not," Aleandro said. "I know you think it's a crazy proposition, but I have contacts in New York, important contacts who can help, and I have plenty of money, if that's what it takes to get you both out. It is not impossible if we wish it, and perhaps he would wish it, too, if it meant a better life for you and your daughter. So come with me, Eva, come with me to New York. Let *me* love you as I've yearned to do since the day that we met."

"I can't, Aleandro." She reached the last ounce of inner strength as tears streamed down her cheeks. "I can't leave here, I can't leave Budapest when there is still a possibility of his return. He is my husband."

Her words fell between them like a guillotine blade, silencing any further urgings or pleas. Turning away from him and those anguished eyes, Eva went into the front room, where she began collecting her things—her slip, her bra, her dress and stockings—and retreated into the bathroom, needing desperately this small distance.

When she emerged, he was still there, still on the edge of the bed, his face in his hands, the long line of his body arched in a Rodin pose. He didn't move as she walked past him to pick up her shoes near the bed or when she continued on to the door. Only when she reached the foyer did she hear his voice from the other room, broken but determined:

"I will not say good-bye to you. I will not mourn you again."

A sob came from her throat as she walked out of the suite and closed the door against the room and all that it contained. Softly, she closed it against those last words to her.

34

E SHOULD HAVE LEFT DAYS AGO. And he had tried. More than once he'd called his travel agent back in New York to arrange for the next flight; he'd packed his bags, telephoned Rudolf to swear that he would be on the next plane. But each time, he ended up changing his mind. Everything was finished yet nothing was finished, and so he delayed one more day, one more weekend, even though Rudolf had tried to reason a dozen times that his visa would expire and there were bound to be all sorts of problems with his exit. He stayed because he knew that once he left, he would never see Eva again, and couldn't bring himself to accept it. Not with the stain of her lipstick still on his pillow, with the sheets he wouldn't let the maid change still imbued with her scent.

After several days of sulking in the hotel room, he began wandering around town. Walking helped to clear his mind, and so he walked aimlessly—at first in the winding neighbor-hoods of Castle Hill, then venturing across one of the bridges into Pest, walking against the chill of late October, his collar raised, hands in his pockets. He walked past the dress shops on Váci utca, where he imagined Eva shopped in a time when the windows were clean and the displays were arranged against backdrops of velvet; he walked through Heroes' Square, where bullet-ridden monuments spoke of the revolution; he walked along the Danube banks, where the muddy, gray sky seeped into the river and the cry of the seagulls mirrored his grief. He rode streetcars. Endless streetcars in no specific direction, his eyes pinned constantly on the window, subconsciously search-ing for her. He wasn't so naive as to think that he would spot her in a city of two million people, but he couldn't help look-ing anyway, with the hopeless desperation of a sentenced man praying for some last-minute reprieve.

About a week later, his tram broke down in the center of town, and after waiting nearly an hour for the next one, he gave up and visited a coffee shop—a tiny, musty place with Turkish rugs on the walls and wicker chairs in need of a good polish. He needed to warm up and study his map, and when his waiter brought him a watery cup of coffee, he asked him to point out where in the maze of streets he was exactly.

"*Köszönöm*," Aleandro said after the waiter had sat down next to him and given him a detailed explanation of the city as though he were a tour guide, and it made him smile to say it. It was the first word that Rudolf had spoken to him in the camp. In America, the two of them only spoke English now, but he'd missed this language, missed the roughness and sweetness of it, and so he said it again: "*Köszönöm.*"

"Is my honor," replied the waiter, a jolly man with a sprouting of wild grayish hair, flushing with pleasure that he could show off his English, and Aleandro realized the man recognized him somehow, perhaps from one of the billboards for the gallery opening. "This sector, beautiful," he went on, tapping the map. "Operaház here."

He redirected his eyes to the map and felt a flash of warmth spread alongside his spine. He was no more than five, six blocks away from the opera house on Andrássy út. Right near Eva's old childhood home.

Pointless. Pointless to go there, he told himself. There was nothing that he would find. Eva had mentioned in the restaurant that her father had died during the war—surely others, not Eva, lived there now. But he couldn't resist the urge to glimpse her childhood home, the home to which he'd sent his letter, the home where upon her return after their summer together he had been in her heart. Already he was on his feet, muttering an apology for leaving the coffee intact (guiltily, for he knew such extravagances were rare in Budapest) and placed several bank notes on the table.

He was not in a hurry. There was no reason to hurry, and he strolled leisurely, taking in the lavish flats of the opera district, the shell-shaped glass awnings, the intricacies of gargoyles and baroque motifs—astonished that these had been everyday sights for Eva, but sobered at the same time by the realization that he'd been mad to ever aspire to her. That even now, despite his success and money, she was still out of his league. He had nearly turned—perhaps this was enough torment for one day—when the sound of a violin came from a corner park no more than a block away.

He stopped and listened a minute longer. It was a classical melody, something Beethoven or Mozart, something he was accustomed to hearing in his gallery openings or in expensive restaurant lobbies in New York. It was good, too, the sounds crisp, the notes precise, and he couldn't help walking in its direction and entering the gardens.

On a dark green bench, seated on the backrest as if on a stage, violin tucked under her chin, he noticed a young woman. A girl, really, in her very early teens if he had to guess, wearing a red coat, her chestnut hair pinned in a smooth ponytail.

A moment longer, he stood and listened, observing her. Her eyes were closed; she seemed in another world, and something in the way she held the violin, the way in which her eyebrows rose and knitted at the dips and escalations, seared him with melancholy for his Sopron days. Then the bow stilled and her eyes flickered open and she saw him. She let the bow drop to her side, the violin still under her chin.

"You play extremely well," Aleandro said, going closer. "I'm sorry, I was just walking by and I couldn't help hearing."

"I know," replied the girl, slightly annoyed, clipped. It reminded him of how he felt when he painted on the stoop in New York, when someone interrupted him. So he took no offense to it and smiled.

"Well, it's good to be aware of one's talents. Please don't mind me. But I'd love to keep hearing it."

"Well, what do I get for it? I'm not a free show, you know."

He laughed, scrounged in his pockets, but he'd left all of his money on the table at the café, and all he could give her was some loose change, which he thought would be insulting. "I'll tell you what. I will play a tune for you first, and if it pleases you, you can then play something else for me. Only if you don't mind me borrowing your violin, of course."

He had her attention now, although she still regarded him suspiciously. She had remarkable eyes—the rich, prismatic color of turning leaves—a bit like Rudolf's but possessing none of the mildness or glint of humor. Her eyes were intense, a bit feral and somehow mocking. They frightened him a little and also seared him to the core.

"You play?" she said, resting the violin in her lap. "And what do you play exactly?"

"I used to play gypsy tunes. May I?"

The look lingered, an eyebrow quirking as her gaze traveled slowly from his hat down to his shoes. Then her glossed lips curled in indifference, and she handed him the violin, moving over to the far end of the bench, where she hopped back onto the backrest and rested her chin on her hand. "Try not to botch up the strings. I just had it tuned up."

"Yes, boss," he said, something American that was clearly lost in translation, and after thinking about it for a moment, he dove into an old favorite tune that his father used to play, something that he listened to on a vinyl he'd bought in an East Village secondhand shop called *The Sounds of Gypsy Rhapsody*. But to listen and to play were very different things, and, faltering the notes more than once, he stopped and handed the violin back to her.

"I'm sorry, it's been a very long time."

"It's not bad," she replied. "How do you know that music?"

"I used to live in Sopron. A long time ago. I used to play that song once when I was about your age. In the taverns."

"My mother is from Sopron. Well, not exactly, but she used to spend quite a bit of time there when she was little."

"Really?" he said, delighted. "And did your mother like gypsy music?"

There was a scoff. "Hardly. My mother only listens to opera. All that melodrama and vocal bravado. It seems ridiculous to me. True music is in the instruments." She pulled from her coat pocket a loose, shriveled cigarette, which she sparked with a silver lighter. Blowing a ring of smoke into the air, she held it up as if in explanation. "Fringe benefits. She tries to pretend she doesn't smoke, but I know where she stashes them."

"How old are you?" he couldn't help asking.

"Old enough not to get caught," she said and blew another circle. "I'm Bianca, by the way. Bianca Kovaks." There was a tiny flick of her wrist, the limp cigarette going around in a circle. "Yours truly."

"And where do you live, Bianca?"

"Why, do you plan on turning me in? My mom would hardly care, believe me. She works all the time."

"I plan on doing nothing of the sort."

"Well, over there." She waved in the general direction of Andrássy, with its glorious Parisian flats, of which she clearly thought very little, chewing on a short, bright red fingernail. "I live with my mother and my grandmother. Well, sort of my grandmother. My nanna. She, on the other hand, would break my bones."

He had to draw in a breath, the blood swimming in his temples, where he pressed his fingers into the shallow flesh. "And where is your father, Bianca?"

"He's away." Bianca took one last deep drag of her cigarette and stomped it out on the bench, then crushed it with the heel of her galosh for good measure and shot him another penetrating look. "Well, you don't look like much of a Russian crony, certainly not knowing that sort of music, so I will tell you." Leaning in halfway across the bench, she whispered: "We will soon join him in Vienna. Vienna is where I will soon live."

"Vienna?" He looked at the girl more closely for a trace of semblance, but there really wasn't one. This girl looked nothing like Eva, possessed none of her soft-edged, angelic features, but he was convinced that this was her daughter.

"Yes, you know, the birthplace of the great composers?" She rolled her eyes at him. "If you are from Sopron, you would know Vienna. Have you not heard of it?"

"Of course I have. Of course. But . . . what if it wasn't Vienna?" He was venturing into forbidden territory, he knew, but how could he help himself? This was Eva's daughter. He couldn't believe it, couldn't bring himself to believe it. "What if . . . what if, let's just suppose, it was . . . someplace else? Someplace like America? New York, for instance?"

The girl sneered. She picked up the cigarette butt from the bench and hurled it into the grass across the narrow path, scattering a group of pigeons. "No, my father would never go to America. America sold us out. They did it during the war, and they did it again last year, during the revolution. Don't you read the papers? America only cares about America, and he would never agree to live there."

"But what if you were to live there just with your mother? New York is a beautiful place. A place of musicians."

Now she looked at him as if she considered slashing his

throat. Lifted the violin from the bench where she'd set it between them and shot him another murderous look as she slammed it inside her case. She hopped down from the bench, and without further word, she began walking away, the dark swoop of her sleek ponytail swinging behind her.

"Wait!" He ran after her, caught up to her on the boulevard. "I'm sorry. It was just a question. I did not mean to upset you. Please don't go."

She swirled toward him, strands of her hair loosened by the wind whipping around her face, which had turned crimson. "My father will come back for us! He will come back because he loves me and he promised me that he would, and I will live with him in Vienna! In Vienna, with my father, not anyplace else." She drew back, aware of a few passersby, and pointed her varnished fingernail at him. "You, mister, should mind your own business."

Then she turned her back to him and stomped ahead, crossing the street at the next block, and he watched her disappear, precisely as he'd suspected, into the building with the Venus statues.

He should have been devastated. Any reasonable person would have been, yet everything had long slipped beyond reason, and he couldn't help but see it as a sign. To run into Eva's daughter like this, to meet her for the first time as she played the violin in the park—the violin, of all instruments!—could only be a sign! Sure, it hadn't been exactly an ideal exchange, but someday, somehow, she would come to like him. Not like her father, certainly not in the same way, but there were plenty of shiny distractions and indulgences in New York to melt her iciness—symphony orchestra seats, the best violin money could buy, and pretty pendants, things of that nature, which no girl of her age could resist. But of all those things, there was plenty of time to think about later. All that mattered was that he'd found Eva. Miraculously, he had found her, and everything seemed possible again.

35

I<small>T WAS NEARLY DARK BY THE</small> time Aleandro realized that he was lost again. So absorbed he'd been in his thoughts for the past two hours, that he'd drifted away from Andrássy and now found himself trapped in a dizzying maze of backstreets. Luckily, at some point, he ended up in front of the same café he'd stopped in earlier and entered, hoping the kind waiter would still be there to offer directions to the bridge.

The lights were turned down low, and the place, just as in the afternoon, was almost empty. Only one family hovered at a table near the kitchen curtain, a father, a mother, and their two boys blowing tiny bits of paper through straws at each other over empty plates. The adults talked contentedly, enjoying sips of some pale liquor.

"Ah, friend, you back!" exclaimed the man, and when he rose to welcome him, Aleandro saw that it was in fact his waiter. He'd shed his apron, and he now sported a brown beret, giving him the aura of a poet. "This, my family. Come, friend, say hello to family!"

Aleandro smiled, inched closer, as a jumble of greetings met him, enthusiastically by the woman, half-heartedly by the boys, who kept on with their paper battle. "Come sit! You want drink? Slivovitz here, best in Budapest! I promise that!"

"Thank you, I would love one, but I have no money to pay."

"You need not money. You pay sooner, remember?"

He couldn't say no; truly, he could use a shot of plum brandy, so he sat, pulling up a chair at the corner of the table. The shot did him wonders, warming him instantly, and he was grateful that the waiter refilled his glass again without him having to ask.

"Nice boys," said Aleandro, now in Hungarian, and winked at them, made a funny face to the younger one who kept staring at him.

"Aurel, Béla," said the waiter, pointing to each of his sons. "And this beauty here is Adda, my wife. I, Tamás. You have children in America?"

Aleandro shook his head, staring at the nearly empty glass. Tamás, the name of one of his brothers. A sinking sensation accompanied the last sip of his brandy. "No, no family now. But I hope to, someday."

"Family everything, ah?" said Tamás the waiter, who kept insisting on English, even though it was evident they could have a much smoother conversation in Hungarian. "My boys, they give life. My life nothing without these boys." He leaned over to one of them, grabbed his chin, and deposited a noisy kiss on his temple.

"Aye, Papa!" squealed the boy, but Aleandro saw that he was smiling as he wrenched himself from his father's grasp. And suddenly, everything crashed inside him—the name Tamás; the boys, with their childish naughtiness; the events of the afternoon; Eva, who was at home just a few blocks away, yet never farther from him. He had to grip the edge of the table for support.

"Another drink?" asked Tamás, raising his salt-and-peppered eyebrows to Aleandro. His coat collar felt too tight, and he unbuttoned it, then undid the top button on his shirt as well. The sudden longing for his brothers was so overwhelming that he couldn't draw a clean breath.

"Thank you, you're very kind," he said. "I do not wish to overstay my welcome. But there is something I'd like to ask." He pushed back his coat sleeve, and without further thought, he unlatched the band of his watch and set it down on the table. "How much could you pay me for this?"

"This?" Tamás lifted the watch from the table, his eyes widening as he brought it closer to his face. He set it back down gingerly with evident dejection. "This cannot buy. Not money enough for this watch here."

"I don't need much. Let's say . . . a thousand forints in 1950s. Enough for a train to Sopron and back. On the overnight, for which I imagine I might have to hurry. You see, to go back to the hotel now in Buda would be a great hassle, and I'm afraid I would miss the last train. And I expect that I will be quite busy here in Budapest for the next few days, so I must go tonight. It is not something that can wait."

"I cannot take watch here." Tamás shook his head, his hands on his knees, eyes downcast, which he lifted a moment later. Then he held up a finger. "But only to hold, for loan. I give you loan, yes? When you come back to Budapest and get money from hotel, you pay and I restore watch."

"You are very kind, thank you. And thank you for the brandy. *Köszönöm*. It has been my honor," said Aleandro, repeating Tamás's earlier words. "It's been my honor to meet your family." Then, taking the money that Tamás had extracted from a drawer beneath the bar, he handed over the watch and walked back into the street.

———

The Sopron overnight train was only slightly better than what he'd experienced in the days of the war: a darkened, dank, heatless cabin with cracked windows through which a freezing gust of air whistled. On the wooden bench that was his seat (at least there was a seat here), Aleandro, bundled in his coat, listened to the rumbling of wheels, watching the span of darkness where fields unfolded and farmers slept in scattered cottages, and apple orchards lay barren, covered in early frost under the starless sky.

The sun was just appearing on the horizon when he descended at the station. It was colder here than in Budapest, a light layer of snow on the ground, and he walked the two blocks toward the trolley station, only to realize that the trolley lines were no longer there.

An hour later, exhausted, hoping that he could find a place to rest, he reached the main square. His eyes scanned the vastness of the cobblestoned piazza as a chill crept into his chest. The church had been burned—a wing of it lay under a scaffold, windowless, and the entrance had been barricaded with planks of wood. Across the square, past the moss-stained column where Eva had once sat under a balcony of flowers, there was nothing but a gaping hole. No bougainvillea tumbling in a cascade of violent magenta, no balcony, no golden letters in a semicircle on the window beneath which Eva, in her red dress, lemonade at her side, read her books.

More because he couldn't bear the cold than anything else, he left the square and made his way to the end. The intersecting street signs bore new names of Soviet rulers. He walked past the baker where he once collected those stale loaves of bread to bring to his brothers, passed more buildings that had been bright peach and green and were now faded to a sad, muddied pastel. He paused before the tavern where his father used to play and where he'd had his first draft of beer. More wooden planks and broken windows clashed against his recollections. The absence of life was like a noose that had been coiled around his neck. It would suffocate him if he stopped to ponder all these changes long enough.

The road opened up to him again at some point. No Citroëns with summer guests from Budapest zigzagged it now, only a few Trabants, the Soviet cars that also peppered Budapest, their horns weak and exhausted as they bleated for him to get out of the way. From the window of one, an arm emerged and something was thrown in his direction—a scattering of cigarette butts, which he ducked, and a curse spilled through the window as the car rounded the curve.

"Bourgeois ass! Next time I'll run you over!"

He paid it no mind; his sole focus now was pinned only on where he needed to go next, the only place that truly mattered.

He took off his beige cashmere coat to prevent attracting that sort of attention and kept walking until he reached the bend in the road he knew so well.

Soon he stood at the edge of the bluff. As he'd expected, the stretch of land down below that dove into the glassy pond was barren, scattered only with a handful of wooden structures. With his heart silent and obedient in his chest, he walked over to a few old barrels of wine lying in the muddy span, decaying, splintered. Above one of the structures, a sign reading *Bartok Winery* hung askew, the letters faded and adorned in rust.

He walked farther, walked through the ashes of his childhood, walked to the one thing that might still be here, and when he found it, he fell to his knees and embraced the bark. His chestnut tree, the tree that stood in front of the hut where he'd lived with his brothers, was still here. It seemed a miracle, the biggest miracle that he'd ever lived. He ran his hands over the bark, over the grooves cut by a knife, felt the words before he opened his eyes to see them. And he did see them. He steadied his eyes on the words and the childish writing, letting out a sob that seemed to come not from him but from them all—a joint cry rising into the lead sky and echoing back to him: *Tamás, Attia, Lukas.* Their names, still there, where he'd shown them how to carve them. He pushed his face into the bark and wept.

———

Some time later, Aleandro ambled down to the edge of the pond where the children used to splash about in the summer time. The fishing pier rose over the lead glass like the skeleton of a beached whale—white and fractured, the end of it collapsed in the water. Near that pier was where he'd first sat with Eva, but it wasn't her that he was thinking of now, nor of his brothers, but, strangely, of the girl in the red coat. The girl who'd stirred his heart with her violin playing and her stark hazel eyes, and the conviction that her father would come for her.

Sitting on the grass by the pier, he dropped his head between his knees. He'd tried to convince Eva to stay, to be with him, to bring her daughter with her. He thought if he persisted long enough, her eyes would close, and she would be his again. What he'd been too blind to see until now was that in severing a child from her father, a father from his child, he would be inflicting the same intense pain he'd just felt under that tree. He'd be causing a loss not all that different than he'd endured at the hands of the Nazi guards.

The sun had set. It was nearly dark again when he rose from the grass and began up the graveled path toward the main road, yet it wasn't with heaviness now, nor with sorrow, but with the knowledge of what he had to do.

I'm going back to see if, after all this time, there is still a chance for me to start living in the full sense, to become that man you can be proud of in every way, he'd written in his letter to Rudolf, and perhaps now, at last, if he had the strength, he could fulfill that promise.

At the bend in the road, as he'd done many years ago, he turned and looked behind him one last time, imprinting the landscape of hills and the brassy indigo of the setting sky, the tiny white structure at the top of the hill that had been Eva's summer villa. A whole life was engulfed in this landscape. A life in which he'd played his music and found his art and danced and loved.

"Good-bye, my beautiful, enchanting, battered Sopron," he whispered to himself. *Good-bye.* Then he walked on, scrunching his shoulders against the chill.

36

My dearest Eva,

Of all the injustices that both you and I have endured, I
believe the greatest one on my part has been to interject myself
once more into your life. You see, for all of fourteen years, since
I last saw you, I've lived in a world of my own making in
which you and I never stopped. I walked the valleys with you,
I sat holding your hand under the stars, I made love to you a
hundred times as I had that first time in the cellar the night
before the fire. And I came to Budapest to find you, to take
back at any cost what I believed was rightfully mine.

Selfish, I know, to think that your life couldn't resume
without me, even though I knew well enough it would.
Nothing at the time could keep me away; nothing could dull
this blind ambition of mine to have you for myself again.

Then yesterday, I went to Sopron to visit the old gypsy camp and found a tree that still bore my brothers' names, and I realized that in this hopeless pursuit I lost something that was important to me.

To put it in not so many words, I lost my honor.

So I leave you with one final token of my eternal love: the sketchbook of your portraits. I hope you will look at it once in a while, as you did all those years ago when I drew them for you. During my days at Dachau, it was the only thing to give me hope and led me to everything that I am today.

And one final thing. I've decided to donate half of my Dachau collection to the Hungarian National Gallery. I'm told by a reliable source back in New York that this should be sufficient to secure from the Hungarian government three exit visas to Austria. I don't not know how long it will take for this arrangement to come to fruition, only that I've had assurances that it will. Perhaps it will be soon, perhaps in a year. But I do know that the angels will be watching, and faith now is all we have.

In Vienna, should you find your husband, live happily. Live with your family as you've never lived before, laugh, love. Forgive Dora. When I came to leave the sketchbook for you this afternoon, we made our peace, and I believe you should do the same. Sometimes, to protect those we love, we must breach our own hearts, as she so eloquently said, and no one understands that better than me. So let her back into your heart as she longs to be. Let there be new beginnings.

As for me, do not worry. By the time you read this letter, I will already be in the sky, crossing the ocean to the only

home that I have now. A family of my own awaits there—a
father and mother, and a son, whom I intend to embrace in
a way in which I have not and could not before. And at the
end of the day, isn't the love for family worth everything?

Yours,
Aleandro

The letter dropped from Eva's hand.

———

She didn't know how long she sat on the terrace with the
sketchbook, only that it had grown dark and the first snow of
the year fell from the sky. Dora had come out to bring her a
blanket and a hat and had retreated inside to prepare dinner.
Through the narrowly open French doors, she heard Bianca
practicing her violin, and on the boulevard a streetcar clattered
by, its bell fading into the span of the city, toward Heroes'
Square. A family passed underneath the terrace, the mother's
voice telling her children to slow down, to not run, for the
pavement was slippery. There was the smell of roasted chest-
nuts, of burning wood coming from one of the neighboring
apartments, and a dog was barking on a balcony as if startled
by the falling snow.

Someday, she would remember all these surrounding
sounds and smells and sights, and how her fingers passed over
the portraits, as if seeing them anew, as if for the first time. Aleandro would never be far from her life, for in his final gift, he
was making it whole again, and they would always be bound

by his sacrifice as much as by their child, of whom he did not know.

She imagined her life going forward. She, Bianca, and Dora would pack up the house, abuzz with excitement and a little sadness as they prepared their belongings for the estate sale, making plans of things they would do and see when they got to Vienna. They would glance back at their home, with its whitewashed cornices and rounded terrace, holding one another in an embrace before climbing into the car taking them to the train station. They would cry meeting Eduard at the end of the journey—Eduard, who'd gone completely gray in the two years they had not seen him, who would cry on their shoulders, vowing to never let them go again.

There would be bridges to rebuild between mother and daughter, daughter and friend, husband and wife. Walks under the lush canopies of trees, and evenings spent at concert halls where Bianca played. And unexpectedly, they would lose Dora one morning, when she simply didn't wake from her sleep. Eva would have love in her life—tears, too, but mostly love.

But for now, for another hour before Eva would walk back inside and into the rest of her life, there was just her and the sketchbook. She closed her eyes and pressed it to her chest and let herself be carried to a different decade, when a young man had rescued her mother's satchel and spoken to her under the gathering rain clouds.

And it was enough. It was enough for now.

Part IV

TRUTHS

37

*B*ELOW THE BALUSTRADE, TREETOPS DRENCHED IN dew glistened like ornaments in the budding sunlight. All night, Aleandro had watched and waited for the sun to rise over Central Park, wondering why in all these years, he'd never been able to capture its silent, magnificent beauty. Plenty of times he tried, but each attempt left him more disillusioned than the last. For a while, he reminded himself that landscapes were not his strong suit, never had been. It was people he enjoyed painting—people, with their conflicting emotions, their struggles and triumphs. His art had always been about people.

Even that, however, he hadn't been able to pull off in quite some time. How long had it been since he'd last held a brush? How long since he'd exhibited in a gallery? It astounded him each time he opened a newspaper or an art magazine and caught his name still in the headlines. Yet that's how the trouble had started, with an article in *ARTnews*, which Frank, his faithful assistant, had delivered that Sunday morning, along with his double espresso from the coffeehouse down the street.

Still in his bathrobe, he'd sunk into the sofa, and, taking small sips from the cup, he began flipping through the journal. There wasn't much that grabbed his attention, save for an article titled "The Death Effect," which he began reading with only mild interest.

It was a piece of fluff, and halfway through it, he'd set it aside with a flare of irritation. Only the expected names were there—Van Gogh, Gauguin, Lautrec, Monet—the great masters of the nineteenth century who never witnessed a day of their fame. If the author had been sitting beside him, he would have grabbed him by the collar. *What about the others?* he would ask. *If you'd bothered to scratch beneath the surface, you'd have discovered there were many others who sacrificed everything for their art and died before selling a single painting. And what of their names?*

Suddenly, however, as he might have expected, there was his name, at the end of the article. Picking up his glasses, which he'd flung onto the sofa, he leaned in for a closer look. Not just a sentence but an entire paragraph had been dedicated to him.

No one has seen seventy-two-year-old Aleandro Szabó in nearly a decade, leading many to believe that the artist is no longer alive. One could certainly assume that, based on the astronomical valuation set by Sotheby's last week for one of his early Dachau pieces. While this can be in large part attributed to their scarce availability—most of Szabó's works are in the possession of the Hungarian National Gallery or are privately owned by business ty-coon Hans Luben and decisively not for sale—what gives rumors of Szabó's demise most credence is that nothing has emerged from the artist's hands in far longer than he would allow.

He let the paper drop to his side. Throwing his head back, he laughed heartily, without restraint—not at the obvious error but because, in fact, what the article said was true. He was dead, truly dead in the way that most mattered. If the world thought him so, all the better.

A sensation of great relief settled upon him, and that same night he left his apartment for the first time in years, to end up here, in Central Park.

It was past midnight. For a while, it all seemed peaceful enough, and he relished the relative quietness of the city, the fresh air, the chirping of birds in a nearby bush. From his pocket he extracted a Cuban cigar and lit it, then reclined against a bench, relishing the aroma. Beyond the gates, some of the windows in the apartment buildings were still alight, and he watched them with the usual curiosity and melancholy. One of the windows opened, and there was laughter, notes of jazz dropping into the night like a sash of velvet. In another window, he spotted the face of a young child, a larger figure approaching behind her. The girl draped her arms over her mother's neck, and as they retreated from view, the window went black.

He didn't know why these mundane slices of everyday life stirred him so. Perhaps that he'd witnessed them from the outside for far too long. It was his own fault. In the past fifteen years since Rudolf had died, he'd found himself spending more and more time in solitude, losing interest in the lives of others. At first, there had been a few women, and fundraisers for Holocaust victims, which he always attended. There had been Marlena's quiet dinners for the three of them, where an extra place setting anchored them to what they'd once been, and larger parties he only attended out of politeness. And Hans. Hans had been his moon and stars, but eventually, he'd grown up, and Marlena had moved to California to start fresh, and more and more Aleandro had succumbed to the walls of his self-imposed prison. He couldn't help seeing himself for what he truly was: a ghoulish figure like one from his Dachau pieces, lurking in the shadows of late-night Manhattan.

He departed Central Park for home more dismally than he had come.

Later that night, he dreamed of Rudolf. Not quite a dream in his agitated state, but more of a hazy, disjointed catalog of their years together. Rudolf alongside him at every gallery opening, his smile bright beneath a chandelier when they'd gone out after his return from Budapest and he'd seen in Rudolf's eyes the respect he'd always yearned to see. Rudolf so much earlier in the days of their youth, standing guard over him as he painted the scenes of the camp. Rudolf in the infirmary when Aleandro didn't think he would live another day. Rudolf years later in another hospital bed, from which Aleandro was convinced that he would rise, asking Aleandro to take care of his family.

Rudolf, Eva. The loves of his life. He'd loved them both so fiercely. All he'd ever wanted to do was to love them, embrace them, live his life with them, live in their brightness. Yet they'd both skimmed the parameter of his life like shooting stars. Burning, fading into darkness, disappearing.

———

The next morning, after watching the sun soar over Manhattan on his terrace, Aleandro walked back inside and poured himself a tall whiskey. The ice clinked in the glass as he glanced around the living room with a cold, discriminating eye. The place was precisely the way he wanted to leave it: fresh flowers in Chinese vases, bills neatly stacked on the granite countertop, pillows fluffed. Even his letters (few as they were) he'd arranged and rearranged on the foyer table countless times, leaving no chance that they would go unnoticed when later the bellman opened the door with his master key.

The whiskey was warm and comforting, fueling his courage as he began his last task. No thoughts at all occupied his mind as he made his way to the foyer table and ran his fingers over the rich, lacquered surface to the drawer down below. He fumbled inside it, pushed out of the way some old bills and fan letters he'd never opened, a stale Cuban, some loose change. Finally, he found the bottle of pills and extracted it gingerly.

Would he have the courage this time? Would today be the day? He'd gone through this exact exercise a number of times, and each time he'd lost his nerve. Each time he'd taken down the prewritten letters, put the pills back in the drawer, then finished his drink overcome with disgust for his cowardice.

Yet it was what he wanted, he was certain of it. It was.

To be free as he'd once been when the roof over his head was mostly the starry sky. Perhaps he needed a couple more drinks beforehand. It was certainly worth a try, even though it was barely seven in the morning.

Soon he was settled on the sofa, second whiskey now in hand, staring at the bottle of pills before him. Summoning his courage, he reached for them, then a sound ripped through the room. A sharp sound, like a gunshot, which set his heart in a somersault, changing his trajectory. He listened again. A swift relief surged through him, realizing what it was, only to give way, almost instantly, to an intense irritation.

Frank. Frank pounding on that brass knocker as if his life depended on it. Only his assistant could get up here unannounced at this hour, but damn it, today, of all days? Cursing under his breath, he ambled back to the foyer in his bare feet, shoving the pills in his pocket. Drawing in a breath, he retied his robe and wrenched open the door.

"Frank, what are you . . ."

The man on his threshold was facing away, but even before he turned, Aleandro's words trailed off. That stance, those shoulders, hunched forward a little as if he were bracing against some invisible wind. Aleandro would have recognized him anywhere.

"Aleandro, my God. What took you so long? Didn't you hear me knock?" An unsuspecting smile spread over the man's good-natured face. "I tried to call from downstairs. Hell, I've been trying to reach you since yesterday. You had me worried!"

Gripping the doorknob with all of his might, Aleandro scrambled for something to say. "Hans! What are doing here? I thought you were out of the country. I thought . . ."

"Yes, well, I decided to come back early. A deal I'd been working on was falling apart, and I couldn't very well let that happen. Can I come in for a moment?"

There was no reason, no reason at all that Aleandro could reach for quickly enough, and then it was too late. He watched Hans unbutton his jacket, then raise his hands up to Aleandro in an amused, baffled gesture.

"Well, may I? It's early, I know, but I have something to share with you that I think you'll find very interesting. So are you going to let me in now, or do I have to put it in a memo for you?"

———

The expression on Hans's face, the way his eyes flickered with understanding and horror, crushed Aleandro's heart. Such an oversight, he thought now, miserably. Such a stupid, grave oversight not to stash away those letters before opening the door. It took Hans less than a second to spot them. And to notice the one bearing his own name.

Still, for a moment Aleandro could have salvaged the situation. When Hans asked jokingly, in such clear jest, "Are you bidding farewell to the world, Aleandro? Are you finally going to take that long trip?" he should have laughed. He should have replied something just as ironic, not stood there as all the blood drained from his face. Maybe Hans wouldn't have grabbed that letter from the entrance table so quickly.

But now Hans sat across from him on the sofa—still in his blazer despite the heat in the apartment, skimming the letter over and over—and the way he buried his face in his hands was more than Aleandro could bear. Hans, with his mild manner and gentle heart, had never looked at him in such a way.

"Why?" he said simply. "Why would you want to do such a thing?"

No answer came, only a sigh as Aleandro lowered his head and interlaced his fingers at the back of his neck. "Just life, Hans. I'm tired, that's all. I've grown tired of it."

"You're tired? That's it? That's all it takes for you nowadays to even consider something like this?"

A sole tear slid down Aleandro's cheek. "I know this is a hard concept for someone your age to understand, Hans, but all I wanted was to be free. No one needs me anymore here. You have your life, and your mother seems happy enough there in the land of laissez-faire sunshine and hippies. To be honest, I didn't think it would matter all that much. Lately, I've been feeling like a burden, even to myself, and that's the one thing I won't be."

"A burden? A burden, Aleandro? And no one needs you? What's all this nonsense? I need you, Aleandro; I need you! You've been like a father to me all these years; you've given me a start in life! You paid for my schooling, you bought my mother a house in Sonoma Valley, for God's sake! If she is happy now, it's only because you've given her a second chance for happiness. How can you say that no one needs you? Ah, all this self-indulgence has got to stop! Because that's the trouble with you! You hole yourself up in here, inside your memories and your self-pity, you drink, and you lose sight of life, and then you say no one needs you!"

He was angry, and it made Aleandro even more remorseful. "Oh, Hans. It doesn't matter now. It's over. I'm sorry to have upset you."

Hans only scoffed. After a while he got up and took off his jacket, tossing it carelessly on the sofa. "So, where is it? Where is . . . whatever you were going to use. Gun, rope, where is it? I can't even believe I'm asking you these questions! Well, go on, goddamn it, show me!"

"No rope. No gun." Aleandro extracted the pills, handed them over to Hans. "Like I said, it's over now. You don't have to worry."

"No, you're right," Hans said, examining the bottle, and drawing a deep breath through his nose. "You're right about that." He shoved the bottle of pills into the pocket of his jeans. "Because I'm not leaving you here. I'm not leaving without you. Get dressed, because you're coming with me. And please don't even try to talk me out of it. All right?"

"All right," agreed Aleandro, and he sighed, knowing that indeed there was no reason to put up a fight. His resolve had been crippled, and he felt drained all of a sudden, beaten, old. He *was* an old man, no more than that—an old man whose bones hurt and whose heart had long turned to dust—so he shuffled off to his room to gather his clothes. In the doorway, he turned toward Hans one last time.

"Tell me, Hans, why did you come here this morning?"

Arms crossed, Hans regarded Aleandro with that same unabating weariness. "It hardly seems to matter now, but while I was in London, a package arrived at my home. I opened it, and it's a sketchbook. A sketchbook of portraits, of a young girl. Something that looks a great deal like your work, even though they are not signed. None of the portraits are signed.

"There was . . ." Hans slowed as Aleandro ambled back to the sofa and plunked himself down, overcome with weakness.

"There was also a letter, addressed to you. That, of course, I did not open. Ah," he said with a dismissive flick of the hand, "it's probably nothing. It's probably just a copycat, or an emerging artist trying to get your attention. I can't tell you how often people try to dupe me into some fraudulent art scheme, but I wanted to ask you regardless if you'd like to— Aleandro, are you listening?"

"Where did it come from?" Aleandro asked, feeling as though he'd fallen into a cavern. "Who sent it?"

"Like I said, no idea. It came from somewhere in the city, via private courier and with signature required on delivery. But I don't think that's important right now. What's important right now is that you go and get yourself dressed and—"

"Do you have it with you?"

"No, I don't have it. It's back at my place. Look, it's probably nothing to get yourself worked up over, and there's plenty of time to talk about this later . . ." But he was speaking into a vacuum, for Aleandro was already halfway to the door.

"So let's go, then, yes?"

Another sigh came from Hans as he waved his hand around in Aleandro's direction. "You are wearing a robe. You've got no shoes."

"Ah, yes, that's right," said Aleandro. "My shoes." He ambled to his room to fetch them, leaving Hans behind, utterly exasperated.

38

E SAT. SKETCHBOOK IN HANDS, HE sat on Hans's white
leather sofa as the shadows deepened behind him,
turning from gold to azure to darkness. Lights from
the towers across from Hans's penthouse softly illuminated the
contours of the room. It was late. Hans had gone to bed long
ago; Aleandro could hear him snoring softly in the depth of the
apartment. His tea mug was empty when he brought it to his
parched lips, and only a bitter drop lingered on his tongue. He
dared not turn on the light. He feared that it would wake him,
that he would find himself wrenched from a dream.

He realized, in the course of this lingering, that he'd forgotten her face. That time had erased the minute details of
her lips and her eyes, that he'd forgotten the honesty of her
gaze, the shape of her fingernails, the way her smile curled just

slightly to the left, or that she never reclined in a chair, but rather always perched herself on the edge of her seat.

His fingers passed over the sketches, and in his fingers he could see the passage of time. His hands as they once were, when they painted and moved, when they painted her in the square. Time. Time had been his enemy, but also his friend. For had he not wanted to forget all these things?

Another page, the last one. On this one, he pulled another recollection from the dusty corridors. She, in a red dress, her honey hair mussed by the wind, her feet bare, sliding into the sand, into the golden light of a bonfire. The night they thought they were parting. The night that had been their beginning— and end. He didn't realize he was crying until a wet drop landed on the page, right at her feet.

He drew himself back and placed the sketchbook down on the sofa, still open beside him.

There were no more pages. Their story was over again.

The letter was on the coffee table. A simple envelope of regular stock, his name written in a careless handwriting, which he knew couldn't have been Eva's. He picked it up, knowing that he was on the edge of another precipice. And took comfort, strange as it was, that he'd almost not lived long enough to know this moment. It seemed a gift now.

Whatever the letter said, he was ready.

Dear Mr. Szabó,

My name is Bianca Kovaks. I'd elaborate further, out of sheer politeness, but I believe you know who I am. My mother is

Eva Kovaks. Formerly Eva César. And I believe that you, sir, were once in love with her.

I hope you'll forgive my brazenness. But I believe what I'm saying is true.

How to begin. You see, I knew virtually nothing of your role in our lives, until five years ago, when my beloved father, Eduard, passed away. It wasn't until then that my mother, Eva, confided in me that it was your donation to the Hungarian National Gallery that secured our visas to join him in Vienna after we were separated in the days of the revolution. To say that I was shocked would be putting it mildly, but, as she so reasonably explained, we all have our angels. And I'd be lying if I didn't say that if it weren't for your kindness, I might not have fulfilled my dream of becoming a violin virtuoso. As grandiose as that sounds, your gesture gave me the chance to see that dream through, as much as returning my father, Eduard, to me.

Which brings me to the reason for my sending you this sketchbook, along with this letter. When my mother decided to return to Sopron last year, she left it in my possession. There weren't many explanations offered, only that it was the sole thing of value she could bequeath to me, and she hoped that someday, if needed, it would provide a safety net. What my mother never understood is that I never feared poverty nor placed much value in money, and so I thought of it as nothing more than a memento to keep on a bookshelf and share with friends over dinner or wine. (Yes, it does indeed make for a great conversation piece.)

Yet, as I studied the portraits, I became aware that

they connected my mother to a past I knew nothing about.
You will pardon my directness, but even a child could
discern in these portraits that there was more between you
than friendship. I suppose we all harbor our secrets, do we
not? Well, whatever it was that you and my mother shared
before her marriage, it is not for me to judge. As I've made
clear, my allegiances belong, and always will, to my father,
Eduard.

Regardless, as this sketchbook surely means much more to
you than it does to me, I hope in all earnestness that it will
reach you. Yet, should it not, then I am comforted that your
ward and close friend, Hans Luben, will cherish it every bit
as much as you would. Either way, I believe I've done the
right thing by releasing it into his hands.

Incidentally, since the Eastern European borders opened
again the winter before last, I've had the chance to return
to my native Budapest and view for myself the pieces that
secured our freedom. And I have to confess that I was deeply
stirred. It was surely not easy to part with something so
close to your heart, and for that I owe you my gratitude. In
conclusion, think of the sketchbook as a returned favor, and
a thank-you gift.

Yours,
Bianca Kovaks

39

A T THE EDGE OF THE POND, Eva sat with her usual array of objects—a book, a shawl, a thermos of tea, and a large Tupperware container to transport the freshly caught fish back to her cottage. She didn't have to come down here for this. The kind fishermen were more than happy to bring the fish back to her, scaled and filleted, ready to be dusted in spices and plopped into a sizzling pan.

But here was where she spent the best moments of her day, here in the tall, undulating reeds among the smell of marigolds and the musky earthiness of the pond, here in the shade of a willow, watching the fishing canoes bob over the glassy water, where the sun-scorched young men scooped trout out of the water in their nets.

She didn't feel like reading today and found herself absentmindedly running her fingers alongside the smooth spine of her Jane Austen novel, letting the sun warm the planes and grooves of her face. How strange she found it, that in all of her seventy years she'd never stopped long enough to absorb the beautiful emptiness of a quiet moment. Why was it that only staring at the looming finality of life was she able to grasp that contentment could not be chased, that it need not be chased, that if one stilled long enough, it would come on its own accord?

Back in Vienna, her life had been so frantic that she would have found the notion utterly absurd. She still remembered those early days, when she first arrived in Vienna, and how it was no more than a day later that she took a bus through a city she did not know, and showed up unannounced at the clinic that Eduard had opened in her absence with Tamara's help. Eduard had insisted that she get herself settled in first and rest, but she did not need to rest; she needed to get herself in motion again. A year had passed since Aleandro had gone back to New York, a year of waiting for the visas he'd bought with his paintings to actually land in her hands, and now that she was here, she was aching to get back to life, to resume her work. The low-cost clinic, crowded with people and children from the poor sectors of town, proved the perfect opportunity.

And so she had begun her new life in Vienna, comprising at first mostly fifteen-hour work shifts. She analyzed patient files, set Eduard's appointments, stocked the medicine supplies, took lab work, balanced books, which on most days showed just enough profit to keep the lights on. Soon it was her seeing the patients who couldn't get on Eduard's booked calendar, and not long after that, it was her with whom they requested to consult.

Tamara had watched her with her quiet scrutiny, and, of course, to be expected, with some resentment for crossing her turf. But Eva also earned some respect. Something the other woman had only reserved for Eduard.

Despite the fact Eva would never know fully what had been between Tamara and her husband, in the wake of Eduard's sudden passing, five years prior, their relationship began to fuse into one of mutual understanding. Eva, after all, knew what it had been like for Tamara all these years, and in their shell-shocked grief, they found the seeds to what eventually would become a close friendship.

Beyond the walls of the clinic, her life had been no less busy. What she remembered now, between the larger details, was this constant state of running. Running home after dark and picking up groceries on her way, running to Bianca's recitals, running through a flurry of snow to attend some medical lecture that she was always late for. And yet, in all that time, she never experienced a sense of full contentment, this absolute, undemanding peace that only Sopron could offer her— here, now, always.

It wasn't until after the fall of the Berlin Wall, which had opened the borders of the Iron Curtain countries, that the idea of returning to Sopron had come to her. It had not been a rash decision. She'd thought it through for many months, vacillating.

Then, after the diagnosis, she began to give it serious consideration.

What would she leave behind, after all? By then, she'd been retired for five years. Bianca had been constantly on the road, and Tamara had met a widowed architect and spent more and more time with his circle of friends, a fact that made Eva happy. And Eduard. At some point, she'd grown accustomed to her existence without him, without his gentle, soft-spoken voice, his calming presence. She'd long come to know what it was like to wake up alone, to take her dinners at the table they shared for more than two decades while conversing with him in her thoughts. So last fall, she'd finally sold her flat in Vienna and she'd bought Dora's cottage from the Hungarian government with the money. It had cost less than she expected, and she'd been happy to still have a modest sum to put in the bank.

Now she watched her favorite fisherman, Pálos, pull his canoe in at the edge of the water and lift his fish in a heavy metal bucket, which he began to carry toward her.

"Good fishing day?" Eva smiled from under her huge straw hat, bending the edge of it against the sun.

"It always is when you come down here, Miss Eva. You must be my good-luck charm."

She laughed. "More like an ancient relic dug up from petrified ground. Well, come on, show me. Let's see what you got. My mouth is watering just thinking about it."

She knew it would make Pálos happy to hear that. Truth was, since yesterday, she hadn't had much of an appetite. Yet she refused to think about it, refused to think this was the beginning of the downturn she'd been warned about back in Vienna, when she'd decided against treatment. Well, she knew just enough from her years of experience what was in store with that sort of treatment, and she had chosen life.

Life to be lived on her own terms, as she always had. There was beauty after all in the exercise of acceptance. There was beauty in returning to one's roots, in planting flowers, in fixing one's cottage, in a warm cup of tea sipped at sunset, in watching fishermen fish. Her remaining time, whether it was a month or a couple of years, would be spent in peace, in beauty.

"You sure you don't want me to bring this to the cottage for you in my truck?" Pálos asked, his smile flashing brilliantly in a way that stirred a blurred recollection. "I'd hate to have it stink up your car. I'm happy to drive it over for you."

"As usual, I've come prepared," Eva explained, brandishing the huge Tupperware box. "And I don't mind the smell, really. It reminds me of the old days when I lived here. But thank you, Pálos. I'll see you again next week."

———

A half hour later, Eva pulled up in town at the post office, double-parking her car as she marveled at how much the town had changed in just over eighteen months since Hungary rejoined the Western world. Suddenly, there were tourists everywhere. Mostly they were from neighboring countries like Romania and Poland, which had also witnessed the crumbling of the Soviet Bloc with great jubilation. But there were Austrians, too, and once she'd heard French. The town was on the verge of a renaissance, and each time she caught a glimpse of it, she was gripped with both happiness and regret that she wouldn't see it bloom fully.

Today, there was nothing from Bianca—not that she heard much from Bianca when she was touring—so she collected her handful of bills and penny papers, and made her way back to the beat-up Ford she'd bought through a local ad, eager to get home to unload the fish.

Just as she opened the door, she saw from the corner of her eye a strange figure. A tall man, elderly, yet firm in his walk. He came directly toward her. He raised his hand in a gesture of hello, his face a play of shadows underneath the straw fedora hat. A foreigner needing directions, Eva thought, someone not from this town, given the crisp white suit and the flash of an expensive watch. Then he took off his hat.

Behind her, some kids scampered by, their voices no more than a distant, incongruous humming. She watched the man approach her, scrunching his hat in his hand, and her heart drummed and turned, and turned again too rapidly. God, she was too old for this sort of emotion. The car door was thankfully there to support her, and she grasped it tightly with her hand. She blinked. It couldn't be. Blinked again. It was.

But she had expected that she'd see him again, hadn't she? Hadn't she dreamed that he would come one day just like this, walking up that old familiar road of their youth with his hat in hand? Even in Vienna, after she'd reunited with Eduard and understood that in his gift to them he'd let her go for good, hadn't she still deep down believed this moment would come?

Here he was, and she couldn't think of a thing to say. She couldn't even utter his name.

It was him who spoke first.

"Eva. It's you. Is it really you?"

The question caused a strange reaction in her. She bent down to the driver's seat and grabbed her own hat, a misshapen, inelegant thing she shoved firmly onto her head. The desire to hide her face from him was unbearable. She hadn't even taken the time to gather her hair this morning in the usual bun, and it had been weeks since she'd done anything else to her face besides washing it with soap and water.

He smiled, as if amused by this gesture, and she, too, felt a thin thread of shock at how time had a way of carving a beautiful face into pieces that were no longer congruent, how his still-perfect teeth seemed displaced in his thinning, bluish lips. Then he did something she couldn't have ever expected. He came closer and removed her hat, tossed it into the street, across the stream of traffic.

"Let me look at you. God, let me just look at you. How beautiful you still are."

His eyes on hers. All she could see were those eyes. They bore the same expression she'd grown accustomed to glimpsing in magazine articles over the years. Filled with unrest. They were unchanged.

"That was my favorite hat," she said.

"It doesn't do you justice," he said, drinking in every contour and recess of her face. "You're better off without it. Plus, we can buy you another. If you care to join me for lunch."

She laughed despite her tears, their joint tears. "What brings you here, Aleandro? Are you visiting?"

"Visiting? Not exactly." A long silence. He cleared his throat. "Your daughter . . . I suppose you could say that your daughter sent me here. Not exactly, not directly. But she peppered the road here with bread crumbs, you might say."

"You met my daughter, Bianca? In New York? At one of her concerts?" She felt confused and slightly panicked. How had Bianca found him? For years, she'd been following the papers, and was very familiar with accounts of his deep seclusion, the rumors of his supposed demise. Yet here he was, smiling in her face, asking her to lunch as if this town were the French Riviera.

"No, I didn't actually speak to Bianca."

"I don't understand. Then how did you know I was here?"

At this, he reached inside his knapsack and extracted the sketchbook. It trembled slightly in his withered hands. "Does this look familiar to you?"

A flash of heat bloomed beneath her skin, and she drew back from him abruptly. "I see. Well, since you've come all this way, perhaps you might tell me exactly what my daughter has told you. About me."

He cleared his throat. "Like I said, we never actually spoke. She wrote to me; she sent me a letter along with the sketchbook via Hans, my best friend's son. She said she felt it was important to return it to its rightful owner. It was a nice letter. Also, it just happened to mention that you'd come back to Sopron last year. Alone."

"Is that all?"

"Is that all? Isn't that enough? Well, it was enough for me to jump on the first flight out of New York, catch the train from Marseille to Vienna, rent a car, and drive straight through. I thought I'd come into town to get a room, change, before I went out to look for you. But here you are. Here you really are. The gods have taken pity!"

"Ah," he said, holding up a hand to bar her objections. "Nothing could have kept me from coming. Once I knew where to find you, once I knew that you were on your own, that you've been on your own for five years, I would have paddled across the ocean to get here." He grinned as though he were a boy. "Although I have to say that I'm starving. So can we go have lunch, then?"

"Oh, Aleandro." Her eyes blurred with tears. He did not know. Did not know why she was here; it was plain on his face in the way he was looking at her with such unvarnished happiness. She shook her head, not knowing what to say, and he lifted his hand and cupped her cheek, held it there. It felt like a slap, the mere contact of it making her jolt, yet she couldn't help leaning into his palm. *Like before.*

"Aleandro, why?" she whispered. "Why couldn't you leave this alone? I mean, look at me. Look at us. Perhaps we'd have been better off with just our memories."

"Yes, it will make for a nice, lengthy conversation over lunch. We have much catching up."

It made her laugh. "You are incorrigible. And undeterred."

"Stubborn as a mule. As always. Now," he said, turning to scan the street behind them, "let's see what culinary adventures await. I hear the Hungarian fare has much improved. I hear they now serve French fries with goulash. Surely a welcome delight for the tourists."

———

They found a sidewalk kiosk, the only thing open at two in the afternoon, and sat on a plastic bench with Coca-Cola bottles and some soggy cheese pastries between them. The sun was hot; they were both perspiring, but neither one of them really minded the heat, nor the flies buzzing around their paper plates folded into the shape of tiny boats. The town was quiet, for while much had changed, the afternoon siesta was still strictly observed.

"We must stop meeting like this," Aleandro commented,

taking a final bite of his strudel, dusting off the powdered sugar from his hands. "Last time, at least there was some wine involved. Ah, what I wouldn't give for a glass of wine, to celebrate."

"Celebrate?"

"Yes, celebrate. You and me finding each other." He smiled. "Yes?"

She looked at him, at the gusto with which he picked at the last phyllo crumbs and popped them into his mouth, unaware of the white dusting on the tip of his nose, at the way his eyes sparkled in the sun.

She'd never felt happier—or more miserable. It would always be like this with him, a few joyful moments crammed into the folds of their larger reality. Of her life, his life.

"Aleandro, I have to tell you that I won't be here for the long term."

"No? So where are you thinking of going? If you want to travel, now that the borders are open we can go anyplace you want." He crossed his hands at the back of his neck and tilted his face to the sun. "I rather like the idea. Of traveling with you."

From her lips, there was only a sigh. He wasn't going to make this easy. She didn't want to tell him, dreaded having to tell him, but she could see now that there was no other way. She stood from the bench, came to sit next to him, took his bony, sugary hand, and squeezed it between hers.

"There is something that you should know, Aleandro. Something important."

"Don't tell me you've remarried. Who is he? Because this time I don't intend to handle things as peaceably."

"Stop it." She was laughing, and she leaned into him, put her head on the lapel of his jacket, felt the rising and falling of his chest. Closed her eyes. "I have . . . I suffer from what you might call an incurable illness. The reason why I came here is because my time, you see, is quite precious. Dramatic, I know, the way I made that sound, because in fact, the end . . . well, it won't be right away. It's still early, and I feel fine, but even with treatment, not a whole lot would change. Prolong, I'm assured, but not change. And I didn't want to spoil the good moments. I wanted to go on my own. That's why I came here. To enjoy the good, while I can. You understand?"

He didn't cry out, didn't wrench his hand from hers, but when she looked into his eyes she saw they'd gone dark. "I'm sorry. I didn't want to tell you. But you rather forced my hand." Silence. "Please say something."

He spoke finally. "I knew it had to be something like this, Eva. I knew from Bianca's letter. Something she said. That you left the sketchbook with her because it was the only thing of value you could bequeath to her. Those were her exact words. It could have meant anything, but somehow, I knew. There would be only one reason that you would come here. One reason only why you'd part with our sketchbook. So, you see, I'm not shocked."

She yanked her hand away. "So why did you still come, then?" She felt angry suddenly, exposed, vulnerable. "If you know me at all, then you would have figured out that I didn't want to be found. That when I sold everything back in Vienna and came here, it was because I didn't want anyone's fussing, anyone's pity. Especially not yours."

"Pity? Dear Lord, Eva, of all the things that this tired old heart of mine is capable of feeling for you, I assure you, pity isn't one of them. Let me explain something to you," he said and stood, and despite her resistance, he pulled her into his arms. "Let me explain in case you're thinking of sending me away again. Only three days ago, I wanted to end it all. It had all become too much. I saw no beauty in anything any longer, not even in my art, and, God, I was so demoralized for such a long time. But then in the course of one evening, everything changed. Just like that, with one letter, it all changed.

"You want to know why I'm here? Well, I'll tell you the truth. I'm here because since I lost you, Eva, all of thirty-four years ago, I've been half a person. I tried to be more, and perhaps for a little while, when Rudolf was still alive, I was. But after losing him, after losing both of you, there was so little left, and no success or money in the world could fill the void. So do not think that I'm here out of pity, nor out of some misplaced romanticized notion. I am here because it is myself I'm trying to save."

Then they were weeping fully, both of them, and it occurred to her what a spectacle they must be, two old people standing in the middle of the busiest street in town, sobbing like little children.

"So you've come so we can say good-bye again? How many times must you and I say good-bye?"

"No, I'm not here to say good-bye. Not this time, my love. Because just like you, I've come home. I've come home to stay."

40

THROUGHOUT THE REST OF THAT SCORCHING, dry summer, which would leave Hungary in a drought for a decade, Eva and Aleandro saw each other every day. Aleandro continued to lodge at the inn downtown, giving Eva the privacy she needed. After so many years of not seeing each other, after so many years of solitude, they both needed to be (at least for a few hours each day) what they were in their prior lives. In the afternoon, they took walks down by the water and went into town for supper once in a while, although most of the time Aleandro cooked for her in the tiny kitchen of Dora's cottage, where on a cassette player he would play Nina Simone's "I Put a Spell on You," and Frank Sinatra's melancholic songs in which their own lives were sung and revisited—every pain and joy and triumph and downfall relived.

It was blissful and quiet, the smell of fried fish, wine, and candles making Eva forget that she might not see the hillsides covered in green the next year, or that they'd lived apart for thirty-four long years. There were silences, too, many silences when they sat out on the porch with blankets and watched the sunset, and it was in those moments when Eva felt they could continue like this, growing old together—he with the aching bones in his hands, which he rubbed endlessly, she with her waves of fatigue, which came more often. The two of them, just watching the sunset on the whitewashed, sunbathed porch.

And yet one thing still stood between them. One thing she could no longer hide from him, for she was growing too weak for secrets, and the reasons for keeping it had long slipped away. So, one morning at the end of August, Eva grabbed the scrapbook of family photographs she'd made for Bianca and hadn't had the chance to send yet, and placed it inside a picnic basket alongside a bottle of wine and some cucumber sandwiches she'd prepared the night before.

He came at half past noon as he did every day in the silver convertible Bug he'd rented at the train station in Vienna, and she jumped in, covering her head with a scarf. He leaned in and kissed her lips lightly, in the way he always did, as though she were made of porcelain. "And what shall we do today?" he asked while smiling, his eyes deep and dark, vivid in the stark morning light. "What is the queen of my heart in the mood for this afternoon?"

It was the usual thing he would say to her, but today was a different day, a day unlike the ones before, so she turned to him brazenly. "For starters, your queen would for once like a proper kiss."

She leaned over the steering wheel and kissed him in the

way she wanted to be kissed, with a full open mouth, as she had kissed him once when she was young. "For a second thing, I thought we'd take a drive. Down to the pond. You know where. Our old spot by the pier."

"Are you sure?" he said, flushed under his straw fedora hat, taking a moment to regain his voice. "Are you sure not someplace new? We could drive down to Lake Fertö, to Burgenland. There is a beautiful little winery with a charming café right on the water that I think you would love. Do you remember how we once almost went to Burgenland together?"

"No, not today. I think today is a good day to revisit our old spot. I would say, quite necessary. Besides," she said, gesturing to the picnic basket, which she'd placed in the back seat, "I packed your favorite sandwiches, and you can't refuse my labor of love."

A half hour later, after they spread out their blanket and lunch things and he opened the wine, she reached into the bottom of the basket for the photo album.

"What's this? Don't tell me you're finally ready to introduce me formally to your illustrious family?"

"You might be surprised. Go on, open it."

The photographs revealed the trajectory of Eva's life backward in time. There, floating beneath the glare of the first sheet protector, was Eva, perhaps just a few years younger than she was now, her hair softened with gray and piled into an elegant chignon, her arm around the waist of a young, dark-haired woman with eyes so direct they seemed to pierce right through the film. They were standing on a sidewalk, and the woman was leaning her head on Eva's shoulder with her arms splayed wide as if to ignite the bright lights of the Vienna Philharmonic behind them. In the photograph below, she was wearing the same black dress and had her arm linked through that of a blondish man in a tux, who held up a violin of his own as they kissed for the camera.

"Bianca. This is Bianca?"

"Yes, my daughter. And that's Sebastián, her ex-husband. At the time they were married, but I guess you can say they were both more committed to their craft than they were to each other. It didn't last, but they are still friends, still tour together once in a while. Well, go on, keep looking."

Bianca's adolescence and childhood were then revealed in the form of endless recitals. She bore the same look of concentration playing her violin, which he had witnessed that day a long time ago in the Andrássy park. Her at a picnic table many years prior, drawing with a cup of crayons at her side, her dark curls pinned back from her face with two huge ladybug barrettes. Her again, no more than a toddler, riding on the shoulders of a man who had to be Eduard—older than Aleandro had pictured him, temples dipped in gray, glasses askew as they both grabbed for an apple from the tree underneath which they stood. Dora was there in the album as well, precisely as he remembered her when he'd come to deliver the sketchbook in Budapest: silvery hair pulled back severely, though her face was etched with doting affection, blurred slightly behind a huge cake lit with candles.

A whole life had been captured in these photos—moments, occasions, like pearls on a string. Eva's life. A homage to what

Eva's life had been, a homage to her daughter. His hand slid away from the sketchbook, dropped limply in the space between them. It seemed impossible to go on.

"I know." Eva's voice pulled him back from the wash of dejection. "I know this must be hard. But please keep going. Let's get to the end. We're almost there."

How could he say no? How could he say no to this one simple thing she was asking of him? It was plain to him that this was important to her, and so he picked up the album again, forced himself to turn another page.

The last one. This one, shot in black-and-white, yellowed with the passage of time. In it, Eva's face greeted him, the face he knew in his own youth: her full lips curved into a half-smile, her eyes bright and alert, though with a toughness he'd not seen in their earlier time. In her arms was a swaddled bundle, the whisper of a hand-knitted bonnet peering over the blanket. A younger Dora, exuding country robustness, was also in the picture, standing above the sofa where Eva sat, one hand on the baby, one on Eva's shoulder. Beneath it, a date had been inscribed.

June 1944.

A shadow passed over his face, a tremor, something Eva couldn't quite read, although she could see well enough that the date had made an imprint. *June 1944.* Less than a year after the fire. He looked at her, tears rising, begging for understanding. All she could do was nod through her own tears.

"I wanted to tell you, Aleandro. God, how I wanted to tell you. But when I saw you in Budapest, there was so much at stake, so much I could have lost by telling you. Then after that, after Eduard died, I looked for you, wanting to at least send you a letter, but you had disappeared. Everything was a dead end. Then I read in some article that you might not be alive at all, and by then Bianca was a grown woman, and there seemed no reason to tell her if she wouldn't even know you at all. So I sealed this secret inside my heart, became at peace with the fact that I would take it to my grave."

A cry left his lips. His face came away from his hands, and they were wet with tears. He looked up to the sky, where two hawks zigzagged under the white swirls of clouds, but he couldn't speak, and neither did Eva. They just let the silence enfold them.

"Oh, Eva, how could I have not known?" he said after what might have been an eternity. "I think I must have known all along. I think, deep down, I knew when I met Bianca in Budapest. I was just too blind to see it."

It was her turn to sound astounded. "In Budapest? But you said you never spoke, that you two never met."

"No, not in recent years, but yes, in Budapest, when I was there for the exhibit in fifty-seven. It was in the days after you left my hotel, and I was so confused and stunned, really, and to be honest, not ready to go back to New York. So I took walks, and somehow, once, I got lost near the Operaház. That's when I met her. It was in a park, right next to your home on Andrássy. She was playing the violin, and my God, I'd never seen a child play quite like that, not even the Romani children, so I approached her. We spoke for just a few minutes, but instantly I knew she was your daughter. I just knew. She touched my heart, and for a few moments that day, I thought there could still be a possibility for us, that perhaps my running into her like that meant that we should be together. Even though she spoke about her father with such deep attachment and told me how much she wanted to be reunited with him in Vienna, I still believed it. I don't know, I think I so much wanted to.

"But then, the next day, I came here. I came to see what remained of my old life, and I saw my brothers' names carved in a tree, and it was in that moment that I understood, truly understood, that no person could alter the way she felt for him, because it's what I'd felt for my brothers. That nothing I could offer her would ever replace him. And I felt so ashamed, Eva, that I'd considered this so little before." He was winded, yet there was more he needed to say, so he kept going, needing this unburdening. "I knew then that she would always belong to him. And she always did, didn't she? Despite everything, it is him whom she's always loved."

"Yes," said Eva, her own voice breaking. "Bianca in a way will always be Eduard's daughter, and nothing on earth will ever change it. But don't you see, Aleandro? There is always time for new bonds to form, always time, at the very least, for new friendships. There is always a way to let a new person into your heart, to love and accept, to embrace, as I have with Dora, as you have with Rudolf, and with his family. Blood ties or no blood ties, in the end all that matters is our capacity to love.

"Now show me your tree," she said, and she stood from the grass, reaching for his hand.

—

The tree was there, and afterward they sat in the grass by the water, watching the sun dip into the pond, ripples forming on the golden, glassy surface. It was the end of summer, summer as it would be again a hundred, a thousand times, when they would no longer be here to see it.

The land behind them was no longer barren, nor was it scattered with the old wine barracks that had been the remnants of a failed wine venture after the Soviet occupation. A golf terrain was sculpted in its place. The villa at the top of the hill, which had been Eva's summer home, lay under a scaffolding, the facade stripped, the window casings replaced to maximize the view of the vineyards when it opened as a luxury hotel at Christmas. There, across the strip of water, a restaurant with pure white walls in the style of a Greek-isle casita would soon be built, and red umbrellas would pepper the tiled terrace in another year's time. And here in the grass, there was just the two of them.

An eyewitness might have suggested that amid all the changes, they represented the end of an era, but how wrong that person would have been. For they were not at the end; they would never be at the end. They were only just beginning.

EPILOGUE

*H*ANS, HERE SHE COMES. HERE SHE comes."

Silence fell over Salle Pleyel Paris and its rows of red velvet peppered with suits and gowns and fans, the art deco balconies gleaming in all their polished starkness under the dimmed light behind them. Leaning forward in his chair, Aleandro struggled for composure, stifling the desire to shout out. It was not exactly the right venue for that kind of behavior, so despite the hammering of his heart, he reclined in his seat, seeking Hans's arm for support.

It wasn't the first time he'd felt this way, his heart tightening in his chest in the moments before she would walk onto the stage. He'd followed her around the world for nearly three years, seen more than a dozen performances, and this was a common thing. Stuffed in that old tuxedo or stodgy suit he'd always hated, he'd sat just like this many times, gripping his knees for dear life in the front row. But tonight, Hans was here with him, and he felt a little less on edge, his heart a little calmer. Tonight would be different, or so he hoped. God, how he hoped.

The silence stretched on, laden with anticipation. Not a single whisper was heard. The conductor appeared and bowed before taking his place on the podium, facing the black-clad orchestra members. Then, a second flurry of applause erupted as *she* came on, stunning in a long green velvet gown, her dark hair cropped into a glossy pixie, the first signs of middle age visible in the creases around her eyes and her smile, a softness underneath her arm as she held up her violin and took a bow of her own.

Everyone was on their feet. He, too, stood with Hans's help, who doted on him in the usual way, even though his eyes were only on the virtuoso, smiling as though the sun had broken through the rain clouds. Dear God, it was worse than he imagined. Hans was utterly lost to him. He knew that look better than anyone, and as they resumed their seats, he sighed in resignation.

Just six weeks prior, when Bianca played in New York, Aleandro bought Hans a front-row seat along with a premier membership to the New York Philharmonic, hoping this would be enough to get Hans backstage access, where he could try to persuade Bianca to meet with him. All he wanted was a cup of coffee, a walk in a park, no more. All he wanted was the simple chance to speak with her, but several hours later, Hans had returned with no answers, but rather a seeming lack of recollection of why he'd been sent there in the first place.

Bianca Kovaks, Hans had bubbled effusively, was charming,

funny, confident, direct, and kind. She was beautiful. And would Aleandro mind if he sent her flowers or chocolates?

Did he mind? he recalled asking. *Did he mind?* Well, if he minded or objected, it was evident it would have made no difference, so he'd only shaken his head, realizing that in the course of this battle tactic, he'd lost his best foot soldier. Then, at the last minute, he'd invited Hans to join him in Paris. If things didn't go his way again, he figured, Paris was no place to be alone at Christmastime.

Now, pinning his eyes back to the stage, Aleandro watched Bianca glide to her gold-plated seat on the conductor's left. The Stradivarius in her hand gleamed under the lights. He watched her lift the violin, her eyes distant, turned inward, half-closed. She raised her bow—

And then, beauty. So much beauty in those sounds that Aleandro felt needles in his chest and thought that he might die in this very chair, and how inopportune that would be, because he did not intend to die in Paris, nor New York, but in Hungary, where Eva was, where they would always be together, where they'd shared in the course of twenty-two months more than most couples did in a lifetime. God, how he missed her. How he missed waking next to her at sunrise and being able to touch her face; to paint her again and not just from memory; to soothe her even in her weakest moments with his zany humor; to hold her, above all, in the light of sunset. And to remind himself of that, he patted at his suit pocket, where every day, next to his heart, two golden bands rested. Their secret bands.

A squeeze of his hand. He opened his eyes, and Hans's gaze was on him now, eyebrows knitted with worry. He hadn't realized he was gripping at his chest. The younger man offered him a bottle of Evian, his gaze tender, authoritarian, instructing. *Please drink this.* Aleandro accepted it and drank, wishing it were whiskey or at least wine or champagne, then after he handed it back, there were no more disruptions of any kind, no more concerned looks, no more water bottles, no more worries over his failing heart.

Closing his eyes, he let the sounds carry him. Across oceans, and decades, and starry skies, over the rumbling of the subterranean trains of New York and Paris, over ponds of the Hungarian countryside and baroque buildings and bridges of Budapest, the sounds carried him.

———

At the end, an explosion of applause brought him back to his senses. He stood from his seat—this time swatting away Hans's fervent hands—and watched Bianca hand her violin to an orchestra member so that she could collect the bouquets carried onto the stage for her. One in particular was large enough to require a cart or a wagon, and as she took it and glanced at the card tucked in the folds of the cellophane, her eyes flashed over the crowd, then came to rest directly on Hans. And she smiled.

Beet red, Hans turned to Aleandro with upheld hands and apologetic eyebrows, as if to say, *It was from both of us, I'm not to blame here*, but Aleandro had already made up his mind.

This time, damn it, this time he would not let her slide away without a glance in his direction, so he stopped clapping. Stopped, while everyone still applauded. Below the edge of the stage, he stood on his old spindly legs, willing her to look at him. *Look at me. You are my daughter. You are my daughter, and you can't ignore me forever. I am here.*

He didn't know what made it different this time. Perhaps it was Hans standing alongside him in solidarity—just two men, one old and one young, connected by their past as much as their adulation for the great Bianca Kovaks. Or perhaps it was just being here in Paris, the city of love.

For suddenly, unexpectedly, the acquiescence he'd been praying for finally came.

From the mad foliage of baby's breath and myrtle and evergreen fern and every flower on earth obscuring her face, a single rose came away. A single red rose as tight as a baby's fist that she placed down on the stage's edge before him. Another look. This one, with a tiny nod, for him, just for him, their nearly identical eyes, save for their color, locked on each other's. Then she strode off with her proud shoulders pulled back, her chin upturned, the green gown's train trailing behind her.

There were many moments in Aleandro's lengthy life that he would never forget—many lessons he'd learned, words that would haunt him. But now it was Eva's words, his love's words, ringing in his head as he collected his rose with shaking, rheumatic fingers.

But don't you see, Aleandro? There is always time for new bonds to form, always time, at the very least, for new friendships. There is always a way to let a new person into your heart.

And she'd let him. Finally, she had let him.

AUTHOR'S NOTE

G ROWING UP IN BUCHAREST, ROMANIA, GYPSY music was an indelible part of my life. In summertime, I'd often hear it emerge from restaurant terraces or busy squares where players would serenade passersby, and I would stop to listen, enraptured by those soulful tunes of loss and longing.

Yet, despite the Romani's unparalleled talent as musicians, I also witnessed far too often the way in which mothers would rush their children along while passing them on the street, the way others would walk right by them without a glance in their direction, as if they were invisible. Why were they treated with such disdain, such suspicion, when they did nothing more than bring some vibrancy to an ordinary afternoon? Why were they seen as outsiders in their own birth countries when they made up such a large part of the population? These questions, even in the years after I'd moved to California, never stopped haunting me.

It wasn't until several years ago when I began researching the turbulent and complex World War II history of Romania's neighbor Hungary that the idea of integrating this little-understood and mystical culture in my new novel solidified. It was important for me to portray not only the bohemian existence of the Romani in times of peace but also their cruel fate during World War II when, much as the Jewish population, they were persecuted, stripped of possessions and rights, and deported in mass numbers to labor and concentration camps. What I found most surprising—and equally disconcerting as my research progressed—is that while a quarter of Europe's Roma reportedly perished at the hands of the Nazis, so little has been written on the subject. Ultimately, my hope is that through Aleandro's heart-wrenching journey and losses, I could shed a little light on what some historians call "the forgotten Holocaust."

While this is a work of fiction, it bears mentioning that many aspects of this novel are drawn from real life. For example, the art of Aleandro Szabó was inspired by that of Latvian artist Kalman Aron, who, after losing his parents when Germany invaded Latvia, was assigned to slave labor and moved through seven different camps in Poland, Germany, and Czechoslovakia. When his skill was discovered by the guards, he was exempted from hard labor and was given extra food in exchange for portraits or replicas of family photographs. In 2018, a *New York Times* article announcing Aron's death at the age of ninety-three quotes him as telling documentary film maker Steven C. Barber: "I made it through the Holocaust with a pencil." After the war, Aron moved to Los Angeles, where he began re-creating his painful memories in a series of paintings that garnered him worldwide acclaim. Today, one of his more prominent pieces, *Mother and Child*, is displayed at the entrance of the Los Angeles Museum of the Holocaust.

Much like Aleandro, Eduard Kovaks, Eva's husband, is inspired by the real-life Dr. András Seibriger, who, during the fifty-two days of the Budapest siege, helped save the lives of thousands of soldiers and civilians in a subterranean hospital buried deep under Castle Hill. Originally, the Hospital in the Rock was equipped to accommodate no more than 120 people, but according to records, during the heaviest days of bombardment, its capacity was exceeded more than tenfold. Beds were pushed together to create extra room for the deluge of patients, while nurses and medics—like Eduard, Eva, and Tamara—endured the harsh conditions themselves, often working without running water or food for days and sleeping only sporadically on vacant stretchers. At the end of the war the hospital was closed, yet when the Hungarian Revolution erupted in 1956, Dr. Seibriger returned to help save the lives of freedom fighters who found themselves under relentless fire by Soviet troops. Unlike Eduard in the novel, Seibriger, who suffered from a heart condition, did not flee Hungary after the uprising (despite imminent danger of arrest or execution), but he did lose the right to practice medicine and was persecuted by the Soviet regime until his death in 1977. Today, the hospital is a museum filled with wax reenactments of those brutal scenes. One depicts a young Dr. Seibriger attending to injured patients during the days of the revolution.

Lastly, while Eva is drawn entirely from my imagination, she embodies the courageous, selfless spirit of wartime nurses and resistance fighters—many from noble families like her own—who stepped bravely in harm's way to fight against injustice and persecution. She perhaps more than any character in the book exemplifies what we are capable of in times of crisis, and how it is that in the most desperate times we discover who we truly are. I hope her story has inspired you as much as it has me.

ACKNOWLEDGMENTS

MY UTMOST GRATITUDE FOR SEEING THIS novel in print goes to:

My wonderful editors, Daniella Wexler and Loan Le, for their faith and close guidance, for the time they so generously dedicated to this project, and for helping me mine this story for hidden gems.

My agent, Elizabeth Copps, for being a steadfast partner through several revisions of this novel, and the esteemed Maria Carvainis for embracing it with enormous enthusiasm and heart.

I'm also hugely indebted to my publisher, Libby McGuire, and the entire talented team at Atria Books who've left an imprint on this novel, especially editorial assistant Jade Hui, Gena Lanzi in publicity, and Raaga Rajagopala in marketing.

And finally, I cannot express enough appreciation to my

family—my sons, Luca and Dominic; my mother, Alexandra; and my sister, Arina. Finishing this book in the tumultuous year of 2020 would have been impossible without your loving support, encouragement, and patience. Philippe, I adore you for your unwavering belief in what I do, for the delicious dinners you serve me at my desk, for burning the midnight oil with me, listening to my writing. Thank you for being my rock and living this dream with me.

ABOUT THE AUTHOR

Roxanne Veletzos was born in Bucharest, Romania, and moved to California with her family as a young teen. Already fluent in English, she began writing short stories about growing up in her native Eastern Europe, at first as a cathartic experience as she transitioned to a new culture. With a bachelor's degree in journalism, she has worked as an editor, content writer, and marketing manager for a number of Fortune 500 companies. Her debut novel, published in multiple languages, is an international bestseller. Veletzos lives in the San Francisco Bay Area.

WHEN THE
SUMMER
WAS
OURS

ROXANNE VELETZOS

This reading group guide for When the Summer Was Ours *includes an introduction, discussion questions, and ideas for enhancing your book club. The suggested questions are intended to help your reading group find new and interesting angles and topics for your discussion. We hope that these ideas will enrich your conversation and increase your enjoyment of the book.*

INTRODUCTION

*H*UNGARY, 1943. As war encroaches on the country's borders, willful young Eva César arrives in the
idyllic town of Sopron to spend her last summer as
a single woman on her aristocratic family's estate. Longing for
freedom from her domineering father, she counts the days to
her upcoming nuptials to a kind and dedicated doctor whom
she greatly admires.

But Eva's life changes when she meets Aleandro, a charming and passionate Romani fiddler with a love for painting.
With time and profound class differences against them, Eva
and Aleandro still fall deeply in love—only to be separated by
a brutal act of hatred.

As their lives diverge and they are each swept into the tides
of war and its aftermath, they try to forget what they once
shared. But as the years pass, the haunting memory of their
romance will reshape their destinies time and again.

From the horrors of the Second World War to the tensions
of the 1956 Hungarian uprising and beyond, *When the Summer Was Ours* is a sweeping story about the toll of secrets, the
blurred lines between desire and loyalty, sacrifice and obsession, and the endurance of the human spirit.

TOPICS & QUESTIONS FOR DISCUSSION

1. At the beginning of the novel as the war escalates and before her intended wedding, Eva heads to Sopron for the summer, knowing it could be her last time there having it feel like "the Sopron of her childhood." Was there a place or vacation in your life where you had similar feelings, when you were intent on enjoying "every languid, unadventurous moment"?

2. When Aleandro first arrives at Dachau, he is forced to reveal his hidden sketchbook in front of a Nazi officer. Were you surprised that the officer, discovering Aleandro's talent, chose to spare his life? Do you think he would have done the same thing if Aleandro was of Jewish descent rather than Romani? Why or why not?

3. From the beginning of the novel, Eva is studying to become a nurse and later continues working in the hospital after the war is over. Discuss if you think Eva's choices went against the societal norm during that time or not. Do you think if the war had not reached Hungary, she would have pursued her medical career?

4. Throughout his time in the camp, Aleandro is tormented by guilt for his brothers' deaths. How does that change when he meets Rudolf? How are his secret drawings of the camp able to free him from that guilt?

5. Do you agree or disagree with Dora's decision to respond to Aleandro's letter after the war has ended, keeping him away from Eva (and Bianca)? Do you think you would have done the same thing in her position?

6. Much of the second half of the book focuses on the revolution in Budapest and the fallout after the war ended. We see Eva and Bianca come upon a protest in 1956 and later Eduard is targeted by the secret police. Discuss how the Soviet occupation was similar to that of Nazi Germany a decade earlier. How were they different?

7. When Eva sees Aleandro again at his art show in Budapest, she is torn between her attraction to him and her loyalty to Eduard. What finally draws her into his arms? What in the end allows her to let him go and move into a future without him?

8. One of the prominent themes of the book is having your own chosen family, as illustrated by the relationship between Eva and Dora, and Aleandro and Rudolf. Besides the losses that brought them together, what do you think bonds these characters strongly enough to maintain life-long relationships?

9. Do you agree or disagree with Eva's choice to keep Bianca's paternity a secret from Bianca and Aleandro until the end of Eva's life? Why or why not?

10. *When the Summer Was Ours* is divided into four parts— "Hauntings," "Roads," "Restorations," and "Truths." Why do you think Roxanne Veletzos chose to structure the novel this way? How did each part contribute to the over-arching narrative?

ENHANCE YOUR BOOK CLUB

1. *When the Summer Was Ours* tackles a popular era for historical fiction, but the primary setting of Hungary and the effects of World War II on the Romani people is unique. As mentioned in the author's note, Veletzos witnessed society's unacceptance of the Romani as a child and wanted to help shed light on what many refer to as "the forgotten Holocaust." Why do you think history has largely overlooked this ethnic group?

2. A major topic in *When the Summer Was Ours* is the medical profession in time of crisis, especially the vital work of frontline medics such as Eva, Eduard, and Tamara. What other World War II novels have you read with medical settings? Discuss how these positions continue to be important in modern society and how their roles have evolved over time.

3. Art and its history has been heavily tied to World War II over the years. Aleandro is spared some of the atrocities at Dachau because he is "a man of arts." Rather than manual

labor, he is tasked with creating portraits of the officers but it is his clandestine depictions of the camp that later make him a renowned artist. Aleandro's Holocaust art was inspired by that of Latvian artist Kalman Aron. As a group, look up some of his work and discuss your favorite pieces.

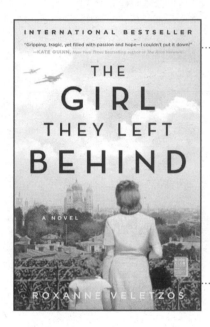